Solemn Vows

OTHER MARC EDWARDS MYSTERIES
BY DON GUTTERIDGE

Turncoat

Solemn Vows

A Marc Edwards Mystery

DON GUTTERIDGE

National Library of Canada Cataloguing in Publication

Gutteridge, Don, 1937–
Solemn vows / Don Gutteridge.

"A Marc Edwards Mystery".
ISBN 0-7710-3675-2

I. Title.

PS8513.U85S65 2003 C813'.54 C2003-902379-6
PR9199.3.G84S65 2003

We acknowledge the financial support of the Government of Canada through the Book Publishing Industry Development Program and that of the Government of Ontario through the Ontario Media Development Corporation's Ontario Book Initiative. We further acknowledge the support of the Canada Council for the Arts and the Ontario Arts Council for our publishing program.

Typeset in Sabon by M&S, Toronto
Printed and bound in Canada

This book is printed on acid-free paper that is 100% recycled, ancient-forest friendly (40% post-consumer recycled).

McClelland & Stewart Ltd.
The Canadian Publishers
481 University Avenue
Toronto, Ontario
M5G 2E9
www.mcclelland.com

1 2 3 4 5 07 06 05 04 03

For Bob and George Clark
and their many enthusiasms

Author's Note

Solemn Vows is wholly a work of fiction, but I have endeavoured to convey in it the spirit of the period and the political tensions that led to the Rebellion of 1837. The statements, actions, and character traits attributed to actual historical personages referred to herein – Sir Francis Bond Head, William Lyon Mackenzie, Allan MacNab, Ogle Gowan – are fictitious, and readers will have to make up their own minds as to whether such characterizations are consistent with the historical record. (For the record, Bond Head did dissolve the Legislative Assembly abruptly in 1836, did campaign vigorously in the ensuing election, and generally ignored advice from the colonial secretary.) All other characters are the invention of the author, and any resemblance to persons living or dead is coincidental.

While Danby's Crossing is fictitious – as are the taverns and domiciles of the characters – the streets, landscape, and public buildings of Toronto in 1836 have been depicted as faithfully as my research would allow. Of particular value in this regard were: Gerald M. Craig, *Upper Canada: The Formative Years, 1784–1841*; Sir Francis Bond Head, *A Narrative*; J.M.S. Careless, *Toronto to 1918*; G.P. de T. Glazebrook, *The Story of*

Toronto; William Dendy, *Lost Toronto*; and Lucy Booth Martyn, *The Face of Early Toronto*. Any errors of fact in the novel, deliberate or otherwise, are my own.

Acknowledgements

I would like to thank the members of my "focus group" for their encouragement and sustained support: Gene Burdenuk, Bob Clark, George Clark, John Gutteridge, Stan Atherton, Gerry Parker, Ian Underhill, George Martell, and Jean McKay.

Thanks are also due to my publicist, Mariska Gatha, and my editor, Dinah Forbes, for her insightful and patient attention to detail.

Finally, I owe a debt of gratitude to my literary agent, Beverley Slopen, who at times had more faith in this project than the author.

Chapter One

June 1836

Marc Edwards wiped the sweat off his brow with the sleeve of his tunic, but not before a rivulet of it had slid into his left eye and two greasy drops had plopped on the shako cap cupped between his knees. The afternoon sun of a cloudless June day was pouring a relentless heat down upon the hustings and its well-fed, overdressed occupants. Surely, Marc thought, the grandees of Danby's Crossing (or pompous old Danby himself) could have had the foresight to erect the rickety political scaffolding under the shade of the maple trees drooping at the northwest corner of the square, or at least close enough to Danby's Inn for its two-storey veranda to provide some shelter. Such was not the case, however – here or anywhere else in the backwater province of Upper Canada, where, it seemed to Marc, elections were considered life-and-death affairs, and high seriousness and bodily suffering prime virtues. And such sufferings invariably included a shaky platform groaning with dignitaries, each of whom managed to "say a few words" in as many sentences as were consonant with their social standing or the patience of the throngs.

At the moment, Garfield Danby, the self-appointed chairman of the day's proceedings, was droning away at what he took to be a stirring introduction of the guest speaker, Sir Francis Bond Head, lieutenant-governor of the province, who was seated next to Marc directly behind the podium. As Marc gazed out at the dusty square and the several hundred people gathered there on a sweltering Tuesday afternoon in the middle of the haying season, he marvelled at their perseverance, their dogged insistence on hearing every word offered them, as if words themselves might somehow right their many grievances against the King's representatives, grievances that had bedevilled the colony for half a generation.

Not two days ago, many of these same folk – farmers, shopkeepers, dray men, and their wives or sweethearts – had stood in this same spot to listen to platitudes from politicians of both parties, Constitutionists (as the right-wing Tories were now styling themselves) and left-wing Reformers. And today they had come back to hear the most powerful man in the province, King William's surrogate in this far corner of his realm. They came to listen and, from what Marc had learned about them in the twelve months since his arrival in Toronto, to judge. Hence their willingness to stand quietly during Danby's ill-grammared maundering. Sir Francis *would* speak, eventually – if the heat didn't liquefy them all before sundown.

Marc could hear the Governor shuffling the several pages of notes he had prepared with the help of his military secretary, old Major Titus Burns, and of Marc, who was now his principal aide-de-camp, even though this speech, like all the others over the past week, would simply repeat his unvarying themes: public order before any redress of acknowledged grievances; a stable government to assure justice and to effect lasting reforms; a purging of extremists of both left and right (Sir Francis being, after all, a Whig appointment in a Tory domain); reiteration of

His Majesty's opposition to republicanism and the "American party" led by William Lyon Mackenzie; and a direct appeal to the common sense of the yeomen who peopled the colony and whose roots lay deep in the soil of the motherland. With Major Burns's rheumatism acting up more frequently, Sir Francis had been calling more and more upon Marc, whose days as a law student had left him proficient in English, to help him in speech writing and, on occasion, to draft official letters to the colonial secretary in London, Lord Glenelg.

While Marc had chosen the action of army over the tedium of law, he was happy to sit at a desk and write because he was by and large in agreement with the Governor's sentiments and strategy. Even though Marc knew that the grievances raised by the ordinary citizens were valid, mainly as a result of the winter weeks he had spent at Crawford's Corners and Cobourg, where he had carried out his first investigative assignment, he had little sympathy for the reformers. He believed, as did Sir Francis, that because these grievances were of long standing and had been exacerbated by the sudden influx of "republican" immigrants from the United States, the first priority was to calm the waters, reassert the King's authority with a firm and fair hand, and then one by one deal with the people's complaints in an atmosphere free of partisan rant and rhetoric. This message, cunningly couched in the non-partisan rhetoric of regal prerogative, seemed to be having a positive effect on the electorate. (That the lieutenant-governor was by tradition supposed to be a neutral in election campaigns was being conveniently overlooked.)

On the bench directly behind the Governor, Langdon Moncreiff – the newly appointed member of the Executive Council – slumbered noisily. Above Danby's drone and the rush of a sudden breeze through the far maple trees, the Councillor's snores rose as strident and nozzling as any hog's. Sir Francis shuffled his papers again: Danby appeared to be running out of inspiration. The crowd below fidgeted in anticipation.

Remembering that he was on the hustings to ensure the Governor's safety, Marc put his shako back on, leaned forward, and scanned the village square. He knew that immediately behind the hustings, where the path south began, two junior officers stood watch, their horses tethered nearby. Marc swept his eyes over the Danby Inn, where the entire entourage, like a royal progress, had arrived at mid-morning with flags flying and carriage wheels clattering. Ensign Rick Hilliard, fresh-faced and keen to please, stood stiffly at the door and gripped his Brown Bess tightly. The platform dignitaries – including three merchants, a brace of lawyers, and a rotund banker – were less than twenty yards from the balustrade of the inn's upper veranda. Hilliard gave Marc the briefest of nods. Beyond the inn, the wide corduroy road that led west to Yonge Street was fringed on the north with several tall maple trees, now sporting a dozen youngsters who had climbed among the branches to "get a gander" at the viceregal personage or simply to make a happy nuisance of themselves. Opposite the hustings, the general store and a sprawling livery stables merited only a cursory glance. On the east side, the smithy was now fireless and quiet, and in front of the harness shop next to it, the proprietor and his family stood in the sun, smiling as Danby wound up his introduction. Above the harness shop was an apartment with glass windows and, higher still, a gabled garret. Marc spotted nothing unusual.

Half-throttled by his own snores, Councillor Moncreiff let out a gasp and a purging cough before the snorts started up again. Marc suspected that the other self-invited platform guests were likely dozing as well. It was not yet three o'clock, but everyone here had already put in a full day. For those travelling in the Governor's retinue – Ignatius Maxwell, the

Receiver General and veteran Executive Councillor, his ample wife, and his debutante daughter, along with Langdon Moncreiff and the Governor's physician, Angus Withers, and their escort, Lieutenants Edwards and Willoughby, and a company of eight mounted and fully armed junior officers – the day had begun at nine o'clock outside the garrison at Fort York. After a lurching ride up dusty Yonge Street, past Blue Hill, Deer Park, Montgomery's tavern at Eglinton, they had travelled the quarter-mile east to Danby's Crossing.

Upon arrival, Sir Francis and the Toronto worthies had been greeted by the local gentry and their ladies (from as far away as Newmarket), several of whom had got into the Madeira sometime earlier. Danby had laid on a stultifying midday meal, with wine, several desserts, and cigars. If Sir Francis had been shocked by the presence of the ladies throughout the meal, by the ingratiating speeches of welcome, or by the port-and-cigar aftermath, he was too well mannered to show it. Marc and his second-in-command, Colin Willoughby, had led the troop into a back room, where more modest fare awaited them.

Willoughby had given Marc a look that said quite plainly, "Did we really leave England for *this*?" which made Marc grin. He liked Willoughby a lot. The young man had arrived with the Governor in January, suffering terribly from a luckless love affair. Sir Francis had taken Colin under his wing and had asked Marc to assist him. Marc found it easy to sympathize with the pain of unrequited love, as his own attempts to win over Beth Smallman, a widow he'd met in Cobourg, had had little success. None of his letters had been answered. Marc now glanced down at Willoughby, whose scrutiny of the crowd in the square was as keen as Marc's had been upon the peripheral buildings. When Marc caught his eye, Willoughby nodded reassuringly and turned his eyes back to the crowd.

"Ladies and gentlemen," boomed Dunby at last, "I present to you this afternoon, Lieutenant-Governor Sir Francis Bond Head!"

A gust of wind swept across the platform, and one of the sheets of notes fluttered out of the Governor's hand just as he was about to stand. He reached down to retrieve it before it reached the floor, as did Marc. There was an embarrassing collision of heads, followed by a loud cracking sound somewhere beyond them, a muted thud close behind them, then silence. Marc turned to see Councillor Moncreiff sit bolt upright and flick open both eyes – eyes that saw nothing. The old gentleman was already dead, his blood and lungs beginning to ooze through the gap in his waistcoat.

Marc froze. Then everyone seemed to move at once. Angus Withers threw his bulk over a crouching Sir Francis, the other dignitaries flailed for cover, Willoughby vaulted onto the platform, and Langdon Moncreiff's body slumped to the floor. The confusion of noises struck Marc a second later: women screaming, men shouting, the Governor hissing to his protector to get the hell off him.

"He's dead," Marc said to Dr. Withers and Sir Francis as they untangled.

Beside him, Willoughby went pale and the whites of his eyes ballooned. Marc steadied him, then leapt up onto the bench and peered across the crowded square. The throng had not yet panicked; they were either too shocked or too curious to move. The members of Marc's contingent appeared to have recalled the training he had given them before the Governor's patriotic rallies had begun a week ago. Several of them were already mounted and scanning the crowd and buildings for the source of the gunshot or some glimpse of a fleeing assassin.

They had not long to wait. A man's cry, sharp enough to carry over the excited mutterings of the crowd, soared out of a treed area on the northwest corner of the square. This was followed by the sounds of branches snapping and a body hitting the ground. Marc looked over in time to see a rough-clad farmer stagger to his feet, gaze around him with brilliant, stunned eyes, and then scurry towards the general store. In his right hand he carried a large hunting gun.

"There he is!" Marc yelled to two of the ensigns who had just ridden up to the hustings. "Apprehend him!"

The crowd now turned to face the latest commotion, and they, too, began screaming for someone, anyone, to block the assassin's flight.

"Stop that man!"

"He's getting away!"

But no one stopped him as the assassin dashed past the general store and down the side of the livery stables towards the trail that led into the back townships of York County. He had tied his horse just behind the stables and now he swung into the saddle and, gun in hand, raced away into the bush.

"Detail. Form up and pursue!" Marc called out to his men. "Willoughby, bring up our horses and we'll follow."

Willoughby was trembling. Marc gave him a furious shake, anxious that the Governor not see what looked like cowardice in the face of danger. Willoughby was no coward: Marc would have staked his life on it. "We've got to go, Colin," he whispered fiercely. "*Now!*"

Fortunately, Sir Francis, Dr. Withers, Ignatius Maxwell, and others on the platform were still crouched around Moncreiff's body, and Marc was able to pull Willoughby away from the hustings. At last the frightened man began to take gasping breaths.

"I'm all right now," he said to Marc as Ensign Hilliard trotted up beside them with the horses in tow.

"Then let's be off," Marc said as he hit the saddle. "We can't let him get away." That the fate of the province might depend on them was too awful a thought to be expressed.

When Sir Francis had given Marc the task of forming a guard for his political forays into the hinterland, he had spared no expense. Marc had chosen eight young and eager subalterns from his regiment at Fort York (Colin Willoughby was put forward by Sir Francis) and armed them with Brown Bess muskets in addition to the traditional sabre and pistol. The horses now galloping along the trail the assassin had taken no more than a hundred yards ahead of Marc were the best that York County could provide. The pounding of their hooves around the next bend could be heard clearly.

"They'll get him soon at this pace!" Hilliard shouted excitedly over to Willoughby.

"If he hasn't swung off the trail into the forest!" Willoughby yelled to Marc.

"I hope to Christ they know enough to keep an eye out for that," Marc said more to himself than to Hilliard or to Willoughby, who seemed to be dropping back. But there was no chance of slowing down to wait for him.

A few seconds later, Willoughby came abreast at a rapid gallop. "Some of the townsfolk are following us!" he shouted.

Eager to be in on the kill? Marc thought. Or hoping to obstruct justice in some way?

"There they are!" Hilliard shouted.

The rumps of the Governor's prize horseflesh came into view as Marc dashed around yet another S curve. He dug both heels in, and his mount – a chestnut mare – responded with a burst of speed that brought Marc alongside Ensign Parker and the others.

"Where is he?" Marc cried.

"Still ahead, sir. We can hear the bugger even when we can't see him!"

"We need to be sure he doesn't deke into the woods. If he's a local, he'll know every deer-trail in the township."

"We thought of that, sir, but the trees are too thick on either side for a horse to get through. He'd have to go on foot, and then we'd spot his horse."

"Good thinking, Ensign."

"I think he's panicked, sir. I think he's beating his mount flat out, and it won't be long before it dies under him."

"I hope so. We can't push our own animals much farther at this pace."

As Hilliard and Willoughby joined the main group, Marc took the lead, raising his hand to signal the others to remain nine or ten strides in his wake so that he could listen to the hoofbeats of the assassin's horse up ahead. The cadence of its gallop was distinctly audible, and it was beginning to flag. A minute or two more and they would have him. Marc's heart was racing in a cadence of its own, driven by anger, excitement, and the sheer thrill of the chase. This was what he had abandoned law and the Inns of Court for! He had traded words for action, and here he was thundering into danger (the man ahead had, after all, just murdered in cold blood and doubtless would not hesitate to do so again if he found it necessary), careless of his safety, hazarding all for his monarch.

Coming around a sharp turn in the trail, Marc at last caught a glimpse of the felon: a mane of grey hair flying in the wind, the glint of the sun on the gun barrel, the pinto beginning to fail under him.

"Halt! In the name of the King!" Marc cried, but it was too late. Felon and mount had swerved into the tangled bush.

Marc swore and reined his horse in as brutally as he dare. If he were to follow the assassin into this narrow passage in the woods, those coming up behind might charge on past him, unaware. It was only seconds, however, before Willoughby and the guards arrived.

"He's a local, all right," Marc said, catching his breath and stroking the chestnut's neck. "He's gone in there. There must be a track of sorts or else he's trying his luck on foot."

Marc eased the horse between two stout pine trunks and entered the humid gloom. As he had suspected, they were on a deer-trail that wound tortuously through the dense woods. There was no need to wave the troop into single file.

"We're right behind you, sir!"

Farther back, he could hear the commotion of the camp followers from town as they, too, stumbled into the woods. One of these fellows, with a stentorian bellow, kept calling out "Stop! Stop!" as if mere repetition would shame the fugitive into giving up the chase.

In the dim light, Marc could easily make out the felon's passage, for the trail itself had been unused since heavy rains a few days earlier, and the pinto's hoofprints were registered clearly in the boggy ground, every stricken step of the way.

"That horse can't last more than a minute or two longer in this morass," Marc called back to Willoughby. "You'd better get your pistol ready. We may need it soon."

The trail arced steeply upwards, and with a sidling lurch, Marc found himself out of the forest entirely and partly blinded by the sun. Ahead lay an extensive clearing – the back field of a farm, most likely – lush with timothy. He could not see the fugitive. Then, as his eyes adjusted, he spotted a rocky, spruce-topped ridge on the eastern edge of the field. At the base of it, not more than fifteen yards away, the pinto pony lay on its side, wheezing, dying. Behind it and rising slowly was the fugitive, with his grizzled chest-length beard and wild shock of grey hair and mud-splotched overalls. He was barefoot. All this Marc saw in a single moment, along with the musket that was pointed straight at his heart. He had been given no time to evade or to retaliate, or even to cry out: the trigger was already being squeezed. What he did feel, in the moment before his certain death, was a twinge of animal terror, then an eerie calm. If he had to die here, at least his courage would have been tested, and found worthy.

The shot did not come. Instead, the felon turned, scrambled up a path of sorts towards the top of the ridge – and vanished. Perhaps the troop coming up out of the woods behind Marc had decided him against pulling the trigger.

"Are you all right, sir?" Ensign Hilliard asked as he and Willoughby reined in beside Marc. "I saw him pointing the gun your way. I was sure he was going to shoot."

"He thought better of it," Marc said calmly. "He's on foot now, climbing that hogback."

"Let's get after him, then," Willoughby said. Marc noticed that the young man was now looking flushed. There was nothing like a fox hunt to get a gentleman's blood up, Marc thought.

"I think we'd be better off waiting here," Marc said.

"Why, sir?" Hilliard said a bit too forcefully. "We can fan out on either side of the ridge and run him to ground."

"Some of the townsfolk are coming up through the woods," Marc said. "At least one of them will know something about this terrain that might help us get our man and save us time and energy."

"Whatever we do," Willoughby added, "we need to remember that he's got a gun and is quite prepared to use it."

"Nevertheless, I am ordering every one of you to make every attempt to capture this man alive. The odds are that the murder was politically motivated, and the Governor will need to know who was involved and why. Anything less could throw the election, and the colony, into chaos."

"We'll do our best, sir," Hilliard said.

The first of the townsfolk following the official posse now emerged into the clearing. His name, he announced when he had stopped panting, was Alvin Chambers, a farmer from York Township. Marc addressed him sharply.

"Where does this hogback lead?"

"It's the height of land hereabouts and runs up that way for pert near two mile," Chambers said.

"Are there farms on both sides?"

"Here and there, with lots of bush in between 'em."

"If you have any idea where the gunman might be heading, I command you in the name of the Governor and the King to tell me."

Chambers winced at the authoritative tone of Marc's voice. "We do better 'round here when folks ask us politely."

"Are you refusing to co-operate with the King's guard, sir?"

"Nope. I wouldn't want to offend Sir What's-His-Name, now would I?"

Ensign Hilliard made a move to thrash the insolent man, but Marc held up his hand. "We'll find the blackguard without your assistance, then." He wheeled his horse towards the ridge.

"There's an old trapper's cabin up there about a half-mile through the scruff and rock," Chambers drawled. "No need to go straight up here, though."

Marc paused but did not look back.

"Just ride on north along the base of the hogback till ya come to the bush and a small crick just inside it. There's a path there that goes straight up to the cabin. I didn't see who we was chasin', but some of the fellas ridin' behind me figured –"

But Marc had already given the signal to move forward, and whatever the farmer had said was lost in the thud of hoofbeats. Alvin Chambers was soon joined by his friends, and they followed the Governor's guard on foot, many of them gesticulating frantically, Marc noted when he glanced back.

"I think we had better keep that rabble well away from us when we catch up to the gunman," Marc said to Willoughby.

"It's hard to tell whose side they're on," Hilliard added.

Less than five minutes later, the troop came to the bush again, and they could hear the creek tumbling down the ridge nearby. "Well, they didn't try and deceive us about this landmark," Marc said.

"So far," Hilliard said.

A minute later, Willoughby called out, "I've found the track!"

"Tie your horses up here," Marc ordered. "Ensign Parker will stay with them and make sure these locals don't get any farther than this. The rest of us will proceed with caution, on foot, up to the cabin. Bring your rifles and have them ready to fire. I'll lead the way. No one is to make any move until commanded to do so. Lieutenant Willoughby will walk directly behind me and cover me, should I come under fire."

Ensign Parker sighed theatrically, while the seven other ensigns eagerly followed Marc's lead. After a long winter of gaming, grouse-hunting, and wenching – relieved by endless hours of idling – they were primed for action.

The path was steep and stony, following the line of least resistance. Scrub pine and barbed bushes blocked any view of what might lie above. Ten minutes of laboured climbing saturated the officers' uniforms with sweat. There was nothing in sight except more bush.

"We could be headed into a trap, sir," Hilliard suggested.

Marc did not reply, and the ensign decided he had offered enough unsolicited advice for one day.

A few minutes later, they clambered awkwardly up over a projecting ledge. Marc whispered, "There it is," and signalled for silence.

Perched on a rocky outcrop at the highest point of the hogback was an ancient log hut, windowless and scarcely big enough to confine one medium-sized bull. A hole in the roof was the only chimney, but no smoke drifted out of it into the steamy afternoon heat. The ground immediately around the cabin was bare, making it impossible to approach it under cover. Between Marc and what appeared to be the only door in the hut, the slope was precipitous but dotted with scrub trees or overgrown bushes. With luck he might be able to crawl up close enough to negotiate with the killer without getting shot before he could begin.

A shadow moved in the doorway. Their quarry had come to roost.

Marc turned to his men, who had all come up behind him and were peering anxiously upwards. Several began loading their Brown Besses. Willoughby's pupils were the size of the buttons on his tunic. Half an hour ago he had seen a corpse with a gaping hole in it for the first time; now the muzzle of a loaded gun might well be aimed at him. Suddenly Marc felt the full weight and responsibility of command: decisions that he would have to make in the next few minutes could put in jeopardy both his own life and the lives of those who trusted his judgment. He took a deep breath.

"I'm going to sneak up as close as I can to the cabin," he said quietly. "I want you to cover me in case I'm spotted. But do *not* fire at the fugitive, merely send a volley over his head to keep him lying low inside, and then only when I give the signal by raising my sabre or uttering a command. If I am shot, then Lieutenant Willoughby will take over the unit and issue orders. Even so, if you must shoot, try to wound him only."

"Understood," Willoughby said, fighting for breath.

"Will he not try to escape by running back along the ridge the way he came?" Hilliard asked timidly.

"Perhaps," Marc said, "but I think he's decided, one way or another, to make his stand." That such a decision clearly put Marc's life at risk was a grim possibility. They felt it to a man.

Without further ado, Marc set out. He moved quickly between clumps of brush, pausing at each to squint upwards at the hut. Three-quarters of the way there he realized with a sigh that his feathered shako and scarlet tunic would make him visible even if he had had a granite boulder to hide behind. But the gunman had made no move to warn him off or to put a bullet through his head. Perhaps in his exhaustion and remorse, he had decided to wait for Marc's arrival and then throw himself upon the King's mercy.

Marc was now about thirty yards or so beyond his men and no more than fifteen yards from the hut itself. It was, he could see now, a hovel: crumbling and pathetic in its slow collapse. The stench of offal and rotted vegetables was overpowering, even at this distance. Suddenly, the gunman appeared in the doorway, his eyes, deep in their sockets, gleaming feverishly. He still held the gun, an aging hunting musket, in one hand.

"Put the gun down, sir," Marc shouted gently in his direction, "and no one will get hurt. I represent Lieutenant-Governor Head, and I need to talk to you."

The old fellow moved the gun as if to drop it, but it seemed permanently morticed to his right hand, and, instead, it began to rise alarmingly upwards. But something in the man's startled stare caused Marc to relax his guard. He stood up slowly and, without taking his eyes off the gun, raised his arm and barked out a single order: "Hold your *fire*!"

Marc took a step forward. "I won't hurt you," he started to say, just before a volley of explosions from below rocked him.

He had to grab a nearby branch to stop himself from tumbling back down the slope. The sting of cordite filled his nostrils and stung his eyes. What had happened? Had he been shot at? Hit? For several seconds he sat on his haunches beside a bramble bush, in shock.

"Are you all right, sir?" Hilliard was beside him, and Willoughby and the others were staggering past him towards the cabin. There was no one in the doorway.

"I'm fine, Ensign," Marc said through the ringing in his ears. "But why did you shoot? I ordered you to *hold* your fire."

Hilliard gasped. "We heard you call out 'Fire!' "

Marc stood up and brushed past him, joining his men, who were crowded around something on the ground in front of the doorway.

It was the old man, dead, with half a dozen bullets in him. Willoughby was turned away from the corpse. He spoke to Marc without looking at him. "I take full responsibility for this," he said in a trembling voice.

"But you were the only one who didn't fire," Hilliard said.

"That's because I wasn't sure what you had ordered," Willoughby said to Marc with some emotion. "It sounded like 'Fire,' but I couldn't be sure because your back was turned. I – I just froze. I couldn't open my mouth. And when I did, it was too late. With that gun pointing right at you, the men did their duty as they saw it. They fired."

"And saved your life, if I may say so, sir," Hilliard said.

Marc sighed. "You may be right," he said. He turned to Willoughby. "It is my responsibility to give unequivocal orders. If I had been brave enough to turn away from the gunman long enough to face you and give the order clearly or if I had drawn and raised my sabre as if we were on a battlefield, this wouldn't have happened. In the circumstances, Colin, your reading of my command was the correct one. Even so, while I was still upright, you had no authority to interpret it either way, and no cause to give independent orders of your own."

Willoughby looked visibly relieved. One of the ensigns, not quite as young as Parker, went over to the nearest bush and retched.

"Perhaps we saved the crown the bother of a trial and the cost of a gibbet," another offered, keeping his gaze well away from the body.

Finally Willoughby glanced down at the corpse. The face had been smashed by one of the bullets, and several others had ripped through the torso and abdomen, which were now oozing blood and innards. Wherever the man's eyes were, they no longer gleamed.

Willoughby sat down suddenly and put his forehead on his knees.

"Remember, Colin," Hilliard said consolingly, "this fellow here put a bullet through Mr. Moncreiff, an innocent gentleman who wouldn't've harmed a mite if it was biting him."

Marc was bent over the body, trying with some difficulty to pry the gun out of the old man's death-grip. He stood up with the offending weapon in his hand. The look on his face was grim. "And this man, gentlemen, may be as innocent as Moncreiff himself."

"What do you mean?" Willoughby said.

"This gun has not been fired," Marc said. "Not today and, by the look of the barrel, not in my lifetime."

Chapter Two

"What the hell have you people gone and done?"

It was the man with the troll's bellow. He and six or seven others were scrambling up the last few yards of the slope towards Marc and his men. Their gaze was upon the body, crumpled on its own threshold. The farmer with the big voice took two threatening strides towards Marc, then stopped, not because Marc's right hand had gone to the haft of his sabre, but because he had caught a close-up glimpse of the victim's smashed face.

"Sweet Jesus," he cried. "You've gone and killed Crazy Dan. You've gone and massacred him!" Behind Marc, his men shuffled and tried not to look – all the fight suddenly gone out of them. They glanced about, more bewildered than angry.

"That crazy old fellow raised his gun and pointed it at Lieutenant Edwards," Ensign Hilliard said, stepping up to their accuser. "His finger was on the trigger. We had no way of knowing it was not primed and loaded. The lieutenant here risked his life trying to talk the man into surrendering. We had no choice but to fire off a volley." Hilliard spoke formally, as if he were rehearsing what he would say in his deposition to an investigating magistrate.

"But Crazy Dan wouldn't hurt a flea. Everybody 'round here knows that."

"We're not from around here, sir," Marc said. "To us he was a man with a gun fleeing a murder scene."

"But the shot came from the other side of the square!"

"What is your name, sir?"

"Luke Bethel. I got a farm farther up the hogback on the Tenth Concession."

"What happened here, Mr. Bethel, is a tragic misadventure. There will no doubt be a proper inquest, and you and your companions may well be called as witnesses."

"How can we be certain, sir," Hilliard said, "that the old geezer didn't hide the murder weapon in his cabin or toss it away somewhere in the bush? We don't know for sure that this old crock of a gun was the one he had in his hand when he fell out of the tree."

"Yes," said Willoughby, a burst of hope rising in his stricken face. "If he was really crazy he might have –"

Luke Bethel cut him short. "Crazy Dan hasn't taken that musket out of his right hand in the past twelve years."

"What do you mean?" Marc said, glancing down and noting that the dead man's fingers were still seized in a gripping rictus.

"Crazy Dan come into these parts in 1816, after the war with the United States. He homesteaded about a mile south of here. Never married. Kept to himself, but was never unfriendly. He was said to be some kind of hero at the Battle of Lundy's Lane. One day he come into the general store – not in Danby's Crossing but the one on Yonge Street below the tollgate – and said he'd killed fifteen good men with the gun he was totin'. He swore he wouldn't ever kill a livin' thing again, not a steer nor a chicken, and he vowed to carry the musket with him everywheres – unloaded and detriggered – to remind people of the evils of war."

"My God," Ensign Parker exclaimed from the rear where he had been violently sick. "We've shot a hero of Lundy's Lane!"

"He was fightin' on the American side," Bethel said.

"Well, then, if *every*body knew this, why were people in the crowd yelling at him to stop and egging us on after him?" Marc said, suddenly confused.

"Only a few of us in this region actually knew Crazy Dan. Even after he give up the farm and moved out here five or six years ago, whenever he did go to town – which wasn't often 'cause his old neighbours brought food for him up here – he went to the Lansing junction up north on Yonge Street. Everybody up that way knew the old guy, and knew he was harmless."

"Then how on earth did he get to Danby's and climb a tree while surrounded by a hundred people?"

Bethel shrugged. He turned to the others. "We don't rightly know. Maybe he just followed some of the youngsters and joined them up there in the tree. He sometimes borrowed old Frawley's pinto, so that's how he got himself into town. He coulda been there all night. There wasn't any rhyme or reason to what he might do or what might've got into his head. Me, I figure that gunshot spooked him. He might've thought he was back at Lundy's Lane or the ghosts of the men he killed were comin' back to get him."

"But *you* were there!" Marc said. "Why didn't you warn us?"

"That's just it," Bethel said. "I did. I was yellin' 'Stop' at you from the minute you left the square. But your horses were too fast for us. We couldn't catch up to you."

Marc sighed. "We did hear you, but we assumed you were shouting at the culprit."

"We're used to havin' our opinions ignored," someone from the group of farmers remarked. It was Alvin Chambers, who had hung back until now.

"But *you*, sir," Marc said sternly to him, "were standing three feet away from me at the edge of the bush back there, and failed to inform me of what or whom I might expect to see when I arrived here. I demand that you explain yourself."

Bethel gave Chambers a puzzled look before the latter replied: "We are not in the habit of takin' orders from the military or the grandees of the Family Compact, especially when they're given in a patronizin' tone. We don't tug our forelocks in this province – *sir*."

"I could have you haled before a magistrate," Marc snapped.

"And I'll tell him I was in the process of informin' you about Crazy Dan when you hopped on your high horse and galloped away."

"Well, I only hope you're pleased with the results of your umbrage," Marc said, glancing pointedly at Crazy Dan's bullet-ravaged body.

"Sir, I still think we ought to have a look inside the cabin," Hilliard said. "Just to be sure."

"You're right, Ensign." Marc nodded to Bethel, and the two of them went into the old fellow's hovel.

It was a stinking shambles. Marc's gorge rose as they picked gingerly through the detritus and ruins of one man's life. There were no guns or bullets or powder or any indication that there ever had been. No animal skin adorned the floor or walls. No bone had been gnawed and discarded: the rotting food was entirely vegetable. Crazy Dan had kept his vow.

"Look at this, would ya?" Bethel whistled under his breath.

Marc came over to him. On a stump table in one corner lay five pieces of hardwood in various stages of being carved. Marc picked up what appeared to be the only finished figure: no bigger than a baby's fist, it was an exquisitely rendered bird in flight. He held it up to the light in the doorway. "It's a dove," he said.

"For peace," Bethel said.

As Marc and Bethel left the hut, Willoughby and the others looked at Marc. He shook his head slowly. Then he turned towards the farmers: "I'll report everything that happened here directly to Sir Francis, and he'll take matters into his own hands. Will you see that this man is given a proper burial?"

"We will," Bethel said.

"Damn right," Chambers said. "Out here, we take care of our own."

As the Governor's guard rode back towards Danby's Crossing less hurried and much less assured than they had been riding out, Marc's mind was in turmoil. Within the space of an hour, he had witnessed a respected citizen and member of the government murdered; he had organized a pursuit with dispatch and discipline; he had drawn judiciously upon the advice of his men and the local folk (with one forgivable exception, perhaps); he had improvised a plan of attack-and-capture that failed only because no one could have foreseen that the musket aimed point-blank at him was not really lethal and its possessor not really a suspected assassin; he had put his own life on the line twice; and, alas, he had contributed to the death of an innocent man, a harmlessly demented veteran of the wars who carved miniature doves.

Marc's heart ached, not because he would soon have to face his superior and make his awkward explanation, and not because he would have to bend the truth just a little to protect his men, whose own motives could not be questioned, but because at the last millisecond before he thought the old fellow was about to pull the trigger, Marc had *known*. That was the tragedy of it all.

Not the least of his problems now was the bald fact that someone other than Crazy Dan had murdered Langdon Moncreiff. Not only was the felon unapprehended, but in their haste to pursue the obvious suspect they had given the real assassin more than an hour to make his getaway. Moreover, any clues he might have left around the square were certain to have been trampled by the curious spectators. The trail would be stone cold. And because Moncreiff was a member of the Executive Council (and all the controversy associated with that body and its relations with the Governor), such an arrogant and outrageous assassination could not go unpunished. What is more, time would be short, for the first polling in the upcoming election was less than two weeks away. Marc dearly wished to curse the Fates, but he knew it would be a waste of good breath: the fiasco of the afternoon had been of his own making.

When they rode up to the hitching posts in front of the Danby Inn, Marc noticed right away that the Governor's carriage was gone. He looked quickly over the square. Fewer than a dozen people remained, most of them moving purposefully from shop to shop or gathered on the wooden sidewalk, gossiping. A few youngsters of indeterminate gender hovered about the deserted hustings: curious and delightfully appalled. Marc waved his weary troop towards Danby's saloon, and then entered the lobby of the inn proper.

Angus Withers rose from one of the settees and greeted Marc with a gruff smile. "Did you catch the bugger?"

"He's dead," Marc said.

"Good. Save us all a lot of trouble."

"I'm afraid not, sir."

Marc led him back to the settee and briefly sketched out the near-farcical events regarding the shooting of Crazy Dan.

"You'll have to tell Sir Francis immediately," Withers said with a snap of his jaw.

"Why did he leave?" Marc said.

"He felt it was his personal responsibility to inform Mrs. Moncreiff of her husband's tragic death. Maxwell went with him – and in such a godawful rush he left the women behind. I stayed, of course, to give the body a careful going over."

"Why did Mr. Maxwell leave his wife and daughter out here?"

"Well, he *is* Moncreiff's brother-in-law, you know."

Marc raised an eyebrow.

Withers grinned thinly, though it was not apparent why. His thick, permanently arched brows gave him a look of perpetual irony – part amusement and part censure. "Didn't know, eh? If you're going to serve the panjandrums of the Family Compact, as I do, then you'll have to get to know who's related to whom on the royal tree and who *wants* to be related to whom."

"I'm learning, sir."

"Anyway, to answer your question, the Receiver General had urgent business in the city, beyond consoling his sister-in-law. More to the point, he often finds Mrs. Maxwell and his daughter more ballast than he needs for most occasions. He practically leapt into the viceregal carriage onto the Governor's lap. But don't look so worried. Mr. and Mrs. Danby have been entertaining the abandoned females, in a pathetic effort, I presume, to compensate for the social catastrophe of the afternoon."

"How will they get home?"

"Old Danby has offered to take us in his barouche to Yonge Street, where, if his horses are as well bred as he claims, we'll arrive in time to catch Weller's coach from Newmarket."

"And the body?"

"Sir Francis will arrange everything in that regard. I shouldn't be surprised if the dear old soul is given a state funeral – considering the circumstances." He arched his brows to their limit. "By the way, even though he assumed that you would capture the assassin, Sir Francis did ask me to convey his distinct wish that you, and you alone, were to be put in charge of all matters pertaining to Moncreiff's death. Furthermore, he wants a full report from you tonight, even if you have to have him wakened."

"I see," Marc said, though he wasn't sure that he did. There were city and county magistrates and, he had heard, a special Toronto constabulary modelled on the London "bobbies." "This is surely not a military affair, sir?"

"Ah, one more thing you have yet to learn. Although he was barely robust enough to lift a pen or his wife's skirt, Langdon Moncreiff was a major in the people's militia, that vast weaponless fighting force that alone stands between us and pandemonium in the radical townships."

"Well, whatever the reason for the Governor's trust in me, I still have a murder to solve, don't I?"

"I'm afraid you do."

"Then I'd better get at it."

"Before you do, Lieutenant, our 'Ariadne' and her offspring desire you to pay them your respects. They're in the sitting room, through that door."

"Ah, it is so kind of you to see us, under such dreadful circumstances." Mrs. Maxwell beamed at Marc from her reclining position on a sofa. "Chastity, my dear, you will remember Lieutenant, then Ensign, Edwards from the Governor's Ball at the Grange last, ah, when was it?"

"October," Marc said, bowing slightly to acknowledge the younger woman.

"My, what a prodigious memory you have, young man, doesn't he, sweetie?" Mrs. Maxwell turned up the beam in her dark eyes slightly, then dropped her gaze to her extensive bosom in a parody of coquettishness.

"Miss Maxwell and I danced the galliard, as I recall," Marc said.

"So we did, Lieutenant," Miss Maxwell said without a blush or dropped eye.

"In what way may I be of assistance in this tragic business, Mrs. Maxwell?" Marc said with more politeness than he felt. "I have just learned from Dr. Withers that Councillor Moncreiff was your brother-in-law. Please accept my sincere condolences."

"Thank you, sir," she replied, and pulled a lace hanky out of the folds of her elaborate skirts, but it found no tear to wipe away when it reached her left cheek. "And do call me Prudence, otherwise I shall begin to think myself old, and beyond those pleasures reserved inexplicably for the young."

Chastity quickly changed the subject. "We thought you might wish to ask us a few questions about dear Uncle Langdon." Her voice caught in her throat, and cracked. Marc offered her his own handkerchief, and she sat down wearily on a sofa across from her mother. Chastity Maxwell was as lithe as her mother was sumptuous, with pale-grey eyes and flaxen hair. Her angular features, like her father's, revealed more character than beauty. Last October at the Grange she had tripped her way through the intricate galliard with Marc, and though not truly attracted to one another (who knew why in such matters?), they had enjoyed the pleasure of the dance. Unfortunately, Marc's card had been filled, as it invariably was, and they had not danced together again.

Marc turned to Prudence and soon became aware that the blush on her cheek was not only rouge but also the after-effect of drink. Behind her on a tea trolley sat a near-empty decanter of red wine and a single smudged goblet. The Danbys had been entertaining the visiting grandees with vehemence.

"What I need to know, ma'am –"

"*Prudence*, please – though my mama always said I had none to speak of."

"Do you know of anyone who might wish to kill your brother-in-law? Did he have political enemies? Rivals who might be jealous of his recent appointment to the Executive Council?"

Prudence Maxwell laughed, a snorting sneeze of a laugh that she belatedly turned into a ladylike cough, which gave her a plausible excuse for waving her hanky about. "No, no, you won't find anything in that direction. And even though Chastity and I have seen little of him and my sister Flora in the past few years – now that's another story and one that has no bearing on the dreadful events of this day – I did know him very well in his youth. And it is my considered view that Langdon could never work up an opinion strong enough to make a monkey fart, let alone a decent enemy or two. Now if it'd been my Ignatius shot, God forbid, I could've given you a dozen names."

When Marc looked shocked at this, she added with relish, "How else do you think the bastard got rich and feared by lesser men?"

"Mother, please stop. You're overwrought."

Prudence turned to her daughter, squinted grotesquely, as if she had momentarily lost her sight or had failed to recognize the young woman across from her. Marc saw now that she was very drunk, but just as he stepped over to offer her some assistance (like holding her chin off her chest), she winched her eyes wide open and leered up at him. Her voice was a loud slur: "Hell, honey, I ain't been wrought over in a long, long time."

Chastity was up instantly, her tears forgotten. "I'll call Mrs. Danby and the maids," she said briskly to Marc. "We've got to get her to a bed. Our coach arrives in less than an hour."

"You'll be all right?"

"I'm used to it."

Marc was seated on the front bench of the hustings exactly where he had been sitting when Moncreiff was shot. The platform was no more than four feet above ground. And though Moncreiff had been snoozing upright in the second row, he could have been seen by any marksman at or above the level of the hustings floor. Luke Bethel out at Crazy Dan's cabin had claimed the sound of the shot had come from the other side of the square, which must mean the eastern side. The boardwalk that surrounded the square was a foot high, and at least a dozen people had been standing on benches in front of the shops: that extra elevation could have been enough. If so, then anyone near the general store, the livery stables, the blacksmith's, or the harness shop – or in the alleyways in between – might be a witness. He would need to question every merchant and tradesman about who had been standing within or near their shops at the time of the shooting. Even then, the presence of so many strangers could easily make any interrogation fruitless. Add to the mix the probability that ninety per cent of the onlookers were Reform sympathizers who would be disinclined to answer questions from Tory investigators about the death of a Tory.

While Marc was willing to take Prudence Maxwell's dismissive description of her brother-in-law at face value, she was unlikely to know much about his political or financial affairs – or his personal peccadilloes for that matter. Like it or not, he would have to probe into the man's life in a manner that was sure to enrage the power-brokers in the Family Compact (of which Moncreiff was a nominal member) and ruffle feathers just about everywhere else.

"Would you care for a smoke?" Angus Withers sat down beside Marc and offered him a cigar similar to the one he was puffing on.

"No, thank you."

"I find a good smoke helps me think. Either that or it just anaesthetizes the thought processes to the point where I don't give a damn any more."

"I wanted to ask you, Dr. Withers, about the wound, if you don't mind."

"That's why I came out. The ladies and I – well, only one of them can be legitimately termed so – have to be off for Yonge Street in half an hour."

"What was the angle of entry? It might help me determine the vantage point of the shooter."

"Unless the poor devil was lying sideways on his bench –"

"He wasn't. He was dozing, but otherwise perfectly upright."

"Then the bullet struck him just under the right shoulder, broke through a couple of ribs, ripped out his lungs, and exited through the fleshy muscle above the left kidney. Only the lungs were hit, no other organ."

"So he had to have been shot somewhat from the side, the right side."

"And from a point considerably above where we are now perched."

While Dr. Withers worked on his cigar, Marc scrutinized the eastern edge of the square. There was only one place the gunman could have been for that trajectory, and, even then, he would have to have been a crack shot. If indeed Langdon

Moncreiff had been the target. That he might not have been was a thought too terrible to contemplate.

"Thank you, Doctor. At least I know where to begin."

And with that, Marc strode deliberately towards the harness shop.

CHAPTER THREE

"Good afternoon, Sergeant," the harness-maker boomed cheerily, coming out to greet Marc on the wooden walk in front of his shop. "We been expectin' someone like yerself to come callin', haven't we, Sarah-Mae?"

Sarah-Mae, as tiny as her husband was gargantuan, poked her bonneted pink face out from behind her better half.

"I'm Phineas Kimble, harness-maker to three townships for twenty-two years." He threw out a hand the size of a pig's rump. He towered over Marc, who was himself almost six feet and accustomed to peering downwards when he talked.

"How do you do, sir?" Marc said. "I'm *Lieutenant* Edwards, and I've been asked by Governor Head to discover who committed the heinous murder of Councillor Langdon Moncreiff earlier today." Kimble's handshake was surprisingly gentle, the fingers as supple as the leather he worked for a living.

"I don't reckon the Governor does too much *askin'*," Kimble grinned.

"Do you want to come in, Lieutenant Edwards?" Sarah-Mae said in a soft, musical voice. "I've just made some tea."

"Officers in the British army don't sip *tea* at five in the afternoon, Sari-girl. Why don't you just whisk on into my study and fetch us a bottle of the best brandy?"

"Nothing, please," Marc said. "I merely wish to ask you and your wife some questions about the shooting. It will only take a minute or two."

"Well, sir, we saw it all," Sarah-Mae volunteered. "Didn't we, Phinn? The whole, horrible thing. I near to fainted right here on the walk."

"I caught her just in time, though, as you can see fer yerself, there ain't much to catch!"

"We was standin' here watchin' the proceedin's from about two o'clock onwards, Phinn and me and our three eldest."

"We closed up shop like everybody else on the square," Phineas added. "We got a better view by standin' on one of our benches."

"And a lot of others did likewise," Marc said. "There must've been about three dozen people around the edge of the square with a bird's-eye view of the murder."

"Surely, then, somebody saw somethin', Sergeant," Kimble said. "All *we* could see from here is the old fella rear up like he'd been rammed you-know-where with a hot poker and then crumple backwards with a big swatch of blood under his arm. Then all hell broke loose."

"Did you see the old fellow run past the general store with a gun in his hand?" Marc said quickly, then stared intently at Kimble's raw-boned face as he reached for an answer.

"Well, now, funny you should ask me that," he drawled. Was he stalling? Marc wondered. "Sarah-Mae didn't see a thing fer several minutes, but when I looked up from steadyin' her, I did see the old geezer sprintin' fer Bill Frawley's pinto by the stables. Looked to me like Crazy Dan, though I ain't seen him in a dog's age." He paused and returned Marc's searching stare.

Marc hesitated, then said, "It *was* Crazy Dan. But he didn't do any shooting."

"I thought not. Still, I found it awful puzzlin' at the time."

"Oh, why is that?"

"Well, Sari here figured she heard a crack like a gunshot somewheres nearby, but the baby'd started to cry back inside the shop and my boys was makin' a considerable racket and the crowd was just startin' to applaud, so she wasn't sure – but then when I seen Crazy Dan doin' his act and everybody and his aunt hollerin' at him to stop . . . well, I just figured she must've been wrong about it."

Sarah-Mae was bobbing her pink chin in agreement.

"Did *you* not hear the shot?" Marc said to Kimble.

"Can't say as I did."

"Phinn don't always hear too good in June," Sarah-Mae said by way of explanation.

"Hay fever and devilish terrible sinus," Phineas explained. "Plugged up like a constipated cow." To Marc, his ears looked as if they were too big to be plugged by anything.

"Well, you'll not be overly surprised, then, to learn that we have good grounds for believing that the assassin's bullet came from the opening up there in your garret."

Harness-maker and wife looked up slowly, in tandem and in joint puzzlement. "You mean the attic?" Phineas said.

"Yes."

"But there ain't been nobody up there since Cecil was born ten years ago," Sarah-Mae said in what appeared to be genuine surprise.

Marc turned to Phineas: "Would you be kind enough to take me up there?"

"If that's what you want. We're always pleased to be able to help an officer in King Billy's service. Ain't we, sweetheart?"

Sarah-Mae bobbed her chin, then added, "But you may have to *fly* there."

As Marc stared upwards at the back of the establishment, he saw the problem. The shop rooms of the business occupied the first floor, and the Kimbles lived in the apartment that comprised the second floor. A rickety ladder led up the outside wall to a small Spanish-style balcony that had long since lost its ironwork.

"When Sarah-Mae and me first come here, that ladder was the only way we could get from the shop to our bedrooms and parlour," Phineas explained patiently. "After one arse-freezin' winter, I cut a hole and built a proper set of stairs inside the house."

"What about the attic room?"

"You got up there through a hatch in the parlour ceiling. We used to store saddles and extra harnesses up there, but so many bats and raccoons got in that after a while I just sealed up the hatch and plastered over her. And as far as I know, nobody's been up there since. Even the coons seem to have found better spots to batten down in."

"How would you get up there if you really had to?"

Kimble looked at Marc as if he thought this were a trick question. After a pause, he said, "Can't ever see why I'd want to do such a fool thing, but if ever I did, I'd use that vine growin' up alongside and hoist myself up to the back window there. The vine's as thick as Sari's wrist and there's never been glass in that window."

"Then that's what I'll do."

"'Course, the balcony could crumble as soon as you put yer big toe on it."

Marc took this as an example of the man's humour. "We are positive that the shot came from that room, so I must examine it carefully."

"Then I better go with you," Phineas said quickly.

"Suit yourself," Marc said.

They moved over to the foot of the ladder.

Marc whistled. "Someone's been on this ladder recently. That break is fresh."

"Coulda been one of the boys, or the neighbour kids."

Marc ignored this and stepped onto a sound rung. Once on the balcony, he immediately spotted, in the inch-thick dust on the plank flooring, unmistakable signs of bootprints, though they were smudged and gave no indication of what boots had made them. But they were man-size, and fresh.

"It wasn't a youngster who made these," Marc said as Phineas crawled up beside him.

"And it sure as hell wasn't me!" Phineas raised a giant boot into a smooth patch of dust to make his point.

"And now we shinny our way up *there*," Marc said, grasping the vine and giving it a trial tug with both hands. In this sort of gymnastic, he had only to draw upon his innumerable childhood experiences playing pirates or crusaders on his adoptive father's estate. Within seconds he had scaled the wall and hauled himself through the paneless window of the garret. Then he turned to give the floundering harness-maker a hand up.

While Phineas was surveying a room he had obviously not seen for some years, Marc went immediately to the opening on the far wall. The late-afternoon sun poured into the dusty room and illuminated every detail there. Smudged footprints led directly to the rotting sill. Marc ran his fingers along the ledge and paused.

"Could be a groove left there by a musket barrel," Phineas said, peering over Marc's shoulder. "Or any other kind of tool."

"Perhaps, but *this* is used in only *one* kind of tool," Marc said, holding up a wrapping that had been bitten off a paper-sheathed bullet. "And here's the mark on it."

"You can tell the kind of gun from that?"

"That and several other things," Marc said. "The shooter, as you can see, was a good fifty yards away from the hustings as he knelt here and rested the barrel of the gun in the notch on the sill. No smooth-bore gun would be accurate from this distance, so our assassin must have used a rifled bore, which would account not only for its accuracy but for the damage it did to Moncreiff. The marking on the wrapper suggests that the rifle is of French design, a *modèle* of some recent make copied by the Americans. I'd hazard a guess that this is a U.S. army rifle manufactured within the past five or six years."

Phineas took a minute to absorb this series of lofty deductions. "So you're tellin' me that some Yankee freebooter climbed up into *my* attic while Sarah-Mae and me were standin' no more'n ten feet below on the sidewalk and blasted the bejesus out of the Councillor?"

"I expect that he was counting on the general hubbub and every eye being directed at the hustings. No doubt that is why he waited until the precise moment that the Governor was about to rise and make his speech." Or, Marc thought, the owner of these premises had become conveniently and temporarily deaf. "Also, at three o'clock, this window would still be in the shade of the overhang. With dark clothes on and the gun rubbed black, he would be hard to see. And he could be out that back window and down the vine to the ground in ten seconds. I expect he broke that rung in his haste to get away."

"With nothin' but bush behind us," Phineas said.

"And it would have to have been somebody, wouldn't it, who knew this place was here and never used, and was readily accessible."

"With a hundred-dollar Yankee rifle." Phineas began to sound doubtful.

"Well, that does narrow down the possibilities. But fifteen minutes ago I was contemplating the prospect of going house to house in search of a needle in a haystack."

The two men made their way back down the vine and ladder. As he stepped to the ground beside Marc, Phineas said, "Well, at least you found the haystack."

Marc was already studying the thick bush that began not more than ten yards behind the harness shop. For someone who knew the area, it would provide the perfect escape route. The assassin must have known both the terrain and the idiosyncrasies of Phineas Kimble's three-storey establishment. A new thought struck him. "By the way, do you have anyone helping you with your harness-making?" he called after Phineas, who had turned towards the corner of the building.

Phineas paused, or froze: it was hard to say which. He swung his huge body around and by the time he was facing Marc his face was lit up by a grin. "Now there's a good question, Sergeant. I am real happy you asked me that, 'cause somebody along the square would've told you sooner or later, and I'd have looked the darn fool fer not rememberin' it myself."

"Then you do have hired help."

"I *did* have hired help, and that's why it slipped my memory somewhat just now."

"How long ago?"

"A fella with the odd handle of Philo Rumsey worked as my assistant fer two years – up to last winter. He was a dandy worker, mind, but not rcliable."

"He drank?"

"No more'n anyone else 'round here, though that's plenty, I reckon. But he wouldn't show up much of the time – 'specially when the deer was runnin'."

"He was a hunter?"

"And a damn fine one: he could pick a fly off the wall of the livery stable from this very spot."

"What kind of gun did he use?"

"Well, it wasn't no Yankee bluestockin', I can tell you that. It was an old musket from one of the wars long past. Rumsey's as poor as a church mouse, with a woman and six kids to feed."

"Yet you fired him last winter."

"Indeed, I done just that. But then I took to feelin' sorry fer his missus and the bairns, so I let him come in now and again and do some piecework for me when I got more orders than I can handle."

Marc asked the next question and held his breath for the response: "Then Philo Rumsey is still hereabouts?"

"Of course he is. He lives in a cabin about a hundred yards that way, straight into the middle of the bush – where he likes it."

"Why didn't you tell me all this at the outset?"

Phineas Kimble grinned again, and this time he let the twinkle remain in place. "Well, now, how can I answer a question before it's asked?"

Trying to contain both his irritation and his rising excitement, Marc peered into the shadows ahead of him in the bush.

"All you gotta do is step between them two birches," Phineas called after him. "The path is as plain as the pestle on a pig. Walk straight on and keep an eye out fer the chiminey smoke."

"Thanks for your help."

"You're welcome, but I oughta mention that Philo himself ain't likely to be at home right this moment."

"What?"

"I heard he went down to visit his dyin' mother – last week."

"Down *where*?" Marc barked. "Dammit, man, tell me where!"

Phineas was unperturbed by the shift in tone: "Down to Buffalo, where he was born."

Margaret Rumsey was perched on the edge of a log stool like an emaciated sparrow watching an owl measure it for the kill: wary, fearful, resigned. What she was particularly afraid of, Marc wasn't sure. The spectre of an officer in tunic and feathered cap standing – however politely or diffidently – in the sanctuary of one's home was enough to strike terror into the most innocent heart. But, when Marc had first entered the gloomy, smoke-filled single room of the Rumsey cabin, its mistress had seemed more flustered than scared, more embarrassed than awed. The symptoms of her impoverishment and misery were everywhere evident: the grimy, runny-nosed children who clutched at her apron and dared to peek up at the uniformed stranger, the barrenness of the room itself. Marc could see only a few pieces of stick furniture, half a dozen vermin-infested straw pallets, and a charred kettle that had fallen into a sputtering fire. Between ineffectual attempts at keeping her two eldest from sidling up to Marc and brushing at his jacket as if it were a cardinal's robe, Margaret Rumsey had been, at first, as curious as she was guarded. She had even managed a smile when Marc had reached down and ruffled the hair of one of his admirers. Marc had winced inwardly as he realized with a shock that this woman, gaunt and pale in dirt-streaked rags, had once been pretty – and happy. But as soon as he had begun asking questions about her husband's whereabouts, her pinched brown eyes drew back into their hollow sockets. Did she *know*? Or was she merely afraid of what she didn't know but strongly suspected?

"You say your husband left for Buffalo to be with his dying mother?"

"Yes, sir, last week. Elmer, don't be touchin' the gentleman's sword!"

"Do you remember the exact day he left?"

Margaret Rumsey paused, as if thinking hard. "I lose track of the days of the week. With these young'uns one day is t'same as the next."

"Was it before or after the last Sabbath?"

"Oh, we don't go to service . . . no more." Her eyes widened. "But they're all baptized! *I* saw to that."

"I was merely trying to help you recall when Mr. Rumsey left for Buffalo."

"'Twas Tuesday last, I remember now, 'cause Mr. Danby, God bless 'im, had me over to the inn to help with the clean-up. He calls on me when there's a gentlemen's gatherin' or lodge meetin'." Marc looked skeptical, and she added with a blush that brought some colour into her grey pallor for the first time, "I don't go over to the inn lookin' like this. Mr. Danby give me a uniform." Then as if further explanation were called for, she said, "No sense in puttin' on anythin' decent 'round this dump. The littl'uns'd just puke or slobber all over it."

"That would make it exactly a week ago, then," Marc prompted.

Margaret nodded. Then with a trembling lip she said, "But you ain't told me yet why I haveta answer all the Governor's questions."

"A man was murdered this afternoon, in the square. Did you know that?"

Some of her fear drained away, and Marc could see that she was relieved, though still wary. "I heard about it. Everybody has. But Philo couldn't have had nothin' to do with that awful thing, he's been gone since Tuesday last."

"And you're certain he hasn't come back?"

"His mama's dyin' of womb cancer or somethin'. All his family lives in Buffalo. He said he'd be gone fer two weeks or more. He's left us no food, and I've gone and spent the last of Mr. Danby's pay on medicine fer the baby. If he'd've come home, these young'uns wouldn't be whinin' fer their supper, now would they?"

Marc thanked her and turned to go. "You will let Mr. Danby know the minute your husband comes home. I will need to talk to him." If Philo Rumsey were indeed in Buffalo – and until that was verified independently Marc was going to assume that his prime suspect had contrived an alibi for himself – then it was quite possible that before leaving he had passed along crucial information regarding the set-up of his sometime employer's unused attic and was, therefore, at least an accomplice to some degree or other. Accomplice or assassin, Philo Rumsey was undoubtedly the key to solving this puzzle.

At the door Marc thought of a final question. "Did your husband own an army rifle by any chance?"

"Philo's a good huntsman, sir, the best in these parts, else we'd starve. But he uses the Kentucky musket my daddy give him when we got wedded. And he makes his own bullets right here in this room."

"Philo was never in the army, back in New York?"

"No, sir. He was only eighteen when he begun courtin' me, and we left Buffalo to come up here and start a new life. But Philo weren't much fer farmin', and we lost the homestead. That's when he took up harness-makin' and brung us here."

"Well, thank you once again. If you'll be kind enough to inform Danby of your husband's return, he will pass the news along to me."

"Philo's brothers're in the army, though. They're doin' real good, I'm told."

My God, Marc thought, I've found the murderer or murderers in a single hour of careful investigation! He grinned from ear to ear, and the children, seeing this, joined him. Marc reached into his pocket and pulled out a handful of pennies, then tossed them joyfully upwards. The children jumped up to grab them, giggling and hysterical with delight. Marc bowed to Margaret Rumsey and strode away through the bush towards the square.

His heart sang. Then it sank. Suddenly he was shaken by a surge of helpless, nameless rage.

Dr. Withers and Maxwell *mère* and *fille* were gone by the time Marc got back to the inn. Briefly he asked Garfield Danby to relay any news of Philo Rumsey's reappearance in the township, bade goodbye to him and Mrs. Danby (who looked as if she had suffered shell shock at Waterloo), and made his way to the saloon.

Seven of the young officers were gathered in a semicircle around the bar singing lustily with charged glasses. On Marc's arrival they stopped singing in mid-phrase, until, at an approving nod from their commanding officer, they started up again and continued until the song was satisfyingly finished.

Marc applauded theatrically, then said to the nearest man, "Ensign, please get the horses from the ostler. We've got to get back to Government House before dark."

"Yes, sir!"

"Where's Lieutenant Willoughby?" Marc asked.

Hilliard blanched, then stepped aside so that Marc could see past the bar to one of the gloomy corners of the saloon beyond. Parker and Willoughby appeared to be slumped comatose across a table, their arms dangling like knackered eels. A quart of brandy – two-thirds empty – teetered between them. The rest of the men, feeling chipper, had wisely stuck to watered claret.

"I wouldn't get too close to Parker," Hilliard warned. "He upchucked even before he started in on the brandy."

Marc went over to Willoughby and reached out to touch his shoulder. He was stopped, however, by a low droning that had been emanating from the two men all along but which he heard only now.

"They've been crooning away like that for the last hour," Hilliard said. "That's why we started singing. It got on our nerves."

Marc leaned over and listened.

"Innocent . . . innocent . . . no eyes . . . no eyes . . . innocent . . . innocent . . ." The words were thick-tongued and breathy but nonetheless distinct.

"I guess they just saw today more than they bargained for," Hilliard said helpfully. "Though Christ knows what either of them will do if we ever get into a real battle."

Marc let his hand rest on Willoughby's shoulder. "None of us knows that, Ensign. And maybe it's just as well."

The officer Marc had sent for the horses poked his head in the front door.

"All right, men. Check your gear and get ready to ride," Marc said.

"What'll we do with *these* fellows?" Hilliard said.

"Tie them to their saddles. A good jarring might bring them around," Marc smiled, and then helped Hilliard haul Willoughby upright. "It's all right, Colin. Everything's going to be fine – just as soon as we get you home."

At least, he hoped so.

Sir Francis had rented rooms for Marc and Colin at Mrs. Standish's boarding house on Peter Street, where they would be at his beck and call. And Marc dropped Willoughby onto that good woman's veranda before waving farewell to his troop as they continued towards the garrison. Then he rode up to King and Simcoe, where Government House stood in its six-acre park. He handed the chestnut mare to one of the waiting stableboys, and ran up the steps into the foyer. There was almost an hour of daylight left. With luck he would not have to wake up the Governor. For although Marc knew that Head would be eager to hear what he had learned about who might have shot Moncreiff, he was acutely aware that first he'd have to tell the Governor about the death of Crazy Dan. He didn't relish reporting this news to a groggy, half-awake superior.

He was met in the vestibule not by the duty-corporal but by Major Titus Burns, Sir Francis's military secretary. The old fellow winced as he grasped Marc's hand.

"Don't mind my rheumatism, old chap, it can't be helped, and what can't be cured must be endured."

"How is Sir Francis, Major? He's had a horrific day."

"So I've heard. But I expect he'll have worse before he has better."

"He commanded me to report on my day's investigative work as soon as I returned," Marc said.

"That would be inconvenient in the extreme," Burns chuckled. "He's gone off to an emergency meeting of the Executive Council."

"Then I'll wait here in my office," Marc said. "I have most urgent news for his ears only."

"I'm afraid the walls have ears in this house," Burns said. "But there's no need for you to wait. Sir Francis explicitly instructed me to send you home to a warm supper and a feather bed. Dr. Withers gave him and me an account of your abortive expedition following the tragic shooting of Councillor Moncreiff. He will want your first-hand version, of course. But there *is* an election pending, and tomorrow he will be tied up in meetings until eleven in the morning. He wants to see you in the inner sanctum at that hour precisely."

"I'll be there."

"So will I, Lieutenant. I'm never anywhere else."

The Widow Standish let her parlour curtain drop discreetly and opened the front door of her respectable boarding house. ("My husband, Chalmers, wouldn't have it any other way," she said more than once, "as he was a very particular gentleman, especially when it concerned the creature comforts of his beloved, God rest his soul." The dear departed had left her a well-built frame residence eminently suited to respectable boarders.)

"Oh, Lieutenant Edwards, it is you," she said, feigning surprise. "I was just putting the cat out for the night."

"Good evening, Mrs. Standish."

"My heavens, but you do look tuckered out."

The cat was nowhere to be seen. "It's been a very long day."

"Your walk from Government House was a pleasant one?" Widow Standish liked to work Government House and any of its doings, however peripheral, into any conversation.

"It's a beautiful June evening," Marc said, following his landlady and self-appointed guardian into the carpeted hallway.

"I've saved you some supper. It's on the hutch in the dining room. Just some cold beef and bread with a bit of cheese."

"I'll nibble at it later, if you don't mind."

"Oh, I see," she replied, lowering her voice and whispering, "He's still on his bed where I left him."

"He saw his first dead man today, I'm afraid, and it was not a pretty sight."

"Oh, I see," clucked Widow Standish. She looked relieved. "I thought it might've been just the drink."

Using a cotton cloth and fresh water from the dry sink, Marc managed to clean up Willoughby's face, and then he got him out of his uniform (which looked beyond rejuvenation, even by Maisie, Mrs. Standish's very dedicated maid-cook-and-launderer). Willoughby moaned now and again, but his eyes remained resolutely shut. Marc tugged a nightshirt over the young man's lean, well-muscled body and let him flop back on the bed. The night air was humid and still: he would need no covers.

As Willoughby's head hit the pillow, his eyes popped open, then closed again. But in the second or so that they remained open, they took in Marc bending over and the darkening room behind him. And what Marc thought he saw in Willoughby's face was fear.

"My God, old chum, but you've had one hell of a fright this day," Marc whispered.

Willoughby, blind and deaf to the world once more, began to breathe regularly and, from the outside at least, peacefully. His was an aesthetic face, fine-boned with fair skin as smooth as a debutante's. The brow was high and delicately veined, the hair – now matted and repulsive – was blond and curly, as his beard would be if he could grow one. Like this, with his eyes closed, he might have been mistaken for an adolescent, all promise and possibility. But when those grey eyes were open, Willoughby looked more like he had seen too much too soon, and Marc was never sure whether his suffering would erupt in words or action, or turn in upon itself.

Marc knew that Colin Willoughby had not begun his manhood years auspiciously. As the second son of a wealthy Buckinghamshire landowner, he was destined for the army or the church, but chose instead a more satisfying life in the gambling dens and whorehouses of London. Papa Willoughby promptly had him hog-tied and returned to the family castle, and after a good talking-to, he was shipped off to military school at Sandhurst. After which Willoughby *père* purchased a lieutenant's commission for him in the army, where *fils* was pleased to discover that dicing and wenching were neither uncommon nor unappreciated.

However, this happy state of affairs was spoiled by the catastrophe of his falling in love with a respectable young woman of high virtue, ample fortune, and great beauty. As Willoughby told the story whenever he'd had three mugs of whisky, his beautifully affluent Rosy ("pretty as a primrose, she was!") had placed unwarranted restrictions on the recreational habits of her fiancé (it had gotten that far, he insisted), and then despite his repeated vows to be forever faithful to her after the nuptials, she had jilted him without cause, explanation, or remorse – after the second reading of the banns! And his father, fearing the worst, wrote to his good friend Sir Francis Bond Head and – presto! – four months later, Willoughby found himself in Toronto, where, he had been assured, the climate was a sure cure for romance.

Sir Francis had realized the need to keep young Willoughby from the temptations of barracks life, and so, having made Marc his chief aide-de-camp on the recommendation of his predecessor, he had hit upon the strategy of appointing Willoughby as Marc's assistant, and renting rooms for the two of them nearby.

From that day late in January of this year, Marc had taken Willoughby under wing, playing the role of older brother and guardian. This arrangement had worked to the benefit of both. So far he had fallen off the wagon only once – at the Governor's Winter Gala when the sight of all those beautiful bare-shouldered young women dancing had reminded him painfully of what he had almost won and then thrown away. He had poured whisky into wine goblets and got himself belligerently drunk before the ball had ended, and it had taken Marc,

Hilliard, and two other burly officers to lug him to a carriage and haul him back to Mrs. Standish's, where he further humiliated himself by swinging wildly at Marc in front of their landlady and uttering a lot of gibberish – the only decipherable parts of which were oaths. Fortunately for Willoughby, the next day he had recalled none of the night's more memorable events. Since then, while he was occasionally sullen about the menial tasks given him around Government House (who wasn't?), his youthful high spirits and keen intelligence had made him an enjoyable addition to the tiny complement of officers at the Governor's residence. As for Marc, he was beginning to realize that he had found something he had not expected after a year in Upper Canada: a male friend his own age.

"But I don't know whether you'll make it as a soldier, old chum," Marc sighed and left the room quietly.

Chapter Four

The Lieutenant-Governor rose to greet Marc as he was shown into his office by a shuffling, sober-faced Major Burns. "Do come in, Marc. And take a seat. We have much to discuss, and I have given orders that we not be interrupted for at least the next hour, barring a catastrophe."

"I think we may have already had one, sir," Marc said as he sat down on the edge of a high-backed brocaded chair and let his boots settle into the thick carpet.

"I was thinking more along the lines of Fort York being blown up – again," Sir Francis quipped, indicating his knowledge of that disastrous event in the War of 1812.

Major Burns smiled at the witticism despite the rheumatic pain that had squeezed his numerous wrinkles into rigid parallels. He turned to go.

"Stay, please, Major. I may have need of your sage advice, and I wish you to take notes." Head sat down across from Marc at his gleaming cherrywood desk that occupied fully a third of the room. Upon it were scattered a dozen thick tomes punctuated by leather bookmarks and innumerable papers, graphs, and maps. Marc recognized the one book that lay open: the blue bound, 350-page *Seventh Report on Grievances*, an anti-government tirade written by a committee of the Reform-dominated Legislative Assembly. Major Burns took a seat off to one side beneath a mullioned window that caught the full force of the mid-morning sun.

"We'll begin with this business about Crazy Don –"

"Dan, sir," said the Major.

Sir Francis hid his irritation in a tight smile. "Crazy Dan, then."

"Would you like me to go over the events, sir?" Marc asked, as several beads of sweat formed between his shoulder blades and began to trickle down his back. "I made notes on them before I arrived here this morning."

"Not necessary, lad. As far as I am concerned, the book is closed on that unhappy adventure."

"But, sir, you have not yet heard my version of the story –"

At that moment there came a discreet tapping at the door and, before anyone could protest, the Governor's personal servant, in full livery, slipped silently into the room, slid a silver tea tray on the desk before Sir Francis, and slipped silently away again.

"Coffee, Major?" Burns nodded. "Marc?"

Marc was about to say no when Sir Francis said, "Of course, you will. I hear that Mrs. Standish serves only weak tea for breakfast." He poured three cups of coffee and placed on each saucer a tiny, jam-topped scone.

"I do intend to hear all about what happened yesterday from your own lips," Sir Francis said to Marc between nibbles on his scone. "From all accounts, it was an exploit worth the telling."

"And there is a perfectly logical explanation for the tragic consequences –"

"That is true. And you will perhaps be surprised to learn

that I already know all I need to know about how and why Crazy *Dan* was shot."

Major Burns, his fingers stiffened by pain, spilled his coffee into the saucer.

"Major Burns and I – who rise with the sun – have been in this office since eight o'clock this morning, closeted with two sleepy magistrates and a clerk who took depositions from each of the ensigns involved. They were hauled from their quarters one at a time and thoroughly interrogated here. Each of them signed a sworn statement relating his version of the events. We had hoped to include Lieutenant Willoughby, but Mrs. Standish told my messenger that he was *indisposed*." Sir Francis frowned over the word, attempted a rueful smile, and continued. "However, as it is apparent that he fired no shot himself and gave no order for the volley to be unleashed, we managed quite well without him."

Marc was about to explain the cause of Willoughby's indisposition but saw that Sir Francis considered it of no immediate relevance.

"The upshot of those interviews and affidavits is that the magistrates came to the conclusion that the death of this wretched creature was unfortunate but, in the circumstances, justified. No blame is to be assigned, and there is no need to drag Withers in for a formal inquest."

"Is that wise, sir?"

For a moment Sir Francis looked nonplussed, then said, "It is not a question of wisdom, Lieutenant, but of justice. A man fled a murder scene brandishing a gun. He had more than ample opportunity to stop and explain himself if he knew himself to be innocent. Upper Canada is not the republic to the south of us, where lynching and vigilante action are commonplace and condoned. This same man, as attested to by eight loyal officers, pointed a musket at you from ten paces. Were they to let him shoot you first, then release their volley? Especially when they swore upon this Bible that the order they heard was 'Fire!' "

"I think the young man is referring to the possible political fallout," Major Burns said quietly as soon as he was certain that Sir Francis had finished.

Sir Francis feigned astonishment, though his features were so nondescript that a casual observer could see only extreme shifts in emotion. Marc had already noted that Sir Francis used the natural calmness of his face and demeanour to telling effect in heated discussions. You had to watch his eyes carefully. "And what political fallout might that be? It was the magistrates who did the questioning, as is proper and customary. The affidavits are public court documents. Later today or tomorrow, you will add your sworn statement to the docket."

"The Lieutenant has studied law at the Inns of Court," Major Burns said.

"What I meant, sir," Marc said, "was that the farmers who followed us, and were in a way witnesses to most of the events under question, might wish to have their say at a formal inquest, even though I am fully confident, as you are, that no other conclusion would be reached than the one made here this morning."

"Purely a waste of time," Sir Francis said with some vehemence, "and you know from our previous conversations and my reports to Lord Glenelg in London that the time wasted here in the past eight years on committees and commissions and grievance petitions and the naming of this member and that in the Assembly has been the principal cause of the current deadlock and the hardening of positions on either side of every issue – petty or important."

"I agree, sir, but my hunch is that these men are supporters of the Reform party, and that they are quite capable of suggesting to all and sundry in York County that the magistrates, as instruments of the Executive and the Family Compact, simply protected their own by denying an inquest and aborting their right to testify."

"Let them feed whatever rumour mill they like! You've seen for yourself over the past week the effectiveness of my strategy of following the politicians of both parties onto the hustings no more than two days after their own nomination speeches or public debates. Grit or Tory, the voters are getting a chance to see the vast difference between, on one side, a politician with all his rant and thunder and, on the other, a statesman who takes no partisan position but, rather, occupies the same wide ground that King William himself would, were he to voyage to this colony – which is, after all, the surrogate terrain of Britain herself. You have seen first-hand how efficacious my direct appeal for loyalty, patience, and trust in their sovereign has been and how well my calm denunciation of all extremism has been received. The fact that most of the extremists are republican and that in that quarter also lies the greatest threat to the Crown does not have to be spoken aloud. Nor would it be proper for me as the King's representative to do so."

Marc nodded, and finished the last of his coffee. It was cold.

"And I fully believe that the fact that I was appointed by a Whig government – and was not automatically accorded membership in that claque of bankers, lawyers, and men of property they call the Family Compact – has made it not only more difficult for the fanatics on both sides, the Orange lunatics and the so-called Clear Grits, to label me partisan but also has given me credibility on the hustings and at the levees."

"Quite true, sir."

Sir Francis leaned back in his wing chair and took a deep breath, aware perhaps that he had just delivered a rostrum speech to two seated confederates in a small room. Then with a twinkle he said, more reflectively, "Oh, I know how many of those who now gather round me and cling to the royal hem once sniggered at my appointment: a half-pay major – down on his luck doing a hack job as commissioner of the poor law – daring to replace the dashing Sir John Colborne, high Tory and hero of Waterloo. But their skepticism then and their sycophancy now neither deters nor influences me. I was sent here by Lord Glenelg with a specific mission. And I intend to accomplish it. Let your farmers in York rant for a while. They'll come onside after the election, you'll see."

But would they? Marc wondered. It was imperative that the Governor have a less fractious Assembly if he were to begin to address the farmers' many grievances, but a Constitutionist sweep at the polls could have unforeseeable consequences. As Marc had learned in January during his investigation in Cobourg, the Upper Canadian farmer was righteously bitter, politically astute, and increasingly willing to take bolder, riskier action.

"Now, Major, if you'll take up your pen, I wish to sit back and hear Lieutenant Edwards's report on the assassination of Councillor Moncreiff. From what Dr. Withers intimated, you were about to follow up several promising avenues as he left you."

With the tragic business of Crazy Dan apparently closed, Marc recounted in precise detail his visit to Phineas and Sarah-Mae Kimble, his search of the attic room above the harness shop, and his discovery of Philo Rumsey's likely involvement. Sir Francis listened without interruption, his face impassive, while Major Burns scratched away with his quill pen.

"That was excellent work, Lieutenant," Sir Francis said when Marc had finished. "Outstanding work. Sir John's opinion of you, I see, was understated."

"Thank you, sir, but I am afraid we're only partway there.

Until we apprehend Philo Rumsey and question him, we cannot be certain that what seems obvious is actually true."

"It usually is, in my experience. But I take your point."

"And while I'm pretty certain it *was* Rumsey who pulled the trigger, or else a close confidant, there is the puzzling question of motive. Why would an out-of-work harness-maker who prefers to hunt deer murder Councillor Moncreiff in such a public place and in such a public manner?"

"A pertinent question, eh? Especially as we are in the middle of an election campaign and the murdered man was a member of my cabinet, so to speak."

"The possibility of this being a politically motivated killing seems likely, does it not?"

"You think the radical Reformers might be behind this atrocity?"

Marc did not reply. While he feared such a possibility for what it might do to the stability of the province, he had an even deeper fear, one that had occurred to him again as he had been making notes this morning in preparation for this interview. "Have you considered, sir, that Councillor Moncreiff may not have been the target?"

Sir Francis leaned forward and Major Burns dropped his pen. "What do you mean? You've just said this Philo fellow was a hunter and an expert marksman with a rifled weapon. Surely he knew at whom he was shooting."

"Well, sir, it only occurred to me an hour ago as I was repicturing in my mind the sequence of events just before the shot rang out."

"And?"

"And instead of rising from your seat as you appeared about to do, you dropped a paper and bent down to retrieve it."

No one spoke for several long seconds. Then Sir Francis laughed. "Nonsense! No one would *dare* assassinate the

King's representative. No British governor has ever been put at such risk, even in uncivilized places like the penal colonies of Van Diemen's Land. It is simply unthinkable – a preposterous notion!"

"I agree, sir, that it is difficult to fathom a British subject committing such an act, but the shooter in this case is a transplanted American with brothers currently in the U.S. army. Moreover, he is poor and disaffected; he may even be deranged. God knows who might have put him up to such a desperate business."

"All of which are relevant points, no doubt. But you are barking up the wrong tree, young man. Meantime, we do have a gentleman dead of a gunshot wound. It was Moncreiff who was actually murdered, so surely it would make sense to begin at least with the *assumption* that he was the intended victim and work out from that not-unreasonable position."

"Yes, sir. I am quite prepared to do just that."

"Good. And let's have no more foolish talk of de facto regicide. It's too early in the morning." His eyes bounced momentarily.

Marc carried on. "What I propose to do, then – with your approval, of course – is to discover if there is any connection between Councillor Moncreiff and Philo Rumsey. Perhaps some action recently taken by your new Executive Council affected Rumsey or his family negatively. Perhaps it was something a previous council did, and Rumsey decided to take revenge at the earliest opportunity. I recall that your itinerary for the York Township address and the names of the accompanying contingent were published in the *Upper Canada Gazette* a full ten days before the event."

"Yes, that was part of my strategy to win the ordinary folk over to the King's side, even before I officially dissolved the Assembly: to publicize my addresses widely and to include selected legislators to sit with me on the platform and share the limelight."

"Rumsey had, then, forewarning and the time to set up his alibi in Buffalo," Marc said. "In that regard, we'll have to have someone, from Fort George perhaps, slip across to New York State and check out Rumsey's dying mother."

"And try to ascertain whether Rumsey had connections with any republican fanatics over there. He might be a member of one of the Hunters' Lodges, the ones I read about in Sir John's report to me of your first investigation in January."

"That is always possible. But from the looks of his cabin and the wretched state of his family, I'd say not likely."

"Nevertheless, I'll send a request to Fort George to have the Rumsey clan checked out." Sir Francis gave a little sigh. "I suppose, though, we'll have to face the fact that if he did murder the Councillor, he may decide to stay in Buffalo or go farther inland where we'll never catch him."

"I don't think so, sir. His wife and six children are near to starvation. I believe he'll be back in the province within the next few days or so."

"But if he is that indigent, then I suppose you'll have to consider the possibility that someone might have paid him to murder Moncreiff."

"In which case there could be a personal motive."

"And that means you'll have to look into Moncreiff's private life." Sir Francis grimaced. "An unsavoury task, and one that will demand the utmost tact. Which is why I want *you* to undertake it. What do you propose to do first?"

"Well, sir, we need to have Rumsey's cabin watched day and night. As a hunter and long-time resident, he knows the area and the bush around it. He won't stroll across the square at Danby's Crossing and wave to his friends. Phineas Kimble, the harness-maker, will need to be questioned again, and anyone else up there who knew Rumsey, to get as much background information on him as we can. I myself will interview Councillor Moncreiff's brother-in-law, Ignatius Maxwell, and discreetly explore the victim's recent personal life and his political connections. And I thought of doing something unorthodox in order to discover how he was viewed politically by the Reformers."

"Unorthodox?"

"Yes. I was hoping to obtain your permission to interview William Lyon Mackenzie."

Mackenzie was the leading Reformer, a rabble-rousing firebrand, and editor of a new weekly, whose pages routinely excoriated the government and its leadership.

Sir Francis flinched. "That man's a fanatic. What he won't prevaricate he'll equivocate. You'd be wasting your time and putting the investigation at risk."

"I met him back in January, sir. In fact, I saved him from a tar-and-feathering, and we had a brief conversation. I know he trusts me, and I believe he will give us a perspective on the Councillor's political status that might prove invaluable."

Sir Francis began to fidget with his coffee cup. The sun had risen close to its zenith and no longer flooded the room. "All right, you may go ahead. And while you're there, I want you to ask him to provide me with the name of a very irritating letter-writer who's been filling the pages of Mackenzie's *Constitution* with tripe and nonsense now for the past month – someone who hides like a coward behind the pseudonym of Farmer's Friend."

"I'll ask him, sir."

Sir Francis detected the note of skepticism in Marc's response. "Tell Mackenzie that I wish only to discuss the issues raised in these letters with their author – as part of my assiduous and continuing effort to understand the long-time grievances."

"I'll do that, sir."

"More importantly, it seems obvious that you are going to need some assistance, especially if you expect to carry out your proposed work within the next day or two. And I'm referring to expert help, not the enthused amateurism of your junior officers or NCOs."

"Where would I get such assistance?"

"When Toronto became a city two years ago, the municipal council established a five-man constabulary modelled on the force that was set up by Robert Peel in London in 1829."

"The bobbies?"

"That's right. While they are still nominally supervised by the magistrates, they act on behalf of the city council, as a unit, as a kind of independent police force, with specific duties and designated territories. I know the chief constable, Wilfrid Sturges, quite well, as he was a sergeant-major in Wellington's army. He spent three years on the London force before emigrating here last year to help establish the Toronto constabulary."

"And you think he'll be able to help us?" Marc said dubiously.

"Indeed. I'm going to send a message to him within the hour and request that he offer his best man to you today, to be attached solely to you and your investigation."

"That is most kind of you, sir, but I feel obliged to point out that the murder took place outside the city limits in the Township of York, where the Toronto constables have no authority."

Head frowned almost imperceptibly. "It is not authority I am interested in, but expertise and local knowledge. I have declared this assassination to be a concern of the military and hence to be placed under the jurisdiction of the military, who in turn take their orders from me."

"I see, sir."

"And, Lieutenant, I hope you can see also that those of us who bear the heaviest burdens of power and responsibility must occasionally ride roughshod over the petty rules and small-minded regulations collected by bureaucrats to keep themselves amused."

Marc smiled. "That is the reason I abandoned the law, sir."

Sir Francis smiled also, but his smile was more like that of the fox that had just surprised himself at his own cunning, as he said, "In the meantime, while we are *quietly* checking out Rumsey and watching his house in the township – the full hue and cry would send him to cover forever – I will tell the Executive Council, who will in due course tell just about everyone else in the province, that we have a prime suspect in our sights, and that it appears he was a hired killer."

"But why tip our hand in any way, sir?"

"Ah, I see, Lieutenant, that you have not yet mastered the fine art of the politician. If, for the moment, the populace believes the assassin to be a *hired* killer – and he may well be, do not forget – then who in the current political context is most likely to be suspected of hiring him to shoot a Constitutionist councillor?"

Marc saw, but he was less than impressed. Not only might the investigation be compromised by the premature release of vital information, but allowing the radical Reform group to be obliquely blamed for "hiring an assassin" was certain to harden, not soften, the divisions between left and right, and could severely skew the coming election. "Perhaps we'll have the blackguard in irons within the week," Marc said with little conviction.

"I want you to take all the time you need, Lieutenant. You are to devote every waking hour to this investigation. While there may be some short-term political gain in having the matter unresolved, any failure of the government, and hence of the Governor, to apprehend the heinous assassin of a respected privy councillor would undo those gains and begin to cast doubt upon my promise to provide a period of peace and stability as the necessary prerequisite to addressing the people's deep-rooted grievances."

"And you yourself, sir, will need to be circumspect in your comings and goings until we know more about the nature and extent of this business."

Sir Francis leaned back. "Then you don't know me, Lieutenant. Not only do I have no intention of curtailing my public appearances, I have already put in train plans for an expanded trip into the London district, beginning next Monday."

"You can't mean that, sir? Those counties down there are the hotbed of radicalism. Half the populace are naturalized Americans."

"Be that as it may, I intend to lead a delegation of concerned citizens to Brantford, Woodstock, and London – where I shall stand tall upon the hustings and deliver my message of hope and reconciliation."

"But, sir, if I am to continue the investigation, then I'll –"

"– not be able to organize the guard for my protection."

"Precisely."

"I will take Willoughby with me. In fact, starting this afternoon, Willoughby will replace you temporarily here at Government House as my assistant military secretary. I have a mountain of correspondence to get through before I set out next week."

"Willoughby is a good man, certainly. He has done much of the detailed, day-to-day work on security . . ."

Sir Francis caught the reservation in Marc's remark. He smiled paternally. "You don't have to be coy about Willoughby, Marc. I know all about his checkered past. I am a friend of his good father, and it was I who agreed to bring him out here with me. He is still young enough, I hope, to find himself as a man, and what better means could there be for doing so than taking on a new profession in a new country? In fact, my original intention was to put him in charge of my security and work him in as military secretary eventually. He is, as you know, well educated and highly intelligent."

"Why did you not do so?"

"First, a few days after our arrival, he got himself disgracefully drunk and ran about Government House frightening the maids and throwing wild punches at anyone trying to restrain him – all this while babbling incoherently about his 'faithless Rosy'!"

"The woman who left him at the altar," Marc said.

"Indeed. Then, while I was reconsidering the matter, I read Sir John's report on your splendid work in the Cobourg investigation and his unequivocal recommendation that I take you on as my chief aide-de-camp."

"Well, Willoughby has begun to adjust nicely in the past few months, has he not?"

"Thanks to you, lad. And to Mrs. Standish's cooking. There's even a rumour that he may have himself a lady friend." Sir Francis raised one eyebrow.

"Truthfully, sir, I've seen no sign of it, but, until yesterday, he *had* seemed much more optimistic and friendly, less given to moodiness."

"Yes, I heard about yesterday from Hilliard, who let the cat out of the bag, I'm afraid."

"It was the sight of the body, sir. Crazy Dan was hit with a full volley. The corpse was a mess. *Several* of the men were sick."

"I know all about that sort of thing, alas. I was at Waterloo – a slaughtering ground. Mind you, I was with the engineers and not in the main battle at all, but I was close enough, nonetheless. He'll get over it, as far as anyone ever does."

"He'll be happy to hear your news, sir. I think keeping him active and giving him more responsibility is just the tonic he needs."

"Then why don't you send him in on your way out."

Marc paused before answering.

"He *is* at his post, is he not?" Sir Francis narrowed his gaze.

"In fact, sir, I could not rouse him before I left at ten-thirty."

Head's blue eyes blazed with a cold, steady fire. "Well, Lieutenant, please return home instantly and inform Lieutenant Willoughby that he is to report to this office by one o'clock ready for duty. If he fails to do so, he will find himself sulking in the brig!"

"Yes, sir!" Marc jumped to his feet, knocking over his empty coffee cup.

The noise woke up Major Burns, who had been peacefully asleep for the last part of the interview – the quill frozen in his arthritic grip.

Sir Francis got up and drew the pen tenderly from the Major's fingers. "I may need *both* you and Willoughby soon," he said to Marc at the door.

Then, as the Governor walked Marc into the anteroom, he snapped at one of his underlings, "Corporal, help Major Burns to his rooms."

Marc ran down the steps of Government House and across the lawn to the winding roadway that led up to King Street. His mind was not bubbling with the details of his new assignment, however; rather, he was wondering how he was going to get Colin Willoughby sober enough to present himself to Sir Francis by one o'clock.

Chapter Five

The Widow Standish, a handsome woman in her mid-fifties, for whom the word *motherly* had been coined, was on the veranda to greet Marc. She was wringing her apron as if to dry her hands, but they had not been near water since the breakfast dishes. "I tried to wake him, sir. Maisie and me both, one of us tugging at either arm, and him in his nightshirt only!"

"It's all right, Mrs. Standish. I'll take over," Marc said as they hurried through the hallway towards the boarders' rooms in back. "If you and Maisie would be kind enough to fill the bathtub and provide some fresh towels –"

Mrs. Standish looked abashed. "Oh, sir, there's not a drop of hot water in the house. It's too warm out for a fire, even in the summer kitchen."

"I think cold water would be more helpful," Marc said, and strode off to Willoughby's room.

When Marc dropped his friend Colin naked and stinking into the bath one of Colin's arms flapped, then the other, then both legs, and finally the whole body thrashed upward. His eyes snapped wide.

"Jesus Murphy, where am I?"

"You're in your own bathtub, but if you don't get a grip on yourself you're going to find your accommodations less accommodating."

As Willoughby grumpily tried to get the soap lathering in the cool water, Marc told him about the Governor's offer to make him temporary assistant to Major Burns and commander of the palace guard for the duration of Marc's investigation. At first Willoughby had difficulty taking it in, due in part to his monstrous hangover, but, Marc sensed, there was something else, something deeper perhaps, that made it hard for him to grasp what had happened. He still looked like a man in shock.

"I'll leave you to your toilette, Colin old chum. Maisie is dusting off your spare uniform, and Mrs. Standish has started a small fire in this wretched heat to boil you some coffee. So quit feeling sorry for yourself and buck up! You've only got half an hour to make or break your fortune." He shoved Colin's head playfully under the soapy water and was pleased to see the troubled young man bob back up – with a wan smile on his face.

During the short walk up to Government House, Marc had time to explain briefly to Colin that the Governor had taken the depositions regarding the shooting of Crazy Dan and had, pending their own statements, absolved the two lieutenants of any blame. This news did not have the spirit-boosting effect that Marc had expected, so he quickly told Colin about the Governor's plans to travel through the London district next week, plans that involved Colin in his new role.

"Do you mean to say that I'll be in charge when we go west?" Colin said, his grey eyes brightening and some colour flushing into his pale cheeks.

"That's right. And what's more, you'll be the Governor's secretary in all but name, as dear old Major Burns is able to do less and less each day."

"And you will be fully in charge of the, uh, investigation?"

They were now stopped on the gravel path that wound its way up to the ornate veranda of Government House.

"It's not a job I asked for," Marc said carefully, "and indeed I was surprised that the Governor insisted on my taking it after the fiasco up at Danby's Crossing."

"Do you have any idea who might have done it? Any trail to follow?"

Marc hesitated. Despite the Governor's own proposal to broadcast selected facts about the investigation, Marc felt that the less said to anyone the better. However, Colin's feeling of complicity in the death of Crazy Dan and the sight of his maimed body had obviously left him shaken and vulnerable – just at a time when he would need to be clear-headed and confident. The responsibilities being offered him could well be the making of him, as an officer and as a man. (The quick capture of the real murderer would do much to ease both their consciences.) And a true friend would not stint in such circumstances by withholding information.

"We think it may have been a disaffected American living up there."

"Has the hue and cry been sent up?"

"Not yet. We're pretty certain he's gone to ground over in New York."

"Ah, then there's little chance we'll ever see him again."

"You may be right," Marc said, hoping against hope that he wasn't.

At this point the duty-corporal at the door waved them inside.

Marc and Colin wrote down their separate accounts of the "tragic incident" (as everyone in Government House had begun to refer to it) and signed them. Marc decided not to delay beginning his own work a moment longer. He set off for Somerset House on Front Street to interview Ignatius Maxwell, who from all accounts was a brutally frank judge of men. He didn't get far. In the foyer, he was stopped and handed a message that instructed him to meet with someone called Horatio Cobb, police constable, at six o'clock in the Crooked Anchor, a sleazy tavern on Bay Street north of Market. Marc was due to have supper with Eliza Dewart-Smythe and her Uncle Sebastian at seven and, as he was beginning to feel he might at last have found a woman who would help him get over his disappointment with Beth Smallman, it was imperative he be there on time. Since he also planned to visit Mackenzie at his newspaper office that afternoon, he decided to stop briefly at Mrs. Standish's for a cold mid-day meal with a glass of warm ale. Then he headed down the half-block to Front Street and walked briskly eastwards under a pleasant June sun. He began to whistle.

The investigation had begun.

Somerset House was by no means the only mansion of note in this prosperous area of the city, where many of its successful merchants, lawyers, bankers, churchmen, and privy councillors lived – as well as a few of those less distinguished members of the Family Compact who, by dint of birth or marriage, managed to maintain both status and the requisite bank balance. But Maxwell's house was the grandest on its block, with an unobstructed view of the bay and the islands beyond.

The building itself was as pretentious as it was presumptuous – all stuccoed quarrystone and slate, neo-Gothic turrets and chimneys wishing they were belvederes, and a carved portico at the entrance to a legendary ballroom fit for princes (should they ever deign to come). Marc walked past the portico without admiring its rococo cherubim, going on to the more plain visitors' entrance off York Street, which was adorned with a morbidly black wreath and an ornate door knocker.

A butler in mourning clothes listened as Marc stated his name and asked to see the Receiver General. After waiting in vain for Marc's card, the butler trundled off down an unlit corridor. It was a good five minutes before he returned and wordlessly led Marc down the same corridor. A door was discreetly opened and, as Marc followed the butler's nod into the room ahead, the servant said in a low, conspiratorial tone: "Lieutenant Edwards, ma'am, as you instructed."

Before Marc could quibble or retreat, the door was closed behind him, and he found himself alone in a sunlit sitting room with two women, Prudence and Chastity Maxwell. Chastity had either just rushed here or was in the midst of working up a rage, for both her cheeks were crimson and her eyes were blazing. Prudence, if she *had* been engaged in a heated exchange with her daughter, had recovered with remarkable speed and aplomb, for she rose gracefully, batted her heavy lashes at Marc, smiled and said, "Good afternoon, Lieutenant. Do come in. Iggy's out just now, but due back within the quarter-hour. I've instructed Jacques to let us know the second he steps through the front door." She put out her ungloved hand – though the rest of her costume was formal enough (as befitted mourning attire) and composed of several layers of cloth that shimmered and rustled gloomily. She turned to Chastity. "You remember Lieutenant Edwards, do you not, darling?"

Chastity blushed just as her cheeks were cooling from

whatever contretemps she had been having with Prudence. "Of course, Mama."

"You are not a gentleman who can easily be forgotten," Prudence said to Marc, and she motioned him to sit. Marc nodded and took a chair across the room from his hostess.

Chastity did not sit. "Please excuse me, Lieutenant, but I was just on my way out –"

"Not to meet that man, you most certainly are not," Prudence hissed without seriously undermining her smile.

Chastity now looked more exasperated than angry. She gave Marc a sidelong glance that implied, "You see what I have to put up with" and said to her mother, "I told you I am meeting Angeline and we are taking her carriage down to the new millinery shop on King Street. I must have a black hat for Uncle's funeral on Friday." Then without waiting for any further remonstrance, she smiled beatifically at Marc and left by the far door.

"What *are* we to do with this younger generation, Lieutenant?" Prudence said to Marc, who she had apparently decided was old enough not to be included in it.

Marc smiled noncommittally. "Is there something in particular you wished to discuss with me?" he asked warily, thinking of several dubious possibilities.

But either Prudence had scant recollection of yesterday's encounter in the Danby Inn or had determined to pretend that it had never happened. She was clearly playing the lady and mistress of the manor. "As a matter of fact, sir, I was hoping to ask a favour of you in regard to my daughter. But first, would you like some coffee, or a sherry?"

"Nothing, thank you, ma'am. I will of course be happy to be of service in any way that I can, though I must tell you candidly that almost all of my time is now taken up with investigating the dreadful business of your brother-in-law's death."

The rouged eyelids dropped down for a respectful second. "Yes, I understand. As you see, our entire household has felt its effects. And while Langdon and I were not close in recent years – you know how families can drift apart even when they live cheek-by-jowl – we are grieving deeply for him and for my devastated sister and my nieces."

"Please convey my condolences to the family."

"Thank you. You are an exceptionally sensitive young man." Prudence opened her eyes wide and gave him a frank, ungrieving appraisal.

Marc cleared his throat. "Since I have you here now, ma'am –" and *sober*, he thought unkindly.

"*Prudence*, please."

"– I was hoping you might give me your insight, as a family member, into Mr. Moncreiff's personality or into any, ah, personal problems he may have been experiencing of late. You see, improper as it is to be probing thus while the family is still in shock, I need to discover a motive for the shooting. People don't kill other people without a powerful reason to do so."

"I understand. And, in fact, I have spent this morning considering what such a reason could be. Many years ago Langdon was a dashing young man, and I was pleased when he married my younger sister, Flora. But for the past ten years he has led what I can only describe as a dull and directionless existence. He has very few opinions and those he has are calculated to offend no one. He does not attend society balls or fêtes and, until Sir Francis begged him to become an Executive Councillor or whatever they're called, he had contributed nothing to the province except two daughters and a disheartened wife."

Marc was not sure how to put his next question. "Was she bored enough to . . . to –"

"– find herself a more accommodating man?"

This time Marc blushed, and Prudence watched him redden

and then pale – never taking her eyes off his face. She gave him a rueful smile. "It does happen, you know, even here a long ways from Sodom and Gomorrah. But the answer is no. And I do know my sister in that regard."

"Thank you for your candour, ma'am." Marc rose. "I'm afraid I have several more urgent appointments this afternoon. Would you tell Mr. Maxwell that if it is convenient, I shall call back at four o'clock. You can send word to Mrs. Standish, my landlady."

Prudence spread one hand across her bosom in either a gesture of modesty or an attempt to call attention to its generous curvature. "But I haven't had a chance to ask that favour of you."

"Oh, I *am* sorry. Please, there is plenty of time for that." Marc remained standing.

Prudence got up and rustled across to him, but there was nothing predatory in her movement. In her face there was genuine concern: "I am positive that my daughter is illicitly consorting with one of the guardsmen up at Government House."

"Are you suggesting that there have been improprieties?" Marc said, taken aback.

"I only suspect so. I can get nothing out of the girl except self-righteous denials, which of course merely deepens my suspicions."

"Has she been seen with one of my men?"

"Not in any compromising situation, no. But she's been hanging about with Angeline Hartley since that creature came here in January and –"

"Sir Francis's ward? Surely you –"

"I don't think anything, but I know she's a wild thing, not yet out of her teens, she has the run of the Governor's open carriage, and the two girls have been seen riding up in College Park with unidentified officers."

"Unchaperoned?"

"Well, not exactly. The Governor's elderly coachman and a groom are always with them, but that hardly counts. It's the secret comings-and-goings that are the real problem. Like this trip to the King Street millinery today, and two or three such 'stories' every week. I'm positive Chastity is having clandestine meetings where she may be getting up to all sorts of shenanigans."

"But if it *is* one of my officers, ma'am, and I have no inkling of any such affair to date, I am certain nothing improper would occur. Indeed, my officers, all of whom I know well, would be honourable and proud enough to present themselves to you and Mr. Maxwell before courting your handsome daughter."

"And I am sure of that, too, Lieutenant. But Mr. Maxwell is *very* particular about who ought to be allowed to 'court' his daughter, as you so quaintly put it. Mr. Maxwell is very possessive of his possessions, and I am afraid that junior officers are not included on his roster of suitable suitors." The look that Prudence now gave Marc suggested strongly that she, too, was deemed one of her husband's possessions.

"Ah, I see. However honourable this suitor might be, Miss Maxwell knows in advance that he would be discounted."

"You have considerable knowledge of the ways of the world," Prudence said and, she did not need to add, *of women*.

"What do you think that *I* could do to help you in this matter?"

"The first thing I need to know is *who*. I am willing to intercede on my daughter's behalf with Ignatius, but only if I know who the young man is, and whether he's worth the trouble it may bring down upon my head."

"Then I will make inquiries and let you know the moment I have found anything out."

"Thank you so much."

Prudence held out her hand and, as Marc took it to give it a mannerly kiss, she squeezed his fingers hard. By the time he looked up in surprise, however, she had turned her face away. At that moment Jacques put his head in the doorway and said, "The master will see you now in his study."

"I can't believe anyone would waste a bullet on dear old Monkee, let alone pay someone else to do the job." The Honourable Ignatius Maxwell, Receiver General of Upper Canada and man of substance, sat in a thronelike leather chair opposite Marc before a flower-filled bay window overlooking York Street. He spoke with the deep voice and easy authority that comes from long years of unchallenged privilege, and every once in a while he took a puff on his cigar, which otherwise he used as a rhetorical prop. He was ruggedly handsome, despite the paunch beneath his silk blouse, with a crop of studiously unkempt reddish-blond hair and a pair of wispy mutton chops that framed his face like pale parentheses. His unoccupied hand rested in the pocket of his moleskin smoking jacket, cut in the latest London style.

"It appears, however, that someone did just that," Marc said, marvelling at how quickly the Governor had begun spreading the news of a possible hired gun.

"So I've been told up at Government House. Some Yankee republican by the sound of it." He flapped at the air with his cigar. "Still, it makes no sense. Even if one of the Clear Grit radicals was mad enough and rich enough to arrange such an assassination in the midst of an election, why would they shoot a harmless codger like Monkee?"

"That's what the Governor has asked me to find out. Was Councillor Moncreiff indeed harmless? A threat to no one?"

"The man had no political ambitions. I'm sure that you already know that the Governor selected Monkee for the council after the disgraceful resignation of those radicals and traitors back in March precisely because, as a nominal Tory but one notorious for holding no fixed opinions, he would be a threat to no cause whatsoever. Nor for that matter would he be of any service to one. He was simply a body to fill up a chair and not open his mouth except to say 'Thank you.' "

"Is that not perhaps being a little too harsh?"

"Harsh, maybe, but true nonetheless. Monkee himself was delighted. That's the whole sad truth of this business. For the first time in years he looked forward to getting out and about. He volunteered to accompany us up to Danby's Crossing." Maxwell stared at his cigar as if he expected it to provide him with an explanation of the inexplicable.

"Then I feel that we must examine the possibility that your brother-in-law was murdered for some personal reason. And since I cannot yet see any connection between him and the man we suspect of actually pulling the trigger, I am forced to explore the hypothesis that someone with a personal grudge did the hiring of the assassin."

Maxwell gave Marc a look of pure contempt, and merely harrumphed. Marc waited patiently. "No one held a grudge against Mr. Moncreiff, unless it was Flora, and she blamed only herself for having been attracted to his good looks when she was old enough to have known better."

"Did he have financial difficulties?"

"No, he did not. He was still living comfortably on the money his father made for him and invested wisely back home."

"Then that leaves the, ah, *personal* aspect."

Contempt flashed again in Maxwell's eye: "Did he have a bit on the side, you mean? Like, for example, the wife of a jealous husband, who, finding he could not compete with our dashing Monkee, paid a mercenary to vanquish his rival?"

"I take your point."

"It is possible, of course, that he had a doxy of sorts he visited on each second Tuesday of the month – lots of men in this town do – but such women do not have jealous husbands or lovers. They're bad for business."

"I agree."

Marc thanked Maxwell and rose to go. Jacques appeared at the door to show him out. When Marc looked back he saw the Receiver General with the cigar clamped tight in his teeth and both hands gripping the arms of the chair – their knuckles white.

Marc walked up York Street to King, passing several of the substantial homes of those who had prospered in a province that had doubled its population over a decade and in a city where fortunes could still be made in ways never dreamt of in the mother country. A recent dry spell after a rainy spring had left the town's roads passable, especially those sections that had been well gravelled, but here and there puddles of watery mud – courtesy of a weekend shower – awaited the unwary walker. Drays and country wagons heading home from the Market Square in Old Town jostled for right-of-way, and weary teamsters urged their horses on with a lick and a *heeya!* Shoeless youngsters hooted and shrieked with laughter, their spirits undulled by a long day of labour (or its avoidance). Jauntily dressed chatelaines and ladies-in-training strolled along the intermittent boardwalk, holding their skirts above the muddy swirl, their bonnets fluttering in the late-afternoon breeze.

Turning east on fashionable King Street, Marc passed a dozen or more elegant shops (by Toronto standards), several with multi-paned bow windows displaying wares tailored to the taste of the discriminating lady or gentleman. (Marc, of course, had seen the originals of these makeshift establishments in the metropolis at the centre of the Empire itself.) He touched his cap to several young women with whom he had danced at various official functions, but if they had not first smiled broadly (or coyly) at him, he would have been hard-pressed to recall their faces or names. Two of them, recent debutantes he thought, giggled and clutched their brand-new hats – purchased, he assumed, from the millinery shop near King and Yonge, the one Chastity Maxwell was supposed to be visiting.

Out of curiosity Marc paused to look down the street towards the shop and was rewarded with the sight of Angeline Hartley, the Governor's wayward ward, emerging from its front door. She moved smartly towards a barouche, with its hood down, where the Governor's elderly coachman and a groom stood waiting with impassive rigidity. The latter helped her climb in and open her parasol. Chastity did not follow. Angeline was alone. The carriage lurched and sped away westward towards Government House.

Marc continued eastward, and as he passed the alley just beyond the millinery and the dry-goods store attached to it, he glimpsed, at the far end where it met the tradesman's lane running behind the shops, a blur of taffeta and military red. Chastity and her illicit beau? Perhaps he should ask a few questions around Government House and the garrison on Mrs. Maxwell's behalf, Marc thought. Ignatius Maxwell was reputed to have a quick temper and, as his good woman had remarked, he guarded his possessions jealously.

As he crossed Yonge, barely avoiding an errant donkey-cart, it occurred to Marc that Colin Willoughby had come home very late in the evening several times in the past couple of weeks, yet in the morning he had not seemed hungover, or inclined to talk about the previous night's exploits. Was it possible, then, that Colin had fallen in love? If he had, he may have chosen dangerously, though it was conceivable that the

Receiver General excluded pedigreed lieutenants from his caste of unsuitables.

As he neared Church Street, Marc noted the imposing two-storey brick jail. Beside it, but set back about fifty feet from the street and encircled by green lawns, sat the matching Court House. (Whether the single design had been chosen by the city fathers for reasons of frugality or a desire to make a public statement about justice in the colony was an open question.) Several carriages drawn by matched teams had pulled up in front of the Court House and were busily discharging or collecting dark-suited barristers and solicitors – the backbone and principal prop of the ruling Family Compact. Somewhere nearby, in one of the many offices attached to the jail itself, Marc assumed, would be the modest quarters of the Toronto constabulary, and he wondered vaguely why he had been told to meet the constable with the arresting name of Horatio Cobb in a tavern. Had the man's father read *Hamlet*, or had he been an admirer of Admiral Nelson, Marc wondered.

Turning south on Church Street, he was soon at number fourteen, the building that had housed the infamous newspaper, the *Colonial Advocate*, for many years, and was now home to the even more presumptuous *Constitution*, both of them conceived and produced by the provincial firebrand William Lyon Mackenzie. Three times this diminutive Scot with the orange wig had been thrown out of the Legislative Assembly, only to be re-elected immediately by the faithful constituents of York County. The frustrated scions of the Family Compact had dumped the *Advocate*'s type into Toronto Bay, but had still failed to stop its weekly insight and invective. As soon as the aldermen and councillors of the new City of Toronto had been elected in 1834, they had chosen Mackenzie as its first mayor. He was, by general admission, the de facto leader of the Reform group on the political left (if not always its preferred choice as standard bearer). He had helped write the *Seventh Report on Grievances* and had spent a year in England lobbying for the many reforms it recommended. He had come back in fighting trim to sit again in the Reform-dominated Assembly (now freshly dissolved by the new lieutenant-governor) and founded an even more radical organ. Marc studied the plain printer's shop and the bookstore attached to it, whose small front window held a dozen neatly displayed, leather-bound tomes and the advertisement: "*Latest titles from New York and London.*" So this was the den of what, from several platforms, Sir Francis had termed "republican demagoguery." It appeared to be both ordinary and respectable.

But Marc had heard the firebrand at his volcanic best in January at the Cobourg town hall, where he had roused the crowd of farmers to righteous fury and where Marc, in spite of himself, had begun to see the justness of their cause. However the Governor managed to shift the balance of forces in the upcoming election, it was imperative that the festering, legitimate grievances of the farmers, tradesmen, and labourers be dealt with immediately.

"Well, well, I believe it's Ensign Edwards, is it not, come to beard the mangy lion in his den!" Mackenzie stood in the open doorway, wiping ink from one of his hands on a smudged apron and thrusting the other out to greet Marc.

"So it's Lieutenant, now. Congratulations." Mackenzie smiled at Marc across the tiny, cluttered office with genuine warmth. From the adjoining room came the metallic sounds of compositors picking and setting type. A bluebottle fly batted against the window-glass half-heartedly in the heat.

"Thank you, sir."

"I presume your promotion was entirely due to the small

service you rendered me and the Reform party last winter in Cobourg?"

Marc smiled, as he was expected to – pleased not only that Mackenzie remembered him but that he felt comfortable enough to tease him. Marc had been told that Mackenzie had a sharp sense of humour, observed less in latter years than when he had first come to the colony. Marc turned the subject to yesterday's tragedy.

"What do I make of it, you ask, beyond regret at the senseless death of a harmless old man?" Mackenzie said. "Well, lad, there are several ways of responding to that question, depending, I suppose, on who's asking it and why. I infer from your presence here that the Governor is concerned about the effect it might have upon the elections."

"That, of course, as well as the importance of finding the killer."

"Rumour has it that the shooter was an ex-patriot American with a grudge or an empty larder."

"Rumour is reasonably accurate, for a change."

It was Mackenzie's turn to smile. Then his chiselled features took on a grave, almost sorrowful, cast. He brushed his wig back unconsciously with his right hand. "A rumour like that could do irreparable harm to the Reform cause in this election. As you know, the Governor is stumping the constituencies and playing up the loyalty theme. The murder of one of his hand-picked councillors by a crazed democrat from the States would play to the paranoia out there and make credible the preposterous claim that the Yanks are mustering for imminent invasion."

"Which is why the Governor wants this man found," Marc insisted.

Mackenzie gave Marc a narrow, appraising glance. "I think you do believe that, lad."

"But surely, sir, you see that, crazed or not, if this killer were *hired*, he could have been recruited by anyone with a reason to do away with Councillor Moncreiff – including someone from his own, ah –"

"– class?"

"Or party . . . which might suggest to the electorate that the Compact and the Tories do not have their own house in order."

"Yes, I do see." Mackenzie began drumming his fingers on the desk, rustling the papers scattered there. "Are you sure you've chosen the right profession, Lieutenant?"

"What I am leading towards, sir, is the question of who might have reason to have Councillor Moncreiff assassinated?"

"Well, then, I'll save you and Sir Francis some time by stating here and now and unequivocally that no one in the Reform party and no one remotely interested in its welfare would have hired an assassin or shot the old fellow himself."

"But there must have been resentment and some bitterness among Reformers when Sir Francis replaced the protesting councillors with even more unpalatable members? Could some, albeit temporarily deranged, Reform sympathizer have hired an assassin to publicly eliminate one of those new councillors, as a message or a warning to the Governor himself?"

Mackenzie gave the question some thought. "Deranged he would have to be, but, yes, it is possible. However, in such a case, Moncreiff could only have been a symbolic target. The old codger had no status as a politician or as a mover and shaker. Remember that Ignatius Maxwell was seated on the same bench as Moncreiff, according to the eyewitness reports my compositors are just now setting to type. If the motive were practical revenge, then that grasping fraud would have been singled out, not Moncreiff."

Marc shuddered. How many of the spectators present at

Danby's Crossing yesterday had already relayed their biased accounts of the events there to the radical press? But if Mackenzie had heard details of Crazy Dan's death at the hands of a less than competent British troop, he had decided not to bring it up. Or perhaps the complicity of Alvin Chambers, one of their own, had given the farmers some pause before spreading the story abroad. But the details, twisted beyond all recognition, would come out eventually and the Governor's crude attempt to smooth over their ugliness would soon become part of the campaign rhetoric.

Emerging from his momentary reverie, Marc said, "I think you're implying that the 'message' was more likely intended for Sir Francis?"

Mackenzie appeared shocked. "If that is so, then it is profoundly regrettable. The Lieutenant-Governor is the representative of the Crown."

Marc hesitated, took a deep breath, and said quietly, "But you are accused everywhere, even by some of your own supporters, of being an ardent republican."

Mackenzie smiled wryly. "Thank you for the 'ardent.' That I am. But if you were to read the many back issues of my *Colonial Advocate*, you would see that I have been from the outset a champion of responsible government – whatever form it must take in the particular circumstances of British North America. And even if that form turns out to be republican in nature, it would not necessarily mean any irrevocable break from the mother country. I have admired people like Edmund Burke and David Hume all my life. What we have begged for and then demanded in Upper Canada is that the executive of our government be chosen representatively from members of the Legislative Council and the Legislative Assembly, and that they be accountable in turn to those bodies."

"But where does that leave the Governor?"

"It leaves him in the position of *viceregal*. For example, to whom is the prime minister and cabinet of Great Britain responsible?"

"To Parliament."

"Precisely – and not to King William. But does that arrangement diminish the traditional and residual authority of the monarch? Not a whit. It's called a constitutional monarchy, and is a uniquely British configuration. That is all we have ever asked for."

"But if the Governor could not govern under instruction from the colonial secretary, this province would become a country of its own."

"Something like that, eventually and all in good time," Mackenzie said, somewhat bemused by the drift of the conversation. "And if we are refused that, then . . . well . . . an independent republic is always possible."

And revolution, thought Marc.

"At any rate, Lieutenant, you do see that it is in the interest of my party to have this assassin tracked down and the truth revealed. You have my word that if I hear – from my innumerable sources – any news of this person or any snippet of gossip pertaining to the tragedy, I will inform you personally."

"Thank you. There is one other thing, sir – the delicate matter of whether Councillor Moncreiff may have had some, ah, personal difficulties –"

Mackenzie chortled. "Sexual intrigue and all that? Low behaviour among the high and mighty?"

"Something of that sort, yes. Naturally his family may be reluctant to discuss such indelicacies, so I was wondering if you, as a journalist, one-time mayor, and long-time resident of the city, if you –"

"Had heard any gossip too salacious not to print?"

Marc blushed, and nodded.

"Not a whisper, and I've heard plenty over the years, most of it true, alas. That brother-in-law of his, now there's a man with a peripatetic codpiece, a roué by any other name. But not Langdon Moncreiff."

Marc's surprise showed. "The Receiver General? But his wife just assured me he was very possessive."

"As he is. Of her and all his chattel. But especially of her, as it is still her daddy's money propping up that hypocritical facade and daddy's power in the Compact keeping Maxwell in office. One where graft, nepotism, and corruption are the norm, I might add." Mackenzie looked sadly at Marc in his bright uniform, the feathered shako cap resting confidently in his youthful hands. "You are still young enough, perhaps, not to realize that the innocent perish more often and more tragically than the wicked."

Marc thought of Crazy Dan but said only, "Thank you, again."

They shook hands.

At the door of the shop, Mackenzie said, "As a party, we are still confident that all the legitimate political and legal means still at our disposal will be sufficient to see justice prevail."

Suddenly Marc turned and said, "By the way, the Governor made a special request of me when he learned I was coming here."

"And we all know the nature of a governor's 'requests,' don't we? What is it, lad?"

"Sir Francis is eager to know the name of the correspondent in the *Constitution* who signs himself Farmer's Friend?"

"Is he, now?"

"He is interested in the stories he tells, despite their implied criticism. He wishes to speak with this person, as he feels such an encounter might be of great benefit to him as he ponders just how to proceed with the grievances."

"I'll bet he does."

"Is that a no, sir?"

"Lieutenant, I would not reveal the name of a pseudonymous correspondent to King William himself. But you can advise the Governor that I do indeed know the writer and that his contributions to the *Constitution* are both authentic and voluntary. As such they may be of benefit to him and the future health of the province."

"I'll do that, sir. Thank you for your candour. I expected nothing less."

"Good luck with your investigation."

And it looked to Marc as if luck would be sorely needed.

Chapter Six

After returning briefly to his boarding house to bathe, change his linen, and shave, Marc walked to Yonge and Bay, where, as a nearby church bell chimed six times, he pushed his way into the smoky premises of the Crooked Anchor. At the bar, amid the din and wonderfully variegated stink of the place, he had the tapster point out the small figure of a man seated at a table and hunched over a flagon of ale and a plate of trout and onions. When Marc sat down opposite, he looked up, one cheek still plugged with a forkful of supper.

"Constable Cobb?"

"Who would like to know?" Cobb swallowed his mouthful without removing his eyes from the intruder.

"I'm Lieutenant Edwards. Governor Head has arranged, through your superior, for you to assist me in the investigation of the murder of Langdon Moncreiff."

Cobb continued forking his supper upwards as if he were pitching hay into a needy manger. In the silence, Marc sized up the man who looked as if he were more likely to spoil the investigation than help it. Cobb reminded Marc of one of Shakespeare's clowns, several of whom he had seen in Drury Lane: Bardolph or Dogberry, perhaps. His nose met you first, a jutting cherry-red proboscis with a single wart on its left side. Set deep within their sockets, Cobb's eyes were tiny, dark, and hard. The hair, which apparently had never seen a brush and seldom a bar of soap, stood up starkly wherever a finger or palm had skidded through it. Cobb could not have been much more than five feet, but the thick knuckles and muscled neck suggested a powerful physique. Marc noted the navy-blue coat and trousers that passed for a uniform among Toronto's upstart constabulary, this version festooned with dried egg and congealed grease. A stiff helmet lay perilously close to the supper plate. Cobb might have been anywhere between twenty-five and forty years of age: he gave the impression that he could have been born looking like this.

Cobb, who had returned Marc's scrutiny in kind, finally opened his mouth to speak. "Would ya care fer a bite of supper? A pot of ale?"

"No thank you, I'm dining out later."

Cobb smiled, though it was hard to be sure because the man's eyes and mouth were not particularly co-ordinated with one another. "Miss Dewart-Smythe is better company, I reckon, than the drubbers and riff-raff in here."

Marc did not smile back. "And what would *you* know about Miss Dewart-Smythe?"

"I know a lot about a lot of things, yer grace. It's what the city fathers pay me fer."

"I'm not a duke, Constable, I'm a lieutenant, Lieutenant Edwards. 'Sir' will do nicely."

"Well, then, Sir Edward, sir, I observed yer young lady on several occasions in the week past – in the course of me duties, I hasten to add. And a *gem-u-ine* looker she is."

"Don't mock me, Constable, and do not speak in that flippant manner of the young woman in question. That uniform will not protect you from a good thrashing –"

"Now, now, don't get yer linens in a snarl. If we're gonna work side by side – and I got the orders from the Sarge loud and clear on that score – we can't go on callin' each other by ten-syllable *sober-quettes*. You just call me Cobb, like the wife does when she's speakin' to me, and I'll call you . . . Major."

Marc relaxed slightly. His experience in dealing with native-born citizens down in Cobourg last January had taught him to proceed cautiously, to take no offence until certain some was warranted, and to proceed obliquely wherever possible. "Very well, then, Constable. Now please tell me how you came to know of the lady and my, ah, interest in her welfare."

Cobb signalled for another ale, and seconds later the tapster hopped over with a fresh, frothing flagon. "They know me here," Cobb grinned, then said, "The lady may not have mentioned that her uncle's stores was burgled two nights ago. Their home and warehouse are on my patrol, so I went up there to see if I could help. The varmints'd skedaddled, of course, with six cases of claret and a tun of port. Shame, too, 'cause it'd just arrived from overseas."

"But I was there Monday evening –"

"I seen ya come out, lookin' particularly satisfied, I'd say. But the old fellow and me was in the warehouse lookin' over the damage at the time. I spied ya prancin' off down Newgate Street through the storeroom window. The lady herself didn't know nothin' about the break-in till later. Things like that tend to scare *aristo-crustic* ladies, I'm told."

Marc knew enough to ignore what was irrelevant. "Did you find any clues?"

"Nothin' except a jimmied back door. The Sarge is in quite a flap about this thievin' of spirits. There's a rash of it goin' 'round. I was called out to assist Constable Wilkie – he's got the east-end patrol – way out at Enoch Turner's brewery near the Don River last Saturday, it was. A dozen barrels of good beer rolled out and loaded quick as a fart onto some schooner or dory, no doubt. Big shots like Dewart-Smythe and Alderman Enoch tend to make the Sarge's breakfast bubble."

"You didn't suppose that *I* was the thief?" Marc said impishly.

Cobb gave him a curious look. "It did occur to me, Major, but you weren't luggin' any casks under yer arm, and I figured you had more interestin' *counter-band* in mind."

"And you had observed me there on other occasions?"

Cobb took a hefty swig of ale, brushed the froth away with his cuff, and said, "We work closely with the watch at night. There ain't much about people's comin' and goin' we don't know about – sometimes even before they do." He laughed, spraying ale over the remnants of his dinner.

"Then your observational skills may come in handy during my investigation," Marc said affably.

"*Our* investigation, Major."

"Have you been briefed on the details?"

"So far, I only know what I hear in the taverns between here and Church Street."

"You spend your time in taverns?"

"Only durin' the day," Cobb said, ostensibly offended.

"But should you not be patrolling the streets assigned to you? In London the bobbies' principal function is to prevent crime by providing a visible presence day and night."

"Now, Major, I do venture outdoors once in a blue moon, just to air out my uniform and stretch the kinks out of my legs. But I find I can learn more about evil-doin' by just sittin' here keepin' my rabbit ears open and waitin' fer my many informants – or snitches as we call 'em – to sashay up and tell me what I need to know, fer the price of half a flagon usually."

"But there are disturbances of every kind out there, surely."

"Surely. And lots more in here. We constables are run plum off our feet, or knocked off 'em, by brawlers and drunks and wife-beaters and the like. Why, if I didn't spend half my time movin' smartly from dive to dive, I'd miss the pleasure of a fist in my face or a knee up the nosebag, so to speak, or the pure joy of smackin' a low-life silly before he pukes all over me. Yessir, Major, us constables've got plenty of hours in a day to do a lot of serious investigatin' – *in* and *out* of the town's taverns. Not to speak of all the happy hours we put in investigatin' whorehouses and investigatin' inebriated gentlemen home to their good wives and investigatin' some mistress cudgelled black and blue by a bigwig fer the sheer sport of it, and investigatin' –"

"I take your point, Constable."

"To give you a fer-instance, it was whispered to me not five minutes before you come in here that the same thieves did over the wine warehouse as did the brewery. Got no names yet. But I will, if it don't take you forever to investigate a simple murder." He drained his flagon, waved it once at the tapster, and said, "So why don't you start things rollin' by feedin' me the details."

Aware that he was in danger of being late for his supper with Eliza, Marc quickly sketched out what had happened up at Danby's Crossing (censoring somewhat the chapter entitled "Crazy Dan"), and even outlined the theories he was considering. Cobb listened without comment, equally absorbed, it seemed, in making his ale last to the end of Marc's tale.

Marc finished but did not wait for Cobb's response – should he have one – for he felt he had sized up his assistant sufficiently and assessed his potential usefulness. "What I'd like you to do, Constable, is arrange for a surreptitious surveillance of Philo Rumsey's cabin. I'm convinced he will return, secretly, to fetch his wife and children or bring them money. He may even use an intermediary."

"You want me to keep an eye on his place without anybody else knowin'?"

"Precisely."

"Well, the best way to do that, Major, is fer me to have a couple of local types act as our eyes and ears up there. That way, no one'll get suspicious or try to warn off this Rumsey fella. I can set that up tonight. I'll have to loan a horse from the Sarge, and take Wilkie with me, 'cause he used to live in that township when he was a tad. We'll ride up there and just pop into the saloon, out of uniform. We'll have yer watch goin' before it gets dark."

"Better still, I'll write you a note to take to the hostler at Government House, and he'll provide you with fast horses –"

"– which'll blow our cover within five miles of Danby's saloon. The Sarge's nags'll do just fine."

"Yes, you're right. At any rate, I'll leave the surveillance to you. But we also need to interview the storekeepers on the market square – discreetly – and build up a picture of the Rumseys and Phineas Kimble, the harness-maker. I'm certain he's involved, because he definitely lied about not hearing the shot that came from his own house."

"If you go up there and take one step outside Danby's in yer fancy dress, the jig'll be up, Major. What I'll do tonight is get good and drunk, so's I'll have to sleep it off on the street or the bush. I'll take some pots and pans along and pertend I'm a peddler, and Wilkie'll be my helper. Then I'll go door to door tomorrow, hungover like, and purvey my wares, whilst pokin' about gently fer any gossip about Rumsey or Kimble. Wilkie'll suggest who we can trust up there as our spies, and take care of that end before he comes home."

"Yes, Constable, that sounds like a superb plan." His

respect for the man was growing with every passing minute. Marc rose.

"Enjoy yer dinner, Major."

Marc hesitated. "Pardon the personal question, but did your father by any chance name you after Admiral Nelson?"

Cobb flinched. "No sir, Major, sir. My pappy named me after some fella in a foreign play."

Sebastian Dewart-Smythe, wholesale wine merchant, lived on Newgate Street near Yonge, not too far from the stately residence of the influential Reform family of William Baldwin. Mr. Dewart-Smythe had one wing of his spacious (but not so stately) residence devoted to the safe storage of tuns and casks of imported wine. In the other wing he lived in comfortable, unostentatious affluence with his niece, Eliza. Only one servant, a butler-cum-valet, lived in. The Dewart-Smythe family of Kensington, England, operated wholesale wine houses on three continents.

Marc had met Eliza the previous November at a harvest fête held in the sumptuous halls of The Grange a few weeks after she and her uncle had arrived to open yet another branch of the family business. He had danced with her once, and afterwards made polite chatter with her long enough to learn that, while her uncle was her guardian, she had come with him principally as a helpmate – her interest in and knowledge of wines along with her fluency in French, Spanish, and Italian making her, she claimed, indispensable. Marc had been aware of her rich, dark, ringleted hair, intelligent brown eyes, voluptuous figure, and attractive, if not pretty, features. But at that time he had not yet recovered from his youthful affair with Marianne Dodds, the ward of a neighbouring landowner back home in Kent. Last November, all the young women at soirees and balls had seemed to him to be frivolous and self-absorbed.

Then, in Cobourg this past January, he had, he was certain, fallen truly in love. The sudden and mysterious death of Beth Smallman's father-in-law had brought him to her farm, and he had been of material assistance to her. While Beth herself had been noncommittal, she had undoubtedly been drawn to him even though their political outlook and loyalties were opposed. But when Beth did not reply to his letters and even the letters from Beth's friends and neighbours stopped coming, he began to accept that there was no hope for him. It was then he suddenly realized just how different Eliza was from the debutantes and husband-seekers among her contemporaries.

In April he had met her by chance on King Street, shopping, and they took up their November conversation as if six months had not intervened. She shocked him, then, by inviting him back to her house for coffee, in the middle of the afternoon with her uncle absent next door and a befuddled butler serving them. But what was most surprising was that Marc found himself completely at ease in her presence. Eliza said what she meant and meant what she said. There was no need to be on guard or to wonder what was going through her woman's mind: her gaze was as candid as it was kind. The only difficulty – and it was one he was loath to discuss with her – was that she seemed to him much of the time more like an elder sister than a potential lover.

But not all the time, and definitely not this evening. Supper itself was pleasant and predictable enough, with Uncle Sebastian steering the conversation back to wine whenever it threatened to veer towards topics he thought too crude for feminine ears, and Eliza having her say on the most arcane details relating to the business here and abroad – while Marc smiled vacuously and basked in Eliza's knowing, grateful glances. Then, despite a solemn promise to Eliza not to do so, her uncle raised the subject of the break-in late Monday evening and proceeded to expound upon the incompetence of the new-fangled constabulary and the superiority of the magistrates and squires of old. Marc decided to remain mum on both themes.

At seven-thirty Uncle Sebastian rose with some effort (he was portly in the extreme) and said deliberately, "Well, I'm off to the Shakespeare Club meeting at McBride's. May I give you a lift, Lieutenant, as it's not out of my way?"

Marc got up. "It's a fine evening, sir, and I feel the need to walk off some of that splendid meal."

"But only when you've finished your cigar and brandy," Eliza said. "You wouldn't be rude enough to rush Mr. Edwards into the street hatless, would you, Uncle?"

"Of course not, my dear. Do stay for a few minutes, sir. I know that my niece gets lonesome with only the day-servants to talk to while I'm working. I'm sure Chalmers will be happy to show you out before he retires at eight." The old man gave Eliza what he assumed was a stern look and headed for the hall.

"He won't be back till ten o'clock," Eliza said with a conspiratorial smile. "They're doing a reading of Act Three of *Julius Caesar* tonight and Uncle, improbably, has been cast as the lean and hungry Cassius."

"Well, I'll certainly stay for a little while. I've had a trying two days, and you're always such a thoughtful listener."

"I'll put my oar in when required," Eliza said.

For the next hour Marc recounted, not always in sequence, the events and emotions and mental debates surrounding the death of Langdon Moncreiff. And though Eliza was not especially concerned with politics, she was fascinated by human behaviour and motive. She interjected, almost tenderly, from time to time to ask a question or to seek further explanation. At last

Marc began to wilt, his broad shoulders sagging, and he slumped against one of the pillows on the settee. Eliza, in a simple blue dress with a dark sash accentuating her narrow waist and full bosom, slipped across the room, fussed with a spray of pink roses for a minute, then turned and settled herself demurely beside him.

"Do you think Moncreiff could have been mixed up in some lovers' quarrel?" Marc asked her drowsily, quite sick of all such unanswerable and futile queries.

"No, I don't. An outraged husband or jealous lover would have done the deed himself or else arranged for it to be done in a less public place. You are wasting your precious time and energy pursuing that line of inquiry."

"So you know a lot about love and lovers?" Marc teased.

Eliza frowned briefly, and Marc instantly regretted the remark. "Oh, it's nothing," she said. "I did love someone deeply, and lost him. But don't you think that sort of experience makes one appreciate the troublesome joys of love itself, that one can become the stronger for it? And more capable of genuine affection?"

Marc was about to agree wholeheartedly but was forestalled by the suddenness of the kiss that neither of them could recall initiating. Marc put his arms around her, and the softness of her breasts pressed against him. He let his face drift into her hair as she gripped his back with clenching fingers.

The hall door banged shut.

The lovers sprang apart. Eliza straightened her hair, patted her dress smooth, and leapt to the dining-room door in time to greet her uncle with a cheery hello.

Then she said with genuine concern, "But you're back early, Uncle. It's only nine-thirty."

"Gastric complaint, my dear. I'll take some salts and go right to –" Uncle Sebastian stopped in mid-sentence, all thought about his balky stomach forgotten. "Young man, what are you doing here at this hour with my niece – unchaperoned?"

Uncle Sebastian tipped forward in his padded chair, pushed his bewhiskered face over his plump and aching belly, and glared at Marc. "What I want to know, Lieutenant – and I wish the candid answer of a true gentleman – is this: What are your intentions towards my niece?"

It was a fair question, and one Marc had asked himself several times before this evening and a dozen times on the slow walk behind Uncle Sebastian as they made their way in stiff silence to his office.

"I am not sure how I would characterize my intentions, sir. If I knew for certain, I would have approached you before this."

"Are you in love with Eliza, sir? I cannot put it more bluntly than that."

"I may well be –"

"What blather and circumlocution! You should be ashamed of yourself. You've been skulking around here uninvited for the past six weeks, stirring up gossip along Yonge Street from the bay to Lake Simcoe! You had the impudence to linger here on Monday evening while I was attending to my ledgers and then again tonight when I expressly indicated I wished you to leave, as a proper gentleman would have done without having to be reminded. If you do not love her and have no intention of asking for her hand, then, sir, you are a blackguard and I am much deceived."

His jowls shook with anger and chagrin, but there was a kind of pleading in his eyes as he stared steadily at Marc.

"You are not deceived, sir. I am truly fond of your niece, and I am in the process of falling in love. That is the truth, upon my word as an officer."

"Then you are considering a proposal sometime soon?"

Marc hesitated – not too long, he hoped – before saying, "I am."

Uncle Sebastian sat back, winced at his rebellious stomach, and attempted to relax. "Do you wish a brandy? Chalmers, bless him, is still afoot."

"No, thank you. I am exhausted from a –"

"Not too tired, I trust, to be asked a few pertinent questions regarding your suitability as a suitor for Eliza's hand."

My God, Marc thought, I must be having a bad dream.

"I must ask you about your parentage and prospects, Lieutenant, because, whether you know it or not, Eliza is the sole living heir of her generation in the Dewart-Smythe family. She stands someday to become a very wealthy woman."

"I did not know that. We talk of many things, but not money."

Uncle Sebastian gave a skeptical cough but carried on. "Money must be talked of or it will speak for itself. Now I understand that you are the adopted son of a reasonably prosperous country squire named Jabez Edwards – whom you affectionately refer to as 'Uncle.' "

Marc wondered where this was leading. "That is right. Apparently I called him that before –"

"And who, then, were your real parents?"

"Thomas and Margaret Evans. My father was the gamekeeper on the estate. They both died of cholera when I was five."

"But you were officially adopted and raised up as Jabez Edwards's own in the County of Kent?"

"I was."

"Adjacent to the lands of Sir Joseph Trelawny?"

"That is so."

"And you are the sole heir to the Edwards estate?"

Marc smiled inwardly. His parentage would have disqualified him as Eliza's suitor except for the fact that he had been given a reputable surname, seemed likely to inherit a minor estate, and had rubbed shoulders with the petty aristocracy next door. "Not quite," Marc said slowly.

"What do you mean, not quite? You either inherit or you don't."

"The land is entailed to full-blooded Edwards' heirs, the sons of his younger brother, Frederick, who lives in France. There was a younger sister, Mary, who would have been my aunt, but she died before I was born."

"So you inherit nothing?"

"Not quite. Uncle Jabez invested his own money wisely in stocks, and I am promised whatever they have yielded, at his death."

"No land, then, and an indeterminate sum of money?"

"That is the case. But you must rest assured that any motive I might have for asking Eliza to marry me – were I to do so in the near future – would not include seeking her fortune."

"Well, we shall see, shan't we?"

"Are you forbidding me to see her, sir?"

"Not at all. But I must insist that you call on her only when invited and then only in the afternoons. There will be no more late-evening tête-à-têtes. Is that clear?"

"Yes, sir." Marc realized that the old tyrant was serious about all this, and that, as a lifelong bachelor, keeping watch on a beautiful and vulnerable heiress (and one he obviously adored) was not easy.

"Now, which of us is going to tell Eliza?" the old man said.

When Marc dragged his exhausted body up the three steps onto Mrs. Standish's veranda, he was greeted by Colin Willoughby peering out the doorway.

"Christ, but you look like a fox who's spent a day in the kennels," Colin said. He was dressed only in his nightshirt, with an expression of immense satisfaction – almost a smugness – masking evident fatigue and strain.

Marc was so tired he could muster only a noncommittal grunt in response.

"Don't shoot the messenger, old boy, but I was instructed by the Governor to command your presence at Government House the moment you returned."

"Tell him I'm dead," Marc moaned.

"Now, who'd want you dead?" Colin laughed.

The uncle of a girl I know, Marc smiled grimly to himself.

Sir Francis was almost as exhausted as Marc, but each went bravely through the motions of doing his duty. Marc gave the Governor a synopsis of his activities at Maxwell's, Mackenzie's, and the Crooked Anchor.

"This Cobb sounds like a crude but cunning devil," Sir Francis said with a nice balance of admiration and revulsion. "Chief Constable Sturges assured me that he was his best man, but then that is a relative statement, eh?"

"I feel that almost everything depends upon his apprehension of Philo Rumsey," Marc sighed. "It seems most probable at this point that Councillor Moncreiff was shot by a hired assassin in order to make a political point of some kind. I believe we can rule out any personal motive whatsoever. Which means, I am afraid, that until we get hold of Rumsey alive, we have no way of discovering who engaged him and for what reason – short of interviewing every malcontent and opponent of the government in Upper Canada."

"Perhaps this Constable Cobb will be able to trace Rumsey's recent movements and link him with the sponsor of this crime."

"From all accounts, sir, Rumsey was a loner, a man who disappeared at will into the bush to hunt – or whatever."

"And you would rule out any direct involvement of the radical left?"

"Yes, sir, I would. Mackenzie convinced me that it would be suicidal for Reformers to have been involved. They may be fanatic, but they are a long ways from being stupid."

Sir Francis suppressed a yawn and turned the gesture into a nod of assent. "While you were there, Lieutenant, did you have a chance to inquire about the identity of Farmer's Friend?"

"I did, and Mackenzie refused to tell me."

"I thought as much."

"But he did say that the writer is a real person with an intimate knowledge of his subject."

"That's precisely the problem, alas." This time Sir Francis let the yawn take its full course. "Come to see me tomorrow afternoon, and I'll explain more about Farmer's Friend. In the meantime, if you see Cobb, you might assign him to make discreet inquiries about the matter. I understand these new constables keep an ear close to the boardwalk."

"Or the bar," Marc said. "I think that's a good idea, sir, provided it doesn't interfere with his duties in the Moncreiff investigation."

"That is understood, of course."

At the door of the office, Marc said casually, "How did Colin get on with his new assignment?"

Sir Francis smiled through his fatigue. "Considering he had the granddaddy of all hangovers, splendidly. He took the bit in his teeth and began planning the security arrangements for our proposed swing through the London district next week and, with Major Burns's heroic assistance, got through a mountain of correspondence before dark. Which left me free to deal with the incredible fuss over the assassination. The funeral is to be held on Friday."

"Military?" Marc said with apparent disinterest.

"As a matter of fact, it is," the Governor said. "The family insisted."

"Well, I'm delighted to hear that Colin is doing well."

"We may bring him back into the fold yet," Sir Francis said. "If so, his father will be the happiest man in England. And I shall be sure to let him know just who did the most to help his son."

"I'm just trying to be a good friend," Marc said with no attempt to be immodest.

"Something we all need," Sir Francis said.

Chapter Seven

Marc spent an anxious Thursday morning sweating in his tiny office at Government House, while the place hummed with activity he could take no part in. By eleven o'clock more than a dozen dignitaries – including Chief Justice Robinson, the Attorney General, the Solicitor General, and the bankers, merchants, and barristers who made up the appointed Legislative Council and the six-member Executive – had paraded into the Governor's suite to report on the state of the State, offer unsolicited advice, and propound exotic theories as to the motive for the crime. On several occasions he noticed Colin Willoughby either rushing past him or else locked in earnest colloquy with Hilliard in the vestibule. It was just before twelve when word came to him to meet with Cobb within the hour – this time at the Blue Ox.

Marc decided to ride down to the rendezvous, as the Blue Ox was a low-life tavern, frequented by sailors and their colleagues, at the east end of Front Street (still called Palace by some) beyond the Market Square at Frederick. He could leave his horse safely at one of the market stalls and proceed the last block and a half on foot.

As soon as he had stepped into the maelstrom of pipe smoke, boozy breath, and raucous chatter, the barkeep caught his eye and pointed to a curtained-off table in the corner most distant from the light of day. Marc made his way through the gloom, drew aside a curtain, and sat down opposite Cobb, who was puffing asthmatically on a short-stemmed clay pipe.

"Too early for ale, Constable?"

"A tad, Major. But I had enough last night to last me fer a while."

"But you were on duty last night," Marc said sternly.

"As I recollect, Major, the purpose of my visit to Danby's saloon was to give the appearance of a drunken peddler too tanked to make it home."

"I recall that stratagem, but –"

"The hardest body to fool into thinkin' you're drunk is another drunk," Cobb said, as if conveying an obvious truth to a particularly obtuse pupil. "And the joint was full of drunks."

"What did you manage to accomplish, then, before you decided to play the drunkard?"

"Wilkie and me spent the early part of the evenin' settin' up our surveillance."

"And?"

"And it's all set," Cobb snapped.

"I require the details, Constable."

Cobb arched his eyebrows, thick as a pair of cigar butts.

"I am expected to make a full report to the Governor in an hour," Marc said.

"Well, then, you can tell him from Horatio Cobb that it's all set: if that bastard Rumsey so much as shows the end of his pecker up there, we'll know what shade o' purple it is!"

"The Governor is not interested in the culprit's appendages –"

"Figure o' speakin', sir. Give the good Governor my regrets, but tell him if I was to give away the details of my spies, agents, and snitches, no criminal of any kind would ever be caught in this town. He'll have to take the word of a lowly constable, and that's the sum total of it. And so will you. *Sir.*"

"There's no need to get agitated; I'll find a way to explain it to Sir Francis. The important thing is that we're prepared to take Rumsey if he returns to Danby's Crossing. And by tomorrow or Saturday we should have some word on how matters stand in Buffalo."

"You figure that's where he's holed up?"

Marc nodded. "Now what about your *morning's* work among the shopkeepers on the square? Did you see Phineas Kimble?"

Cobb may have blushed, but it was impossible to tell. "I didn't quite get around to that."

"What do you mean, not quite?" My God, I'm beginning to sound like Uncle Sebastian, Marc thought.

"I only woke up an hour ago. I found I'd been sleepin' in the bush, beside my horse, thanks be to Jesus."

Marc now noticed that Cobb's peddler's outfit was not only rumpled but littered with bits of stick and grass.

"So you've blown your cover already!"

"Not quite, Major. I simply galloped back down here as fast as I could. I knew you needed to know what Wilkie and me did about the surveillance."

"Well, then, I'll just have to go up there myself. We need to get background information on Rumsey because even if we're lucky enough to capture him, there's no guarantee he will talk."

"You could try a little torture, Major. I hear tell that's what they do down in them dungeons you English folk have tucked underneath yer castles."

Marc glared at him.

"But you won't need to make the trip, Major. I'm gonna get myself some ale and a plate of smoked fish, courtesy of the house, and then I'm headin' back up to Danby's. Nobody's seen me crawlin' out of the bush yet, so that's what I'll do, tryin' my best to look hungover, mind. I'll meet you at the Tinker's Dam way up on Jarvis Street, say, about seven tomorrow evenin'? That is, if you ain't too busy otherwise."

"But that's practically in the countryside!"

"And safe from pryin' eyes, eh?"

Marc smiled reluctantly. "You've done good work thus far, Constable Cobb. I'll meet you there at seven. But there is one other minor matter that the Governor wishes you and me to address."

"And what might that be?" Cobb pulled the curtain aside and signalled to the tapster.

"The Governor is exercised about a person calling himself Farmer's Friend, who writes a weekly letter in Mackenzie's new paper, the *Constitution*. These letters, Sir Francis feels, might be having an adverse effect on the election here in York County –"

"Where Mackenzie just happens to be runnin'."

"That is irrelevant. What I've found out is that the writer is not Mackenzie or one of the other candidates but a genuine farmer. And this seems to be the problem."

"Ya mean he's tellin' the truth."

"Well, his version of it, I suppose. Anyway, it occurred to me that those *sources* of yours might be able to give us a name or a lead to the author's identity. Apparently these letters have stirred up a lot of comment locally, so there may be loose tongues about here in the taverns and –"

"You're hintin' that since I spend some time in them, I might be able to call on a snitch or two?"

"Something like that. But, of course, you still must focus your principal attention on the Moncreiff murder. In the meantime, I'll go up to Government House and report to Sir Francis."

"You don't want to eat first?"

The tapster was heading their way with a tray of drink and food.

Marc stood up. "I'll see you at seven tomorrow." As he stepped out of the curtained stall, he let in a glimmer of daylight. "Constable, where did you get that black eye?"

"Got into a bit of a brawl at Danby's," Cobb said proudly. "Had to make it look real, now, didn't I?"

Marc was back in the Governor's office at two o'clock. Sir Francis sat behind his desk, looking tired but determined. Major Burns shuffled several papers – notes or reports of some kind – then leaned back as far as he dare to catch the slight breeze from the open window behind him.

"Before I hear your report, Lieutenant, I have some interesting news for you," Sir Francis said. "I have just received a deposition from Magistrate Thorpe up in York Township, taken from a farmer named Luke Bethel."

"He was the man I spoke with after Crazy Dan was shot," Marc said with some surprise.

"That's the one. And according to his sworn testimony, Crazy Dan's gun was still in his grip with his finger on the trigger as he lay dead on his doorstep. Bethel admitted under close questioning from Mr. Thorpe that he saw Crazy Dan raise the gun just as he came over the rise below the cabin, but cannot say whether it was pointing at anyone in particular. He says also that, although attempts were made to warn you that Crazy Dan was harmless and the gun stoppered, these were not successful, and therefore the troops could not have known these critical facts before discharging their weapons."

"That is all true," Marc said, marvelling at Luke Bethel's honesty in the face of much temptation to behave otherwise.

"It seems to me you made quite an impression on Farmer Bethel."

"Quite the reverse, I'm afraid."

"In any case, this affidavit will go a long way to justifying my decision not to hold a formal inquest."

While Marc was relieved at this unexpected turn of events and heartened by Bethel's integrity, he was less than reassured by the Governor's cavalier decision not to hold the inquest. Too often, it seemed, the Governor dealt high-handedly with volatile political situations that required insight, diplomacy, and judicious decision-making. Marc brushed aside this thought, however, and dutifully brought Sir Francis and Major Burns up to date.

"Thank you," the Governor said when Marc had finished. "That is encouraging. We'll meet again tomorrow before the funeral, if there is anything further to be discussed, and later on after you've talked with Cobb at seven. Now, Major, would you mind giving Lieutenant Willoughby a hand in his office?"

Major Burns nodded assent, rose stiffly, and left the room.

"I have another matter I wish to discuss with you privately," Sir Francis said conspiratorially, and Marc wondered what was coming next.

"It's about Farmer's Friend."

"Ah," Marc said, relieved. "I've put Cobb on his trail. If there *is* a trail to be found, he'll find it."

"I hope so. But what I wish to do, in the few minutes I have you alone, is explain to you more fully why I think this matter urgent."

"My duty is to carry out your commands, sir, not to question them."

Sir Francis smiled wryly. "Well said. I wish more of the people's representatives felt that way. Nonetheless, I do want to explain to you why I am so serious in my concern over Farmer's Friend. After all, we have an angry, dissolved Assembly, an

Executive that resigned in protest, and a contentious election campaign in progress, not to mention a political assassination."

"Well, sir, I did wonder at the timing of your request."

"As any thoughtful human being would have. But it is precisely the timing that is most significant here. As you know, this Reform mouthpiece" – and Sir Francis tossed last Monday's edition of Mackenzie's newspaper rudely upon the desk between them – "this demagogic puffery is the common currency of journalism in this province. Its gross hyperbole – matched, alas, too often by the Conservative press – is so extreme, so distanced from fact or possibility, and so outrageous that readers of every stripe, supporters or detractors, have become inured to it. That is, as you know, one of the reasons that I decided to take to the hustings myself and deliver to the ordinary, loyal Upper Canadian the kind of plain talk he has not heard now for more than a decade."

"I understand, sir."

"Moreover, the so-called 'letters' sent by the quire to the popular press every week are cut from the same hyperbolic cloth and fall upon the same deadened ears. But five weeks ago the *Constitution* started to include a letter each week from this Farmer's Friend, and what has been different about it – and indeed more compelling – is that it, too, speaks in plain language and gives the dangerous illusion that its author has no political agenda except to recite the facts and have them make their own point unaided by bombast or political cant. What is more, each letter is in the form of a story, a kind of parable, which purports to illustrate the effects of various official policies upon ordinary folk. I have had three members of the Legislative Council in here today complaining of the influence these letters seem to be having upon the very moderate majority we are endeavouring to bring over to the Constitutionist side. Someone, most likely Mackenzie, has begun printing these meddlesome parables as broadsheets and flinging them about the hinterland like snowflakes."

"But if they are not distorting the truth, sir –"

The Governor's eyes tightened. "Dammit, man, they are telling only *one part* of the truth. I haven't the slightest doubt that these 'real-life' tales are true – for that's where their power to persuade lies – but to go on and on about the evils of the Clergy Reserves and the failure of the banking system to support the individual farmer or gripe about money being wasted on the Welland Canal that could have been used to improve roads is to ignore the good our policies have also done: we have to have money to support the Established Clergy, do we not? If they do not get it from the reserve lands, it will have to come from the farmer's own pocket. And if our richest citizens did not selflessly put up their own capital to establish banks, there would be no banks at all!"

"And you feel the letters from a single malcontent could be significant in the election?"

"My task, Lieutenant, is to make certain that by every legal means possible the Crown and the justice it embodies prevails at the polls. I wish to overlook nothing that might be detrimental to our cause. At the moment, for example, the murder of Councillor Moncreiff is working in our favour. There is fear and outrage among people of all classes."

And a convenient Yankee scapegoat, Marc thought, but it was a thought that did not make him happy. "Do we not, sir, have to respect the right of citizens to send letters to the press anonymously, provided they are not libellous?"

"Of course. And as I intimated briefly yesterday, I wish only to invite this person here to have a heart-to-heart talk. I feel that in doing so I may discover, shall we say, more *subtle* ways in which to frame my plain talk as we head into the London district next week. I have no wish to staunch the flow of the letters themselves."

"May I have copies of these letters, sir? There may be some clue or other in them that could lead eventually to identifying their author."

"Indeed you may. I had Major Burns clip them out for you."

With nothing to do but wait for Cobb's report tomorrow evening and for any news from Buffalo, Marc sat in his office and read over the letters penned by Farmer's Friend. As described by Sir Francis, they were written in simple, compelling prose. Each was in the form of a story, complete with touching dialogue and an ending pathetic enough to wring tears out of Diogenes. Each parable focused on one grievance and a single example of its devastating consequences. One letter dramatized the struggle of a farm couple to better their lot by investing their tiny store of hard-won capital in a gristmill. The mill, already serving their township, was owned by an elderly bachelor with no family in North America, who promised the couple that they could "buy him out" when he was ready to retire. When that day arrived last fall, he moved in with the couple and their five children and, on condition that they look after his simple needs until he should die – in addition to a cash payment equal to half of their life savings – he turned the operation over to them. The new miller and his eldest sons immediately spent the rest of their savings on needed improvements to the machinery. What they didn't know until several months later was that there was a lien on the property. The original owner had taken out a mortgage with the Investment Bank of Toronto and had been paying it off in quarterly sums. He assumed this would be no burden to the enterprising couple, but what he hadn't done was read the fine print of the contract he had signed. On January 1, 1836, the outstanding sum became due and payable in full within thirty days. All this usually meant was that the mortgage would be renegotiated at the current interest rate. But the bank, a well-known institution backed by a group of wealthy members of the Family Compact, refused to renew the mortgage and offered no explanation. The couple desperately tried to arrange a mortgage with the other two banks in the province but, again, were summarily and inexplicably rebuffed. A month later the Investment Bank foreclosed and took over the mill. Lo and behold, a nearby landowner, with direct links to the Tory faction in Toronto, bought the mill, appropriated the improvements, and set up a thriving business next door to the beleaguered couple. To no one's surprise, the Investment Bank had provided the mortgage money for the transaction. The disenfranchised couple was left with no savings, no mill, and no intention of turning the old miller into the streets (refusing even to take a cent of the money he offered them).

Other letters told similarly heart-wrenching stories, unvarnished by sentiment or anger. One recounted the familiar tale of a farmer whose pond had dried up and whose only alternative source of water now lay in an adjacent property designated as clergy-reserve land. The description of cattle nearly dying of thirst a hundred yards from fresh water – while a weary farmer and his wife carried buckets of stolen water in an effort to save them – was as touching as it was, sadly, true.

The wretched state of the roads – which the province could not afford to maintain because of the hundreds of thousands of pounds that had gone into the corrupt management of the Welland Canal scheme – was painfully illustrated by the story of a sick child being driven in her parents' donkey-cart to the doctor who lived not on some back-township concession but on Kingston Road. Necessary repairs on several sections had not been carried out because government subsidies had been delayed, in part it appeared, because there was uncertainty over who was to receive the patronage money to do the actual work. Needless to say, the wagon bogged down, the child's condition grew worse, and when a wheel broke off and the donkey collapsed under the strain, the father was forced to run on a shortcut route through swamp and bog – with his daughter whimpering in his arms – in a futile attempt to reach the doctor's house. The child was dead on arrival.

When Marc finished the last letter, he leaned back in his chair and lit his pipe. His hand was trembling, but not because of the obvious tragedies related in these stories and so witheringly told by Farmer's Friend – after all, dreadful deaths among the poor and the abandoned were commonplace everywhere on earth, it seemed, and were, everyone said, the result of God's will. Few people really expected justice from the world. But these tragedies and injustices were preventable, not inevitable: they were the direct consequence of greed, mismanagement, malfeasance, and criminal negligence. And these themes were the flashpoints of the current election. Moreover, the parable-like format made these accounts accessible to anyone who could read, and that included most of the property owners eligible to vote. These letters could be mass produced, and distributed as broadsheets at political rallies and picnics and at the many church socials held during the fine-weather month of June.

It was little wonder that Sir Francis was worried.

Marc's sleep that night was interrupted twice: first by a nightmare in which the scene of Moncreiff's murder was replayed with horrifying verisimilitude, except that the assassin's bullet travelled through the bent neck of the Governor before striking Councillor Moncreiff. The second interruption was less fantastic but more disruptive, as a noisy (drunken?) Lieutenant

Willoughby clattered and thumped his way down the hall, crashed against the door to his room (next to Marc's), and finally pitched inward to the accompaniment of muted curses and breaking porcelain. After that, there was silence. Widow Standish had, mercifully, slept through the commotion. Then, surprisingly, there came a soft whistling from Willoughby's room: a sprightly air of some kind, lyrical and longing.

Willoughby's mood had soured considerably by morning. Marc met him coming out of his room on the way to breakfast. Colin was understandably bleary-eyed and out of sorts, but the look he gave Marc as they almost collided was quite hostile.

"Sorry, Colin, I'm still half-asleep," Marc lied amiably.

"You're never half-asleep, so don't go pretending you are!"

"Hey, don't take your hangover out on me! I'm an ally."

"You're like all the others," Willoughby said, some unspoken resentment seething though his clenched teeth. "You're looking out for number one. You want everything: advancement, women, glory –"

"If I remember rightly, it was you whom the Governor chose to take with him to the London district," Marc said, more puzzled than hurt by Colin's words.

Willoughby's jaw dropped, and whatever he had intended to say was left unuttered. He looked at Marc now as if he were seeing him from another angle. A boyish grin broke across his face. "I'm sorry, Marc. You know I have trouble sometimes controlling my anger. I'm doing my best to forget what happened back in England with my dear Rosy, but every once in a while, all the frustration boils up inside me."

"Apology accepted," Marc said with evident relief. "But you'll need to keep your wits about you around Sir Francis."

"You're right. I think I'll go straight up there now and get the day started."

By the time Willoughby got to the end of the hall, he was whistling.

Marc himself was in no hurry. He had thought of offering to help with the Governor's correspondence but decided against it because he wanted Colin to feel fully in charge. As it turned out, Marc did not have to twiddle his thumbs for too long. Before noon, Sir Francis summoned him to his office.

They were alone.

"I've just received a written report by courier from Fort George," the Governor said. Nothing in his face indicated the nature of the news. When he wished to, Sir Francis could play poker with the best. "Major Emery has outdone himself. I must recommend him for an official commendation."

"They've unearthed Rumsey?"

"Not exactly. But in less than a day and a half they have gathered several bits of important information."

Marc simply sat back and waited.

"First, the story from Mrs. Rumsey about her husband's mother being gravely ill was true. The family is well known in Buffalo, and the people over there are, fortunately for us, loquacious busybodies. A cousin of Rumsey's assured our agent, who was accompanied on his rounds by one of the New York sheriffs, that Philo had arrived the previous Thursday and stayed at his mother's bedside until her death on Saturday. She was buried on Tuesday in a private funeral attended only by family members. They all swear that Rumsey was present."

"And if he were in Buffalo then, he couldn't simultaneously be a hundred miles north in Danby's Crossing."

"But he wasn't at the funeral. A neighbour, who is not particularly friendly with the clan Rumsey, told our agent that Rumsey was seen leaving the house on Monday morning – with a packsack on one shoulder and a large rifle on the other."

"A U.S. army rifle – a gift from one of his brothers, no doubt," Marc said with mounting excitement.

"We won't know that for sure until we catch up with him."

"But if we're now pretty certain that he set out last Monday morning for Canada, how could he have reached Danby's Crossing by midafternoon on Tuesday? A courier could do it in seven or eight hours, but only with fresh horses every twenty miles. Do you think he had that kind of help? Are we possibly looking at a larger conspiracy?"

"I think not," Sir Francis said with more confidence than seemed warranted. "He could have ridden up to Fort Niagara and taken a boat across the lake. Fishing vessels and smugglers abound on the lake, as you know from your Cobourg investigation. A small bribe would bring him across in three or four hours – probably on Monday night. That would give him ample time to reach Danby's and plot his strategy."

"If so, it looks more and more as if the harness-maker Kimble was in on the murder. Rumsey is not going to miss his mother's funeral on the off chance that he might be able to take a potshot at Moncreiff."

"Well, he was happy enough to use her as his alibi. And he couldn't have known precisely when she would die."

Marc nodded in sad agreement. "But he definitely has not returned to Buffalo *since* Tuesday?"

"Not to the family home, according to the nosy neighbours, but it's not likely he would go back there, unless he feels he has not been targeted as a suspect."

"Well, let's hope he's still in the province and not yet aware he's a fugitive." Marc considered the latter possibility doubtful, thanks to the Governor's hasty decision to broadcast the notion that an American malcontent was the likely culprit – but he said nothing further on the matter.

"At any rate, we're making progress," Sir Francis said amiably. "And Willoughby and Hilliard are fine-tuning our travel plans for Monday."

"Yes," Marc said, "Willoughby has even taken up whistling."

The funeral for Langdon Moncreiff – one-time major in the local militia, privy councillor, businessman, husband, uncle, and father – was as solemn and dignified as the rutted streets and intermittent rain would allow. There was much pomp and ceremony, and a sea of crêpe and sackcloth stretched (reported the Tory *Patriot*) for three city blocks. Sir Francis rode at the front, as befitted his station and dignity – proud, grieving, unafraid: "A man of imperial demeanour with the common touch," enthused the *Cobourg Star*. What Langdon Moncreiff might have made of all this hoopla was not cause for speculation in the press, liberal or conservative.

Marc received a written invitation to have supper with Eliza and her uncle at seven-thirty. If Sebastian had read the riot act to his niece, it had been a mild reading – though Marc had little doubt that he and Eliza would be chaperoned for the duration of the evening. Was it possible that her uncle had relayed to her, however garbled in the translation, the nature of her lover's "intentions"? He hoped not. Meanwhile, there was the appointment with Cobb.

The rain had stopped and the sun was shining by the time Marc left Jarvis Street north and nudged the chestnut mare onto the muddy lane that he had been told would take him to the Tinker's Dam. For a moment he thought he was heading straight into the bush, but the thicket of scrub alder and hawthorn was short-lived. Beyond it, helter-skelter on either side of what was now merely a mud path, lay improvised huts and hovels that had never felt a carpenter's square or an iron nail. Nor was there a level spot of green ground anywhere, just middens and cesspools. A few puffs of tired smoke were the only indication that these grim buildings were inhabited. Marc could see no one around except a blackened pig or hairless dog rooting in a garbage dump between two huts. Marc was glad he had buckled on his sabre at the last minute.

Rounding a twist in the pathway, Marc spotted the Tinker's Dam. There was no sign outside, but the fact that it was the most substantial building on the "street" left no doubt. Nor did the blast of raised voices Marc could hear pouring from its paneless windows and one-hinged door. What on earth was Cobb up to, Marc wondered, as he tethered the mare to a tree stump where she could be seen from inside the tavern.

In this tavern, there was no tapster primed to point out Constable Cobb nor was there a bar or table: a wooden plank on two trestles served as the former and three or four tilting stumps provided the latter. The proprietor stood beside an open barrel of whisky, collecting pennies from the customers before they dipped a battered tin cup into the raw liquid. The clientele was a motley collection of men who – from their ragged clothing, slumped posture, and deep-set, sad eyes – looked to be unemployed, unemployable, or simply so far down on their luck that nothing much mattered except the solace of alcohol.

The din of their conversation – vibrant with anger, bravado, pathetic threat – suddenly died. Every eye in the place was fastened upon the uniformed intruder. Marc smiled but kept one hand on the haft of his sabre.

"It's okay, gentlemen, the Lieutenant's a colleague of mine. Go back to your business." It was Cobb, perched on a stump-stool, puffing on his pipe, and back in his constable's attire. Several of the barflies made grudging way for Marc.

"Pull up a stump, Major," Cobb said heartily, as if they were in the Governor's parlour sampling brandy. "Care fer a dram?"

Cobb's wife must have taken advantage of his absence to clean and buff up his uniform, for the stains had been removed from the coat and a fresh shirt peeked out from under it.

Marc eased himself onto a sawtoothed stool and said, "What were you thinking of in calling me out to a place like this? We stick out like a pair of roosters in a fox's den!"

"Now, Major, don't get yer scabbard in a curdle. These chaps may look dangerous, but they'd only stab you if you was alone in an alley with yer back turned, yer flies undone, an' both legs wobbly with the drink."

"But I have to *shout* to hear what I have to say!" Marc yelled into the general roar.

"May be, Major," Cobb shouted back, "but who's likely to be listenin', eh?"

"Couldn't we go for a walk?"

"An' how then would I be gettin' my cup refilled?"

Marc gave in, but only because he realized that he had adjusted to the noise level and that Cobb would, strangely enough, function better here than elsewhere.

"You may find it hard to reckon with, Major, but it's in this dive and in the Blue Ox – where I dined – that I come up with the details I think you'll find interestin'."

"Be that as it may, Constable, I am most anxious to know what you found out about Philo Rumsey up at Danby's."

Cobb sighed, shrugged his shoulders, emptied his cup, and said, "You're the governor, Major. Do ya want me to start with the point where I crawl out of the bush and gather my pots together?"

"I don't need all the extraneous –"

"I know, I know." Cobb got up and went over to the whisky barrel.

Marc was suddenly aware of being stared at. He turned to his left, and no more than three feet away stood a ragged creature with a walleyed gaze and a drooling lip.

"Don't mind ol' Stony," Cobb said, sitting down. "He likes to look, but he's as deaf as a post, *ain't ya, Stony?*"

Stony grinned, and drooled happily.

"Here's my report, Major, sir, with the details whittled away."

Marc acknowledged the witticism, and waited.

"I had no trouble gettin' the wives to chatter on about the Rumseys. Seems they're the talk of the town. Rumsey is a loner. He ain't got a political bone in his body. But since Kimble let him go last year, he's been desperate poor. Kept his family alive by huntin' in the winter and sellin' the meat left over. The gossip is he's beat up his missus or the nearest kid when he's been in an ugly mood – but nobody claims they actually saw this."

"Desperately poor enough to take cash for a little marksmanship on the square?" Marc mused.

"Desperate enough, I'd say. But I don't think it was Kimble put him up to it."

"Why not? It was his house the shot was fired from."

"Maybe so. But Kimble's got debts. He's a bit of a poker player, they told me. He may be part of the set-up, but he's not the money man."

"And his politics?"

"A Reformer, but then everybody up in that township except old Danby and his dame are liberals," Cobb said with some vehemence. "And so are lots of ordinary folk down here." He stared hard at Marc.

Marc carried right on: "Has anyone seen or heard of Rumsey, on the day of the shooting or since?"

"Not up there."

Marc's jaw dropped. Cobb deliberately took a slow draft of his booze, then said, "He was spotted in here on Tuesday evenin'."

"Jesus!" Marc cried. "We could have taken him!"

Cobb smiled. "Not a soul in here would've turned him in – without a fifty-dollar reward."

"Who saw him? Let me question him!"

Cobb sighed. "You don't get it, do ya, Major? I was told by one of my snitches who was told by a pal of the guy who was supposed to've seen somebody who might've been Rumsey."

"My God."

"But he was here, all the same," Cobb sighed again, and began to fuss with filling his pipe. He peered up and said, "He's been spotted in other places, too."

"Christ, man, are the Governor and I the only two people in the province who *haven't* seen him?" Marc was exasperated, but he knew now that in Cobb lay his only hope of solving this crime.

"Keep yer linens dry, Major. I'm just gettin' to the good part. It seems Rumsey was a loner and a recluse up in Danby's Crossing, but down here in town he was quite the dicer and ladies' man. In these parts he went by the name of Lance Carson. His favourite waterin' hole turns out to be the Blue Ox. One of my regular snitches there knew who he really was, though. But in them kinda dives and whorehouses a man is who he says he is."

"And?"

"And so his movements weren't as secret as he figured. Another snitch reckons he may've spotted someone who looked like Rumsey-Carson gettin' off a fishin' boat on the pier down past Enoch Turner's brewery." Cobb paused for a suspenseful puff. "About sun-up on Tuesday. And luggin' a long 'fishin' pole.' "

"I must have that man as a witness."

Cobb said nothing, puffing contentedly on his pipe.

So, Marc thought, Sir Francis was right about Rumsey coming across the lake. And now they had him back in the province on the morning of the shooting and here at the Tinker's Dam a few hours after it. Had he been on his way back to Buffalo? Well, no one had seen him there yet. So there was a chance that he might simply be hiding in the bush until he could figure out how to get his wife and children away with him. But with Cobb's spies watching them closely, that would not be easy. Surely now it was just a question of being patient. There seemed, moreover, no quick way to link Rumsey with whoever had put him up to the deed.

"You want to hear the rest or not?" Cobb said.

"You've got more?"

"A bit, and then some."

"Well, then, get on with it!" Marc snapped in his officer's voice.

But Cobb had got up and was glaring over Marc's shoulder. "Harpie, you get away from Stony or I'll come over there and knock the last of yer brains all over yer face!" He sat back down. "Sorry, Major, where was I? Ah, yes. As I said before, I had supper in the Blue Ox before I come up here. My dinner companion, fer the price of a meal and a flagon, happened to mention that he might've seen Rumsey-Carson here at the Tinker's Dam about a week before the shootin'. In fact, I might've seen 'im myself if I'd've known what it was I supposed to be lookin' at."

"But you've already said that Rumsey-Carson was in the city a good deal of the time he was supposed to be off hunting."

"Ah, but it's who he was spotted with that's downright curious."

"The person behind the assassination?"

"Could be. Could be. Seems that Rumsey-Carson was seen drinkin' here with a stranger – no one'd ever seen him before anyways – and they was talkin' real low and secretlike, and when they finished, some money changed hands. Foldin' money. Big bills you gotta crinkle more'n once."

"This sounds like the evidence we need," Marc said excitedly.

"'Course, it coulda been just a gamblin' debt bein' settled . . ."

"What did this stranger look like?"

"Hard to say. Dressed like a sailor, I was told, with a wool navy cap of sorts pulled way down over his brow – it was ninety degrees in here, I bet – and a bushy black beard."

"But that could be any of a hundred men wandering around the docks." Marc could not hide his disappointment.

"Maybe so," Cobb said, "but he walked an' carried himself like a swell."

Marc's mind was abuzz with facts and theories and might-be's, as he and Cobb strolled over to the chestnut mare. Two naked children, purple with impetigo, were staring at the great beast with wide-eyed wonder.

"There is one other thing, Major," Cobb said, making a shooing motion with his hand that failed to dislodge the children. "Not a big thing, but you did ask me to look into the business of the letters in Mackenzie's paper."

Marc stood with one hand on the saddle. "But surely you –"

"That was the easiest part, Major. When I dropped into the Crooked Anchor to whet my whistle after my bumpy ride home today, a fella there was in his cups and braggin' that he earned himself a U.S. silver dollar every Saturday mornin', and all fer pickin' up and deliverin' a letter to the *Constitution*."

"Did he say who gave it to him?"

"He wasn't *that* drunk. And if I hadn't've still been in my peddler's disguise, he wouldn't've spouted off like that at all."

"Tomorrow's Saturday."

"I believe it is, Major, though we country folk don't pay much heed to the days of the week."

"But that means that –"

"I can kick the old lady outta bed before sun-up and head down to Abner Clegg's place."

"You know this man?"

"He's a dock worker and, if rumour be fact, not always an honest one. I'll track him to your letter-writer like a he-hound on a she-hound's arse."

Marc nodded his approval while failing to hide his amazement. Then he went over to the children and put a three-penny piece in each of their grubby hands. Cobb looked on impassively.

"You've done yeoman's service, Constable. I shall let the Governor and Chief Constable Sturges know of your . . . diligence. And, if you'll keep track of any monies you've paid out during the investigation, I'll see that you're reimbursed."

"We ain't allowed to take fees," Cobb said curtly.

"Would you like a ride home?"

"No thanks, Major. It's a pleasant evenin' fer a stroll. Besides, ya never know how many interestin' people you might bump into along the way."

Marc mounted his mare and waved to the children.

"By the bye," Cobb said, "I managed to sell three of the wife's cookin' pots."

It wasn't until Marc was crossing Hospital Street that he had the sudden disturbing thought that Cobb had gathered an enormous amount of pertinent information in only a day and a half, but not one jot of it had been, or could be, corroborated. Was it possible that he had made some of it up? *All* of it? And if so, why?

It was almost eight-thirty by the time Marc had reached his boarding house, bathed, changed his shirt, and presented himself at the Dewart-Smythes'. The excitement and mental turmoil over Cobb's tidings had made it difficult for him to concentrate on what might lie before him. But it was hard to imagine that Uncle Sebastian's blundering interference could seriously alter the rapport he and Eliza had cautiously established over the past few weeks.

Although he was late, no mention was made of it. Supper was served in the parlour-dining room, and, although Uncle Sebastian kept a watchman's eye on his niece and her suitor throughout the several courses of the meal (the jellied venison was particularly tasty, as were the fresh strawberries), Eliza showed no sign of irritation or concern. They discussed the funeral service, the outlandish dress of this or that country aristocrat, the sadness in the gait of Moncreiff's daughters as they walked from St. James Church to their crêpe-swathed carriage, and the awful moment when the hearse had heaved sideways in the mud of a rain-slick street and nearly capsized. Eliza remarked how closely related were comedy and tragedy, which brought a reproving glower from her uncle, who then turned the conversation into a monologue on the infinite opportunities for the expansion of the Dewart-Smythe enterprise. "New York, now there's a market, eh?" he sighed. Eliza gave him a curious stare.

When the meal was complete, Eliza pushed her chair away from the table and went over and sat down on the sofa. She patted the cushion beside her. "Come over and have a cigar," she said to Marc. And to her uncle, whose remonstrance never got as far as his lips, she said, "Did you not tell me earlier, Uncle, that you were going to check the new stock before retiring?"

Uncle Sebastian huffed a bit but replied, "I believe I did." And he struggled up out of his chair. By the time he was perpendicular, Eliza had taken two slim cheroots from the humidor on the table beside the sofa and popped one of them between her lips.

"Eliza! What would your blessed mother say if she were alive to see you behaving . . . behaving like a –"

"– gentleman?" Eliza said, laughing.

"Don't be impertinent," Uncle Sebastian said, but he hurried off so as not to bear witness to the actual ignition of the offending objects.

Eliza blew pretty smoke rings into the still evening air as twilight descended outside the bay window. "He'll be gone for at least half an hour," she said, leaning against Marc.

For a long minute they were content to let the touch of their bodies speak for itself. Through the open window, the evening breeze perfumed the room with the scent of roses.

"You should know he's been asking me frank questions about what he calls my 'intentions,'" Marc murmured.

"I thought so," she said, but there was only amusement in her face. "He's been trying to find a way to warn me about the dangers of young men without actually spelling them out. I'm not sure he *can* spell them out, the old dear."

"He was quizzing me about my parentage and my prospects. I'm sure he sees me as a fortune-hunter pursuing your money and your virtue."

"Well, you can't have my money!" she laughed.

"I'm serious. In your uncle's view, both my bloodline and my potential inheritance are suspect."

"You mean he would refuse you my hand in marriage?" The dark eyes danced.

"Yes, I believe he would."

"And would you ask for it?"

"Well, I . . ."

"I'm teasing, silly. Let's not spoil a good cigar with that kind of talk."

Marc sighed with some relief. Eliza was unquestionably a remarkable young woman. But when they had set aside their cheroots and slid comfortably into one another's arms and when Eliza began nibbling at his ear, Marc simply held her close and rocked back and forth – his own lips open in pleasure but not in passion.

"Call out the watch! Fetch the constables!"

Marc and Eliza sprang apart, but it was doubtful if Uncle Sebastian noticed their embrace.

"They've been at it again!" he cried. "In broad daylight!"

"Who?" Eliza said.

"The wine thieves, that's who!"

Chapter Eight

Marc had yet another restless night. This time his nightmare took him to the death of Crazy Dan. In one horrific sequence the poor devil appeared with his head sundered from his body and floating above the neck-stump, where it proceeded to cry out a single word, over and over: innocent, innocent! This time when Colin Willoughby clumped in, in the dead of night, and woke him, Marc was relieved. Only in the morning, when he found that Colin had arisen early again and headed up to Government House, did Marc realize that it had been days since he and Colin had had a chance to sit down and talk as friends – which he was certain they now were. He still had not yet reassured Colin that he bore no responsibility for Crazy Dan's death. At least the reasons why he had not had the chance to do so were all in Colin's best interest: his new duties at Government House and, it seemed probable, a newly awakened love life. Well, when all this trouble blew over or was resolved, he would take Colin out on a pub-crawl and bonding expedition.

Before going over to Government House himself to report Cobb's news to Sir Francis, Marc walked briskly through the

Saturday sunshine to Eliza's place. There he found Constable Ewan Wilkie, who had taken over Cobb's patrol area and had returned to the scene of the break-in to examine it in daylight. He seemed pleased to see Marc, probably because he provided a neutral party to place between him and Uncle Sebastian's unchecked contempt. The thieves, whoever they were, had been professional to a fault. A door to one of the storerooms had been jimmied with a minimum of noise or damage. They had chosen an entrance off a shadowy alley and, somehow knowing the merchant's routine, had moved in undetected just after closing time and selected only a few tuns of the most expensive wine. The fresh ruts of a cartwheel suggested they had boldly parked a wagon on the street and, as darkness fell, had rolled the tuns onto it, covering the booty with a sailcloth or such, and then trotting off at a sedate pace for their lair.

Wilkie, a stolid man who blinked a lot, blinked at Uncle Sebastian and summed matters up succinctly: "I reckon, sir, you'll have to get yerself a night watchman."

This advice did little to modify the good merchant's contempt. And Marc decided that it was an inopportune time to ask after Eliza's health. So he and Wilkie left together and walked down Yonge Street. Just before they got to King, Wilkie said, "By the bye, sir, Mr. Cobb wants to see you."

Marc met Cobb at the Cock and Bull on York Street about eleven o'clock. For the first time Cobb looked just slightly abashed. Something had gone wrong.

"You didn't find out who Farmer's Friend is, I take it," Marc said, unable to keep the critical tone out of his voice.

"'Fraid not, Major."

"Did this Clegg fellow show?"

"Yup, just like he said," Cobb replied. "I got to his house down on Front Street just as the sun was comin' up over the

Don. Out he waltzes a few minutes later and starts headin' west into the city proper. I was able to keep myself well hidden behind bushes until he arrived at Market Square, where the farmers'd already begun settin' up their stalls and barrows. It was busy enough fer me to mix in with the crowd, seein' as I wasn't in uniform."

Marc refrained from pointing out that his beet-sized nose, spiked hair, and bottle shape might provide something less than perfect anonymity.

"Well, all of a suddenlike, he starts to pick up his pace, and I do the same. But there's three dozen stalls around us, and people start jostlin' me, and before I know it, Abner Clegg's vamoosed."

"You lost him?"

Cobb looked hurt. "I don't give up that easy, Major. I circled 'round the Market Square, checkin' all the streets in and out. No sign of him or his shadow. So I head up towards Mackenzie's shop on Church Street, duckin' in and out of alleys careful-like, and pretty soon I spot him comin' out of the printin' place."

"He had delivered the letter?"

Cobb ignored the impertinence of the interruption. "So I follow him down here to this dive. I send a message to you, and then wait outside fer him to leave. But all the time I'm thinkin', like I always do, and I reckoned he wasn't outta my sight after the market fer no more'n a quarter-hour, so he must've picked up the letter from one of the houses or shops within, say, three blocks of Mackenzie's."

Marc made no comment on this unhelpful bit of deduction. Finally, he said, "Why all this secrecy? All this cloak-and-dagger manoeuvring? Surely most letter-writers deliver their material themselves or have a friend do it or pay a street urchin a penny to carry it – or, if all else fails, use the mails."

"Beats me, Major. But I don't suppose you're interested in hearin' the actual end to my story?"

Marc heaved a deep and resigned sigh. "I'm all ears."

"Clegg's got a mouth twice the size of his brain, lucky fer us. He starts braggin' in here – in front of my chief snitch – about how he figures he was bein' trailed this mornin', and just to make sure it don't happen again, he's arranged with his client to pick the letter up next Friday instead of Saturday."

"Well, that's better than nothing," Marc said as kindly as he could.

"And I'll be there like a –"

"I'm sure you will," Marc said.

When the duty-corporal ushered him into the Governor's office, Marc was mildly surprised to find Sir Francis seated at his desk next to Willoughby, shoulder to shoulder and obviously putting the finishing touches on one of the speeches planned for the progress through the radical ridings of the London district. Sir Francis glanced up at Marc with his usual welcoming smile and impeccable manners, but Colin was so engrossed in his work that he seemed not to have realized anyone had entered the room. Sir Francis directed Marc to the chair usually reserved for Major Burns (prostrate, apparently, with a rheumatic attack), and the corporal slid another up behind his commander opposite Marc.

"I've asked Lieutenant Willoughby to work into the night if necessary to get the wording of my Brantford speech exactly right. Tomorrow being the Sabbath, we have only a few hours left to get everything perfected for our assault on the western ridings. And as you know, Marc, my success there is critical to the outcome of the election."

"I believe so, sir."

Willoughby's constant scratching and blotting were an irritation, but Colin himself seemed oblivious to the conversation going on no more than ten feet from him. Not once did he look up to greet Marc, and Marc realized with a guilty start that he himself was both hurt and jealous. He wanted Colin to do well, but not well enough to supplant him. He felt that his protégé ought to show some gratitude or at least acknowledge that Marc had played a part in his rehabilitation.

"It is vitally important that we win seats in all regions of the province," Sir Francis was saying. "Our triumph must not be in numbers alone. I want troublemakers like Mackenzie and Peter Perry and Marshall Spring Bidwell driven from the field."

But not humiliated, Marc wanted to say.

"Young Hilliard is doing a splendid job in helping Willoughby with the security of those travelling with me – including my son. You have trained the ensign well, Marc."

"Thank you, sir."

"You'll also be pleased to know that I am taking along in the official party the Receiver General, Mr. Maxwell, and Colonel Allan MacNab. I want not merely to show the flag but to flaunt it!"

Certainly the inclusion of MacNab would have that effect. MacNab was a high Tory, who had been instrumental in having Mackenzie expelled illegally from the Assembly for the third time, in 1832. He was also a symbol of loyalty to the Crown and of the rise to wealth and power of the native-born. He had fought bravely as a militiaman in the War of 1812 and had become on his own merit a successful lawyer, legislator, merchant, and land speculator. The sight of him sitting beside Sir Francis in full regalia would undoubtedly raise hackles and tempers.

"About the investigation, sir," Marc said diffidently.

"My word, yes. Of course, that is why you have come, isn't it?"

When it seemed clear he was to make his report in Willoughby's presence, Marc began. As was his custom, Sir Francis listened without interruption as Marc gave him chapter and verse of Cobb's prodigious discoveries at Danby's Crossing and elsewhere.

"Excellent work, Lieutenant. If all this information proves out, it appears we have identified the man who pulled the trigger and established that he was most probably a paid assassin. This corroborates the edited account I have already released to the public. And when we capture the blackguard, we'll know who is really behind the murder, and why."

"That is what I believe too," Marc said. "But it begs a more serious question. Should we set up a general hue and cry with a warrant issued and all military and police personnel given a description of the man –"

"What *does* he look like, by the way?"

"Constable Cobb did not relay that detail to me, sir, but I am sure he could at a minute's notice."

Sir Francis looked thoughtful for a moment. "I sense you do not wish to raise the alarm immediately?"

"If Cobb is right, sir, the odds are that Philo Rumsey has not gone back to Buffalo but is camping out in the bush. Why he would do so, except that his wife and children are still in Danby's Crossing, we don't know. But if the alarm is raised everywhere, he may well panic and cross the border – forever."

"So we might be better off alerting our people along the border – at Fort George, Fort Erie, Fort Henry, and even Fort Malden – and leave it at that for now?"

"I believe that is the more prudent plan, in the circumstances. There is no likelihood of Rumsey assassinating anyone else, as he himself has no political motive."

Sir Francis watched Willoughby's quill-scratching for almost a minute. "All right, Lieutenant, we'll do just that – for a few days at least. But you do realize that our decision is based on our acceptance of the evidence gathered by one lowly police constable, and uncorroborated."

"I do, sir," Marc said, keeping his own doubts to himself.

"It does seem amazing that this Cobb – who, I was told by Mr. Sturges, comes from a farm family near Woodstock – could have found out so much so quickly."

"Well, he did fail in one respect, sir," Marc said. And he gave the Governor an account of Cobb's misadventure with the letter courier.

"Well, that's unfortunate. I was hoping to come face to face with Farmer's Friend before setting off for the west," Sir Francis said, then added, "Don't you find it odd that Cobb could tease out so much useful information up at Danby's and in the taverns of the town, and then allow himself to be led astray by some nondescript like Abner Clegg – in his own patrol area?"

"What are you suggesting, sir?"

"Only that these constables were not selected from former militia members, who might have brought some experience to the occupation. They were patronage appointments made by Toronto aldermen sympathetic to the Reform party and headed by a Reform mayor."

"You think Cobb may have allowed his political views to influence his duty in this particular case? Because he owes his appointment to Mackenzie?"

"I am suggesting that it is a possibility."

"In this business of the letters, you mean?"

Sir Francis sighed. "I hope to God it's in this instance only."

"I'll do the job myself, then," Marc said quickly, "next Friday morning. I'll have the letter-writer's name for you by Friday noon."

"And with any luck you'll have Rumsey in irons," Sir Francis said warmly. Suddenly he clapped a hand on Marc's shoulder and began leading him towards the door. "Now I have a much more pleasant assignment for you. The coachman I usually employ to drive my ward about town – and to keep a close watch on her – is ill today, and Angeline has her heart set on a shopping trip. I'll have one of my grooms drive the team, but I would feel more at ease if you were to escort her. It will take less than an hour of your time."

"I would be happy to do so," Marc said, suppressing his chagrin as best he could.

At the door Marc turned around just far enough to catch Willoughby's eye. Colin was smiling.

Angeline Hartley, the Governor's ward, was petalled entirely in pink, from her floral hat to her frilled and beribboned frock to her dainty boots and the bloom of her parasol. Even her face shone pink with the first blush of womanhood – a state she wished, devoutly and often, to enter permanently. She was all of seventeen, and nothing set her heart aflutter as much as a young man in uniform. The image of Lieutenant Edwards – tunicked and tall and handsome – was not so breathtaking, however, as to strike her dumb. Quite the opposite. She babbled non-stop in Marc's ear all the way down fashionable King Street. About *what* Marc was not able to decipher exactly, but, then, it was the passion and intensity of her girl-chatter that mattered most. When they passed Bay Street, Angeline stopped talking, sat upright (she had been teetering coquettishly towards her escort's shoulder from time to time), arched her parasol jauntily, and with a gloved hand waved to the throng of onlookers she imagined must be watching in undisguised envy.

"Do stop here, Coachman!" Angeline called, and the young groom drew the open carriage to a halt. "This is one of the shops where I purchase my dresses and gowns," she said to Marc, who had stepped down and offered her his hand. She held it as long as she dared, then moved across the boardwalk to Miss Adeline's.

"I'll wait for you here," Marc said, touching the brim of his shako cap.

"I shan't be long, Lieutenant," Angeline burbled, then twirled prettily and entered the shop.

A minute or so later, the shop door opened, but it was not Angeline who emerged. It was Prudence Maxwell. And if Angeline was a spring flower, Prudence was a late-summer rose or gladiola. She had packed the overblown bloom of her flesh into a low-cut bodice and blinding-yellow skirt. All about her hung an air of over-lush ripeness. When she spotted Marc, she stopped abruptly and aimed a thick-lipped smile in his direction.

"Why, Lieutenant, how nice to see you once again."

"Madam," Marc said, bowing briefly.

"My, what onerous duties Sir Francis puts upon you!" she laughed. "How are your ears?"

Marc acknowledged the reference to Angeline with a slight smile. "They have survived, ma'am – so far."

"Well, I do hope they last until next Saturday."

Marc looked puzzled.

"Good gracious, doesn't that old fuddy-duddy up at Government House tell you anything? The whole town is agog with the news, Lieutenant. We are holding a gala at Somerset House next Saturday evening – to welcome Sir Fuddy-Duddy home from the wars and celebrate the coming triumph in the elections. Every officer at the rank of ensign and above has been invited. Your invitation *must* be on your desk by now."

"That is pleasant news indeed, and I must apologize for not noticing the invitation. But as you can see, I've been kept occupied away from my office."

"Well, so long as you come," she said, feigning a pout. "As

hostess I have taken the liberty of placing your name first on my dance card. I trust you do not mind?"

"I would be honoured to have the first dance with the Receiver General's wife."

"I'll try to make it a waltz," she said with a leer. "It's so much more intimate than a galop or a reel, don't you think?"

"I'm sure you dance well, whatever the form."

She stared at him as if deciding how she should take this remark, then smiled and said in a more serious tone, "Have you discovered the name of my daughter's secret lover yet?"

"I have one or two suspicions, ma'am, but no confirmation."

"Could you throw me a hint? From the blush on Chastity's cheek these days, I feel it may come too late."

Marc replied quickly, almost priggishly, "I could not, madam, compromise the reputation of any of the good men under –"

Prudence frowned and then stepped onto the road, coming up close to Marc beside the carriage. "Jesus, fella," she hissed, "you don't need to spread that mannerly crap all over me. We ain't in Mayfair." A gust of perfume made Marc gasp, as she stretched up and kissed him on the chin, permitting him a frontal glimpse of her barely harnessed breasts.

"That's for being a naughty boy," she laughed, before turning towards her own carriage, which had just pulled up.

Marc watched her leave, annoyed, because, in spite of himself, he had been momentarily aroused.

Angeline came out of the dress shop, unaware of what had just taken place, though the teenaged groom was still gawking. Marc helped her aboard, and they moved off up the busy street. Angeline's chatter about ribbons and furbelows and the hat she was planning to buy today was now pleasantly diverting. So much so that, as they began to slow down in front of the new millinery shop, Marc did not see or hear the pounding of hooves or the clatter of wooden wheels bouncing wildly until it was almost too late. The rear portion of the runaway vehicle skidded into the Governor's carriage and knocked it upwards and over with a jarring collision, pulling its horses to their knees. Marc just had time to grasp Angeline and follow the arc of the carriage as it careened and slammed onto the boardwalk with a murderous thump amid the squeal of terrified animals. He hurled himself sideways and tumbled onto the road, landing in a pool of soft dirt, and breaking Angeline's fall with his own body. Dazed but thinking hard, he peered down the street at the disappearing wagon and saw its driver – in overalls and a straw hat – hauling futilely on the reins and crying havoc. Then surprisingly, the "runaway" team veered neatly to the left down Bay Street, still racing but not without guidance. At least it seemed so to Marc as his head swam and his vision suddenly blurred. As he rolled over to check on Angeline, he saw Ensign Hilliard sprinting across King Street towards them. Where had *he* come from? Had Hilliard been following him? Or following Angeline?

At this point, as a curious and concerned throng began to close in around them, Angeline tried to raise herself out of the only mud puddle on the street, sighed loudly, and sank back in a faint. Marc lunged in time to catch her firmly in his arms, at which her thick lashes opened to reveal pale-blue eyes with just the hint of a twinkle in them.

"Are you all right?" Hilliard panted as he knelt down beside them.

"No bones broken, Ensign. But don't hang about here, get after that wagon!"

Hilliard jumped to the task and hurried away. Marc struggled to his feet with Angeline still limp in his arms. Several sturdy men had freed the horses and righted the carriage. Miraculously, it, too, was in one piece.

"Someone please fetch the lady a glass of water," Marc said just as Angeline swooned again and he had to drop to one knee to catch her. This time she pulled his face down towards her and kissed him lightly on the cheek. The onlookers applauded.

"Would the lady like to come inside our shop and rest?" said a familiar voice. With Angeline still wrapped around him, Marc looked up to see who the proprietor of the millinery shop might be. There, standing over him with an expression of intense curiosity and amused concern, was the face that had haunted him night and day for the three long months of winter.

It was Beth Smallman.

"Fallen in love again?" she said.

Chapter Nine

Beth and an older woman – white-haired, sweet-faced – helped Angeline into the millinery shop. At the sight of her mud-splattered skirt, the girl began to weep. Then her whole body trembled, and she started to sob in earnest. The shop door closed resolutely, and the curious had to be content with watching Marc stagger to his feet, more dazed by the mysterious reappearance of Beth Smallman than by the accident.

"Where's the driver?" Marc said, suddenly remembering the groom, who had been sitting on the bench at the front of the barouche.

"Here, sir," the young man said, brushing off his livery. His face was pasty white. "I'm so sorry –"

"It was not you who struck the carriage," Marc said reassuringly.

"But I saw it coming, sir, and my tongue went stiff as a plank. All I could do was jump and save myself."

"And I'm happy that you did, son. There's no need to wring your hands over it. I saw the runaway myself and just had time to latch on to Miss Hartley."

"But the wagon's ruined!" the lad wailed.

"Not entirely," Marc said. Several burly men had arrived on the scene and were sorting out the tangle of harness and gear, while another stroked the noses of the frightened horses. Marc gave the collapsible leather roof a tug. "This rig won't be keeping off any rain for a while, but I think the creature itself will live long enough to get us home."

Someone came out of the dry-goods store with a pitcher of water and two glasses.

Controlling his own shakes as best he could, Marc was about to leave the groom sitting on the boardwalk with a drink in hand and a mothering woman at either shoulder when he saw Ensign Hilliard come galloping up King Street towards him. An even bigger crowd had now formed, and Hilliard had to force his mount through to Marc.

"Were you able to catch him up?" Marc asked.

"I caught up to the wagon, sir. And the horses, poor devils."

"But no driver?"

"Someone saw him headed towards the docks, but I couldn't find him. Nobody knew who he was."

"That's unfortunate," Marc said, and the same thought lay unspoken between him and Hilliard: Was the "accident" deliberate? And if so, who was the target? "Most likely he saw my uniform and realized he had struck somebody important, and then panicked and fled."

Hilliard nodded dubiously.

"But surely he'll sneak back for his horses and vehicle," Marc suggested.

"Ensign Parker was with me when we saw the collision, sir. We were on an errand for the Governor. I'll have Parker stand watch on the wagon until one of the city constables can take over. We'll find the culprit, don't worry."

"Good idea, Ensign. But don't you leave just yet." With that Marc parted the crowd and entered the sanctuary of the millinery shop.

Inside, the older woman was brushing as much mud off Angeline's skirt as she could while making soothing maternal noises. Beth was holding Angeline's gloveless right wrist gently and rubbing it with some sharp-smelling unguent. The girl's sobs had subsided, and she smiled adoringly at Marc through a scrim of grateful tears.

"She's just shaken up," Beth said. "And bruised her wrist a little."

"I'm fine, really," Angeline said, her eyes still fixed on Marc.

"Are you well enough to travel back to Government House?"

Angeline nodded angelically.

Marc then led her carefully back out onto the street, where few of the spectators seemed to have relinquished their place. Marc called Hilliard over.

"The carriage appears to be drivable," Marc said. "Walk the horses and Miss Hartley back to Government House, inform Sir Francis that there's been an *accident*, and have Dr. Withers examine her."

"Yes, sir," Hilliard snapped, and leapt to Angeline's side to assist her up into the jittery carriage.

If Hilliard *was* infatuated with the Governor's ward, Marc thought, it was just as well he was heading off for Brantford and farther fields on Monday morning. For it was an infatuation that would do his career little good.

"Are you not coming with us?" Angeline asked.

"No, Miss. The groom will sit with you if you feel faint."

The groom was most pleased to accept this responsibility.

"Where are *you* going, then?" Angeline said with a little pout that reassured Marc the girl was recovering rapidly.

"I'm going back into the shop to see a woman about a hat," Marc said.

Marc sat across from Bathsheba McCrae Smallman in a sparsely furnished room that served as an office and temporary retreat at the rear of the shop – much as he had five months earlier sat in the simple sunshine of her farm kitchen in Crawford's Corners. Now, as then, the sun poured lavishly through a south window and backlit the slim figure and copper hair of the woman he had been drawn to from the instant he saw her and heard her speak, like Cordelia, in a voice ever soft and low. Now, as then, she poured him a cup of tea and served him a scone with homemade huckleberry jam – as if long months of separation and silence had not intervened.

Marc could think of absolutely nothing to say other than to mumble a brief and garbled account of how he and Angeline happened to arrive entwined and dishevelled on her doorstep. She listened politely and observed him with the gentle skepticism that he so admired and out of which flowed her humour and her candour.

When he paused sufficiently, she said almost solemnly, "I owe you an explanation, Marc."

"Not at all," Marc said bravely. "You made me no promises."

"I didn't open your letters," she said.

"Erastus wrote me back. He said he thought you just needed time." Erastus Hatch was her neighbour, who had helped Marc during his first investigation into the mysterious death of Beth's father-in-law, Joshua Smallman.

"That is so. I'd lost a husband and then a man who was a father to me. I needed grievin' time. But that's not the real reason I didn't open your letters." She looked across at him until he raised his eyes and held onto her steady gaze. "I was afraid to."

"But after a while *every*body stopped writing," Marc said with just a touch of self-pity.

"I am sorry for that: *I* asked them not to write."

"But why?"

"Because I'd made arrangements to come here and start a new life. I didn't want to complicate yours."

"You've been here since *March*?" Marc was astonished.

Beth laughed. "Only since April, actually. Oh, I knew we would meet eventually. But you must believe me when I say I have not been deliberately secretin' myself away from you."

"Oh, I do."

"But you and I do not exactly move in the same circles here in Toronto."

"But I've ridden right past this place a hundred times since April, and I've overheard women discussing the new bonnet shop more than once!"

"But you haven't had occasion to purchase one . . . ," she said in her familiar half-teasing way.

"Or, until today, to accompany a lady to do so."

"You didn't notice, then, that this shop was next door to my father-in-law's dry-goods store?"

"My God, so it is!" Marc was delighted that his surprise once again brought a smile to her face. Joshua Smallman had operated a dry-goods establishment here on King Street for many years. Since his own arrival here thirteen months ago, Marc had been in the store several times and had met the proprietor. Only now, though, did he remember that Beth – after protracted legal proceedings – had inherited his estate, including the dry-goods store adjacent.

"This shop is part of the same buildin' that father owned," Beth said, as if reading Marc's thoughts. "We leased out the dry-goods section, set up for ourselves in the smaller space, and moved into the apartment above us."

"But you must have seen *me*," Marc said.

"Oh, yes, I did. Many times. Mostly from the shop window as you rode or marched on by."

"Yet you did not –"

Beth's reply was barely a whisper: "I wanted to. More than once."

"My God, why didn't you? You must have known how I felt – feel – about you."

Beth looked down as if contemplating what she ought to say next, or how. Neither had touched their tea. "That has never been a problem, though I do hear you've been payin' court to a beautiful and intelligent young heiress."

"But no one knows about –"

"I'm afraid everybody does," Beth said with a sad smile. "All the great ladies of the town pass through our doors here. And they're mighty fond of their gossip."

"I see. Well, then, what they don't know is that Eliza and I are just good friends. In fact, I like her for many of the same reasons I admire you." Marc realized only as he spoke these last words that they were undeniably true. The principal difference seemed to be that Eliza elicited as much brotherly affection and respect as passion, while Beth evoked affection, respect, and something else he could not put into words.

Beth blushed, her pale Irish skin showing every shade of embarrassment prompted by Marc's declaration. Deliberately she picked up her cup and sipped at the cold tea. When she spoke again, her voice was eerily calm: "I also owe you a full explanation of why and how I got here."

"Yes, I've been wondering what happened to your brother, Aaron, and the farm," Marc said, glad for the moment that the conversation had moved away from its more dangerous direction.

"I'm sure Erastus wrote you that he married Mary Huggan, and that Winnifred got married to Thomas Goodall."

"A double wedding, yes," he smiled.

Mary had been Hatch's housemaid. Winnifred, his daughter, had taken a fancy to Goodall, their hired man. After his experiences in their township in January, Marc considered them all to be his friends.

"Well, the Hatch mill and farm was bound to be a bit crowded with both couples livin' there," Beth continued. "And so when my Aunt Catherine, my father's sister, wrote me from Boston that she had a small inheritance, no livin' relative nearby, and was lookin' to start up a ladies' business of some kind, I made the biggest decision of my life. I suggested we set up a millinery shop here in Toronto, in father's buildin', and run it together. She jumped at the chance. I leased the farm to Winnifred and her new husband – on condition that they let Aaron stay on and help out, like he has since we first moved there. They said yes."

Aaron was Beth's teenage brother, slow of speech and slightly crippled.

"Aaron's very happy. I've been back to see him. And Mary's expectin' her baby in September."

At this point Aunt Catherine Roberts poked a round, friendly face through the curtain and said, "Sorry to interrupt, Beth, but Mrs. Boulton wants to know when the black-widow bonnets are due in from New York."

"Tell her sometime late next month," Beth said. "Better still, pick an exact date and make sure to get her order in writin'."

Aunt Catherine grinned, and slipped back into the shop.

"You've become quite the businesswoman," Marc said.

"And you've become quite the speech writer for a Tory-tinted Whig governor," Beth retorted with unexpected vehemence.

A deep silence hung between them. What had to be said sooner or later had just been uttered. There was no taking it back.

Finally Marc said quietly, "Will you grant me an opportunity to try and explain?"

Beth said nothing. Her face was turned to one side – her expression implacable.

"Please. You owe me at least that. I've been to hell and back since we parted in January."

"All right," she said stiffly. "You talk, I'll listen." And she remained as she was, half-turned away from him, like a stern priest in a confessional.

"I have not relaxed my determination to see the grievances that you and your neighbours showed me to be real and reversible. You don't know just how far I've come in changing my views because you have only the slightest knowledge of how I was brought up to think and behave. My adoptive father was a landowner, and a good Tory. I absorbed his values and attitudes. My two years at the Inns of Court confirmed and deepened these views, as did my training at Sandhurst. Since my arrival here to serve Sir John Colborne a year ago last May, I have been surrounded by, and taking orders from, the pillars of this community, every one of them a Tory of some stripe or other. But after meeting you and seeing for myself what you suffered needlessly as a result of governmental negligence and obtuseness, I came to accept the legitimacy of your complaints. What I told you then about my change of heart was sincere, and is still so."

Marc waited for a response. But none came. The bell over the shop door jangled. Low voices in the next room discussed embroidery and veils.

"Why then, you might ask, am I in the service of a Governor bent on defeating the Reformers at the polls? First of all, I am a soldier, and as such I was commanded, against my will and better judgment, to become Sir Francis Head's chief aide-de-camp. It took some time, but I slowly became convinced that his strategy of appealing to the moderate majority and of dampening down the extreme rhetoric on both sides was right. And this will be just the first step of a multi-step plan to correct, in good time, *all* the legitimate grievances and rooted injustices."

Beth turned her face to Marc and squeezed out a grim smile. "That sounds like one of the speeches he's been givin' on the hustings."

"But don't you see that his plan is at least worth a try? What has been gained since the Reformers took over the Assembly in 'thirty-four? Even with a Whig governor and a Whig colonial secretary, not one grievance has yet been addressed."

"And you trust this Whig gentleman, this commissioner of the poor laws and glorified mine manager, to right all our wrongs?" The contempt in her voice shocked Marc.

"Yes, I do. He is under orders from Lord Glenelg to do so, and I believe in his sincerity."

"You've *seen* such orders?"

Marc stiffened. He had gone a lot further than he had intended. That he was privy to some of the exchanges between London and Toronto was a grave responsibility. His probity in that regard must be absolute: he had sworn a solemn oath.

"Well, the Governor's letters to the *Patriot* are not state secrets," Beth said. "Did you have a hand in writin' the one in today's edition?"

"No, I did not," Marc said sharply. The conversation was not going the way he had hoped.

"Are you helpin' him with the speeches for Woodstock and London?"

"As a matter of fact, no. Lieutenant Willoughby is. I've been assigned to investigate Councillor Moncreiff's assassination. It seems the Governor was impressed with my work in Cobourg and Crawford's Corners in January."

Beth flushed and said softly, "He should be. I'll never forget what you did for me, or how you did it."

"Then, please, let us at least be friends. Let me come and see you."

"No, not for a while. At least, not till the election is over."

"My God, Beth, what in hell does politics have to do with love?"

Beth sighed: "Politics has to do with everythin'."

Marc stared past her out the window, struggling to control his anger.

"You say you're investigatin' the murder of Mr. Moncreiff. That is a good and proper thing to do. He was a nice man. He came in here with Mrs. Moncreiff to help her pick out an Easter hat. I liked them both. Most of our customers are Tories or sympathizers, and I do not hate them. In fact, I've come to like and respect many of them. But when I read the Governor's letter this mornin', I knew why I could never be married to one of them."

"What on earth are you talking about?"

"The Governor suggests in so many fancy words that Mr. Moncreiff was shot by a hired killer from the States, in the pay of a disloyal citizen or citizens, and he don't have to spell out which party they cleave to, does he? But he goes even further than that! He hints darkly that foreign influences are at work, and this isn't likely to be the last violent act we'll see. You know the rest of the argument."

The rejoinder Marc had planned died on his lips. Was Sir Francis actually using the Councillor's murder so blatantly for political purposes? The foreign threat and necessity of unswerving loyalty to the Crown in times of crisis, etc.? Was this the theme the Governor and Colin had been weaving into the speech Marc had seen them collaborating on? Or was he just becoming paranoid?

"I had nothing to do with such tactics," he said lamely. "I do not approve of stirring up irrational fears. I thought that's precisely what we were attempting *not* to do."

"Then have a look at this poster some concerned citizen left on my doorstep this mornin'." She handed Marc a rectangle of stiff paper. He read what was printed there.

Farmers!
BEWARE!
The enemies of the King and the People, of the
CONSTITUTION,
AND Sir Francis Head
ARE DAY AND NIGHT, SPREADING
LIES.
They say Sir Francis Head is recalled –
Sir Francis Head is NOT recalled,
but is supported by the king and his ministers.
They say tithes are to be claimed in Upper Canada –
Tithes are NOT to be claimed in Upper Canada

FARMERS!

Believe not a word these Agitators say but think
for yourselves, and **SUPPORT SIR FRANCIS**
HEAD, the friend of Constitutional Reform.

"This is the very type of rhetoric the Governor is trying to avoid," Marc said with not nearly the conviction he intended to convey. "He would not have approved this. Nor would I."

Beth looked at him sadly, regretfully. "Then shouldn't you do somethin' about it?"

Marc got up. "I am a soldier, not a politician. I must do my duty."

"As I must do mine – to honour the memory of my husband and his father, who both died because of politics."

At the curtains, Marc said, "Do we not have a duty to love?"

"Yes," she said. "That is what keeps us human."

Even as they parted once again – with the gulf between them apparently wider – Marc was certain that she cared for him almost as much as he loved her.

When Marc arrived at Government House – bruised, sore, crestfallen – he found Sir Francis agitated and incoherent. He was pacing up and down the lofty entrance hall, with Willoughby and Hilliard following warily and flinging words after him that were meant to mollify him but were having the opposite effect. Had something gone wrong with plans for the journey on Monday? Or worse? Major Burns was looking stolidly on the commotion from a nearby doorway, either indifferent or too ill to intervene. It was the sight of Marc that brought Sir Francis to such an abrupt halt that Hilliard and Willoughby tottered right past him before stopping themselves.

"Ah, it's you, Lieutenant – at last."

"I came as quickly as I could –"

"You're not hurt, I hope?" Sir Francis said, halfway between threat and concern.

"Not really, sir. Just a bruise or two."

"Well, Angeline tells me you saved her life." The Governor's panic at seeing his ward dishevelled, scraped, and weeping still showed in his face, as if he could not yet bring himself to believe she had not been seriously injured.

"Miss Hartley is recovering?"

"Yes, she seems to be, but I can't tell whether she's crying over her ruined dress or a bruised arm. She just repeats your name over and over."

"Have you caught the blackguard?" Hilliard said to Marc.

"I'll have the bugger horsewhipped and clapped in irons!" Sir Francis cried with such vigour that his eyes bulged. Marc realized with a sinking feeling that Hilliard had not been discreet in his account of the incident.

"It may well have been an unfortunate accident, sir," Marc said. "A runaway wagon is not that uncommon, especially during the Saturday market."

"I have a difficult time believing that," Sir Francis said through clenched teeth, "after what I've been told by Hilliard and my ward and even the groom."

"Ensign Parker has been posted to watch the horses in the event the driver returns for them. The constables will take things from there."

"I want the man brought *here*! Is that understood, Lieutenant Edwards?"

"I'm sure that Cobb and Wilkie will get to the truth of the matter, sir."

Sir Francis uttered a purging sigh. His anger slowly drained away. He put a hand on Marc's shoulder. "You must forgive me, young man. I am overwrought. I've had a terrible shock, especially after what happened up at Danby's. You deserve nothing but my gratitude and my deepest respect. I should be more concerned for your hurts than for my own wounded pride."

"It's been a trying week, sir – for us all," Marc said, wondering what the Governor would say if he were to learn the nature of the hurt now burning its way everywhere through his aide-de-camp.

Willoughby and Hilliard looked as if they wanted to say something helpful but had chosen discretion over valour.

Sir Francis began pacing again. Everyone else stood where they were and watched anxiously. "I don't give a damn for my own safety," he said, picking up the shreds of his earlier anger.

"I intend to walk tall into the lion's den next week. I shall challenge any citizen to strike down the royal surrogate, if he dare. But to prey upon innocents like poor Moncreiff and now my ward, a mere chit of a girl, for whom I am solely responsible, and who has been most abominably abused. I will not have it! *Do you hear?*"

Everyone in the far recesses of the building could hear.

"Perhaps I could find a couple of reliable corporals from the garrison to watch Miss Hartley while you are away," Marc said, then bit his tongue as he saw Willoughby glowering at him: it was Colin who was now in charge of such matters.

"My God, Lieutenant, you're right. I will be gone for four days, and Angeline will be here alone and unprotected." The implications of this remark had just begun to sink in, for Sir Francis stopped in mid-step and glared at the nearest Athenian pilaster as if he would, like Samson, bring it and the house crashing down.

Willoughby decided it was prudent to put his oar in. "Perhaps you could suggest, sir, that the young lady keep indoors for the duration. After all, it's only until next Thursday."

Sir Francis shifted his glare from the pilaster to Willoughby. "That, sir, is a preposterous suggestion!"

Willoughby's head snapped back as if struck. But Marc was pleased to see that he held his ground. "But you wouldn't willingly put her in danger?"

"I have absolutely no intention of putting my ward's safety in jeopardy. But she has expressly conveyed to me her desire to shop for a gown suitable for the gala at Somerset House next Saturday, and on Tuesdays she always takes the carriage to Streetsville to visit a second cousin of hers of whom she is extremely fond, and on Wednesdays she goes riding in the College Park."

"But surely, sir, these are extraordinary circumstances," Willoughby tried again.

"Miss Hartley, provided she is fully recovered by Monday, will continue with her habitual routine. Is that clear to everyone?" The Governor's voice had the ring of royal prerogative in it. No one spoke. "Moreover, she shall be fully protected and armoured against the slightest interruption or irritation. Willoughby, you will choose two reliable men from the barracks to act as bodyguards. You yourself will accompany Miss Hartley wherever she wishes to go, and I shall hold you personally responsible for her well-being as well as her safety."

Willoughby began to tremble, from anger or chagrin, it was hard to tell, and Marc felt obliged to say, "I would be happy to take on those duties, sir. Lieutenant Willoughby will be needed at your side in Woodstock and London."

"That is a magnanimous gesture, sir, and I know you would carry out those duties conscientiously, as you demonstrated this afternoon," Sir Francis said evenly, but his rage – stoked no doubt by guilt and anxiety over Angeline's mishap on King Street and, probably, by Willoughby's mistimed temerity – was not far below the surface. "But Lieutenant Willoughby has already done me yeoman's service this week: the speeches are written. You, on the other hand, have a murderer to catch. Any pressing paperwork here next week can be handled by Major Burns, whom you and Willoughby will assist whenever you can."

"But what about your own safety, sir?" Willoughby said desperately.

"Hilliard will take over the unit. All the basic arrangements have already been made, thanks to you." Sir Francis looked long and hard at Willoughby, who was in a way like Angeline: a ward and a trust, as well as the prodigal son of a friend. He said, not unkindly, "Colin, I am giving you a *very* important assignment. You have acquitted yourself with distinction these past few days. I have already written to your father to inform him of your progress and of the potential I see in you. But you are a soldier and an officer: you took an oath to serve and obey your monarch and those who speak in his name – however you may personally feel about the commands given you. What I am telling you by offering you this assignment is that I have enough faith in you to put Miss Hartley's well-being in your hands."

And with that the Governor wheeled and strode towards his apartments.

Willoughby stood stock-still, clenching and unclenching his fists, a wild, unfocused anger in his eyes. Four days to be spent as chaperone and nursemaid to an overindulged, babbling, flighty, whim-driven ingenue would have unsettled the most dedicated officer. For Willoughby – who had become, however temporarily, the day-to-day aide-de-camp of a lieutenant-governor – it was a crushing blow.

Hilliard made consoling noises, but Willoughby swore at him or the world in general, brushed rudely past Marc, and stormed out.

Major Burns, impassive in his office doorway, said to Marc, "I think you'd better go after him. He looks capable of anything."

Including self-destruction, Marc thought, and headed for the door.

Marc spent the next two hours in a fruitless search of every public house and drinking den within a ten-block area of Government House. Not only did he not find Colin, he found no one who had seen him. At least his anxiety over Colin was keeping at bay the dark thoughts about this afternoon's encounter with Beth. It had promised so much, had seemed so serendipitous – fated even – that the disastrous outcome was all the more unbearable. But bear it he must. It seemed self-evident now that he must give her up. That decision was simple compared with the impossible one: to cease loving her. So he was not surprised to find himself on Eliza's flower-bedecked doorstep – red-eyed, haggard, and seeking any sort of solace. His urgent need for comfort made him blissfully blind to the inappropriateness of wringing pity out of another woman who possibly entertained the notion that he was in love with her.

Eliza took one look and ushered him quickly past a startled butler and her uncle's office into the sanctum of her private sitting room. He slumped onto the sofa there and let Eliza pull his boots off and undo the buttons of his jacket. Seconds later a brandy snifter appeared in his right hand, and he drank.

"Did you get hit by a horse?" she said lightly, but there was deep concern in her eyes. She stroked his brow, and he felt both guilt and ease at the spontaneity of the gesture.

"By two horses and a wagon," he murmured, and realized then that this was the only part of a devastating day he could talk about, the only part of it that he had a right to reveal to this handsome, generous, unjudging woman with the sloe eyes and free-falling, lustrous hair.

"Do you want to discuss it?" she said gently. "Or shall we carry on as we usually do?"

"Let's carry on," he said.

And so they talked about wines and the hazards of shipping and the bad roads that ruptured casks, and about a dozen other idle, tender diversions – always giving a wide berth to the confusions he couldn't talk about and she knew to be more than accidental.

Later on when she kissed him, he kissed her back. And felt like a traitor, though who it was he was betraying most, he could not determine.

It must have been midnight when Marc slipped out of Uncle Sebastian's house like a cat burglar and walked home under a star-filled sky. Once there, he eased open the door of Colin's room just enough to note that the bed was undisturbed. He tiptoed back to the veranda and sat down on the bottom step to wait.

He was just dozing off, his chin in his hands, when he heard footsteps. It was Colin, walking deliberately. He was not drunk, Marc was relieved to see as he stood up to greet him. Colin stopped, squinted incredulously at the shadowy figure on the porch, and then came up to Marc until they were face to face – no more than a yard apart.

In the distorting light of the moon Marc could see a sudden rage take hold of Colin's features, then his body, and finally his fists. "Traitor!" he hissed and swung wildly at Marc's head. Marc ducked away easily and watched, with some bewilderment, as his friend wobbled noisily into the hall.

Well, he was alive and almost sober – that was something, Marc thought; then he wondered what in heaven could possibly happen next to make his own life more miserable.

Chapter Ten

At daybreak on Monday morning Sir Francis Bond Head's viceregal cavalcade trotted out of Toronto onto Dundas Road, with flags flying. For four days the capital would be without its steward, but the countryside west of it would be graced by his presence and treated to the power and authority of his rhetoric. The future of a British colony lay in his hands and in his capacity to persuade. Having a convenient scapegoat – a disaffected Yankee mercenary, for example – was an unexpected boon and too tempting to be resisted. Sir Francis would hammer that plank into every platform on his royal route. And, lest the loyal citizens of Toronto, in his absence, forget the message he had delivered to them daily from the seat of Government House, he left these words on the front page of the *Gazette*:

> I consider that in a British colony, *British interests should be paramount*, and that in these provinces we should foster them by every means in our power, by infusing into the country Britain's redundant population, and by giving nothing to aliens but their bare rights.

Marc spent the morning with Major Burns working on back-logged correspondence. About ten o'clock he heard Colin come out of his office (they had not spoken about the incident on Saturday night) and go back towards the living quarters. If Colin was still angry, he was keeping it to himself. But a morning spent on a shopping expedition with Angeline Hartley would soon put any restraint to the test. A few minutes later, the Governor's second-best carriage was heard rattling along the east driveway towards Simcoe Street.

About eleven, Marc got a note from Cobb to meet him at the Crooked Anchor. He left Major Burns asleep on his desk and walked quickly towards Bay Street. He was eager to hear any news about Rumsey. Sunday had been a long and tedious day for Marc. The Governor was a strict observer of the Sabbath and expected others to emulate his public piety. After church, Marc tried to forget his personal troubles for a while by riding up to the mess at the garrison. Throughout the winter months he had eaten his evening meal in the officers' quarters there at least three times a week – both as a pleasant diversion and as a way of maintaining contact with the regular army. But lately his increasingly onerous duties as aide-de-camp had made these visits less and less common. Last night he had astonished his peers at mess by getting thoroughly drunk and singing bawdy songs he couldn't remember having memorized. But the camaraderie and the drink had worn off by morning, leaving Marc lower in spirits than ever. What he needed most was action – of any kind. A break in the investigation would be just fine.

Cobb was nursing an ale and looking as if he, too, had found Sunday interminable.

"Anything on Rumsey yet?" Marc asked, skipping the preliminaries.

"You don't expect him to pop up in front of us and beg for the leg irons, do you?" Cobb muttered.

Marc waited while Cobb scratched at his wart. His uniform had regained its customary stains. His sweat-soaked helmet and wooden truncheon lay on the table. "His wife hasn't budged from the cabin except to trot off to Danby's to empty the slop pots. The older kids're spendin' a lot of time at Kimble's harness shop. The Kimbles seem to've taken to the Rumsey brood. My spies are suggestin' the Kimbles are just what they seem to be: nice honest folk who vote Reform, as they ought to." Cobb peeked up from his ale to see the effect of this provocation.

"Perhaps Rumsey is content to let the Kimbles take care of his children," Marc said. "He doesn't sound like much of a father. Unfortunately that means he might well forsake them and join his relations in Buffalo."

"Or he's got another reason to hang about."

"Another assassination?"

"Could be. Or could be he's into some kinda fuss with the people payin' him."

"There are just too damn many 'could-be's' in this case," Marc snapped.

"Downed one too many at the mess last night, did ya, Major?" Cobb said.

Marc ignored the jibe (while quietly marvelling at Cobb's seeming omniscience in matters local), and said, "Give me something positive, Constable, something definite. God knows, I need it."

"Well, then, I can tell ya fer certain that the little collision on King Street was most definitely an accident."

"And how do you know that?" Marc said abruptly and regretted the doubt in his voice – which Cobb had picked up instantly.

Cobb polished off his ale, then said evenly, "Wilkie found the driver of the cart. Wilkie's just a country bumpkin like myself, but he does know a horse's arse when he sees one, and in fact he recognized both of the horses. Turns out they belong to a butcher on John Street. So Wilkie had them taken home, where said butcher was most startled to see them and even more startled not to see his driver – one Alfie Foote by name. Seems that Alfie'd lost his regular job as a joiner and talked the butcher into takin' him on as a teamster. Which the kind-hearted butcher did. Only Alfie neglected to tell said butcher that he'd never driven a harnessed team before. He only got a block or so towards the market when the horses reckoned they would go fer a nice trot up Newgate Street. Alfie tried yellin' at 'em, but they figured he was encouragin' them, so they roared along Newgate, wheeled south onto Yonge, and then decided to head fer home back along King Street – where you was foolish enough to get in their way."

"You're certain of this?"

"Wilkie's known Alfie and his folks fer years: dumb, but honest as they come."

"Good work, Constable," Marc said in what he hoped was not a patronizing tone. Then he remembered something. "When did you discover all this?"

"Late Saturday afternoon. We don't walk around with a thumb up our noses, Major."

"Then why didn't you inform me immediately?"

"Now, now, keep yer braces buckled. I left a warm stew and a willin' woman in my house to come all the way to Mrs. Standish's place. But you wasn't home."

"But that was Saturday. You had all day yesterday to get in touch."

Cobb looked horrified. "Major," he said solemnly, "yesterday was the Sabbath."

While Marc was pleased with the news that the collision had not been deliberate – which meant that Angeline Hartley's life was not in any danger – he was angry at Cobb for not letting him know in time to let Willoughby off the hook and to put the Governor's mind at ease before he left. And while it was possible to get a message to Sir Francis at Brantford or Woodstock, he knew the Governor well enough to realize that he would want to hear the facts directly from the source. Nor could Marc leave his duties here to ride west himself. In any event, Colin had been given his orders, and Sir Francis, who saw them no doubt as yet another trial by fire for the wayward Willoughby, would be unlikely to reverse himself. Marc finally decided that he would send a note by courier to the commander at London barracks informing the Governor that it seemed almost certain that no one was out to injure his ward but that, to err on the side of safety, he would have Willoughby continue to shepherd Miss Hartley according to her whim. Nor would he tell Colin: at least the poor bugger now had some reason to think himself useful as the girl's chaperone. If he were to find out that the whole business had been a mistake, he might go off the deep end for good.

Three days went by with no word from Danby's Crossing. Marc sent Cobb back to his regular patrol, subject to instant recall should the need arise. Major Burns's fingers stiffened so much that his pen dropped between them. Marc buried himself in paperwork. Colin fumed and boiled by day and avoided Marc in the evenings by heading out somewhere every night. "The blast of his cologne would've brung a donkey to its knees," Mrs. Standish informed Marc, who was grateful for such news, as it seemed that Colin had found some female company to help him cope with his bitter disappointment (as long as that company wasn't the daughter of a possessive and vengeful Receiver General!). The day trip out to Streetsville had been particularly trying as Angeline's second cousin proved to be an exact copy, and so poor Willoughby had had a giggler at each ear and was paraded about the town like a wooden soldier on display.

"I feel like a goddamn pimp!" he was heard raving to a defenceless duty-corporal.

As for Marc, he avoided Eliza's company for as long as he could, and found more than one reason to pass by the dry-goods store and its adjacent millinery each day. But he didn't go in, and no one he knew came out.

On Thursday evening, the Governor's cortège returned, and everything changed.

Hilliard was bug-eyed with excitement as he recounted to the staff of Government House the succession of triumphant speeches delivered by Sir Francis. Colonel MacNab was ecstatic. Receiver General Maxwell predicted a Tory/Constitutionist landslide, with even Mackenzie going down to defeat in the second riding of York. There wasn't the faintest rumour of a threat against the Governor. Security had been tight, the crowds boisterous but non-violent. The Governor's message had sunk in. Its effect had been palpable.

So when Marc was asked to join Sir Francis in his office after supper that evening he was astonished to find him in high dudgeon. By the time Marc arrived, he had already worked himself into a crimson rage – with the ailing Major Burns as his sole witness. Marc had expected to be asked immediately for a report on Rumsey and another on Angeline and the accident, but the Governor had already chosen his theme.

"I want that bastard's name, do you hear!" he shouted at Marc across the room.

"Do calm yourself, sir," Burns was saying. "You'll do yourself some damage."

"I do *not* intend to be upstaged by some anonymous coward calling himself by the ludicrous name of Farmer's Friend! The people of Brantford and Woodstock and London heard for themselves who is really the farmer's friend. Did they not?"

"I'm sure they did, sir," Burns soothed, and glanced at Marc imploringly.

"Damn right they did!" Sir Francis seemed for the moment to have lost sight of Marc. "But everywhere we went, *everywhere*, those damnable broadsheets preceded us. They were even left on church pews, I was told, on the Sabbath! And supporters of that traitorous Yankee and so-called Reformer, Bidwell, had the nerve to move through the crowd in London handing them out like invitations to tea! Giving them out to the people who had come to hear their *Governor*, not to have their minds polluted with that rot!"

"But, sir –"

"And don't tell me to calm down, Titus!" Sir Francis brayed.

"Are you referring to the letters written by Farmer's Friend, sir?" Marc said quietly.

Sir Francis wheeled and caught sight of Marc near the door. He heaved a huge sigh, and struggled to get his anger under control. When he spoke again his voice was low, but still tight. "It is, Lieutenant. And I'm glad you're here. I want you to drop everything and follow this Clegg fellow from his house tomorrow morning. Don't lose him. Let him lead you to the writer of these scurrilous, seditious letters. Find out his name. Then bring him here to me – by force if you must. And don't tell Cobb. I don't trust that man."

"What about the investigation, sir?"

"Damn the investigation, Lieutenant! I want Farmer's Friend in this office by noon tomorrow! You can tell me *then* why you haven't caught Rumsey."

"But, sir, I thought you wanted to speak to the letter-writer before you left for your tour of the hustings, to help you with –"

"I want those letters *stopped*, Lieutenant. I do not want

anything disrupting what we have accomplished in the past four days. Is that clear? You are to find this traitor and put a stop to his democratic drivel!"

"Understood, sir."

Marc walked towards the boarding house through the soft darkness with a slow and troubled step. He had never seen Sir Francis so agitated, so lacking in control or perspective. Moreover, what he was contemplating was not legal. Even if Marc were to track down Farmer's Friend tomorrow – presuming, of course, that Cobb had not been deliberately misleading them – there was no lawful means of stopping the flow of letters or coercing the author to visit Government House. That some kind of intimidation was being planned Marc found both distasteful and profoundly unsettling. And a good part of his unease had its roots in the disastrous dialogue he had had with Beth Smallman just five days earlier.

He was a block away from home when he sensed that he was being followed. But, when he turned quickly, he could see no one. Perhaps his nerves were more frayed than he thought. He had not slept well all week. Every time the duty-corporal or a courier moved through the hallway outside his office, he had jumped with the anticipation of sudden word about Rumsey from Cobb and the call to precipitate action. It had not come.

Marc felt the breeze of the club descending upon him just in time to duck, so that the savage blow glanced off his padded shoulder and merely grazed his shako cap, knocking it off. But the force of the blow spun him sideways and down. He struck the ground hard, and his bare forehead pitched into the root of a tree. The world swam. With blurred vision he saw a black figure raise the club above him, cocked for the kill. He rolled away. The club must have missed him, for he found himself against the tree trunk, with his skull still intact.

It was several minutes, though, before his head cleared enough for him to struggle to his knees and peer anxiously about.

"Sorry, Major, I lost the bugger. Are you all right?"

"Yes, Constable. I think so."

"That was no robber," Cobb said as he knelt down and helped Marc to his feet. When Marc started to wobble, Cobb hung on to his elbow, and Marc could feel the tensile strength in the little man. "He was tryin' to kill you, and there ain't no doubt about it."

"Then you saved my life, Constable."

"Just doin' my duty, Major."

"But this area's not on your patrol," Marc said.

"So it ain't," Cobb said. "Now we need to stop jawin' and get you home so's the Widow can have a good gander at yer skull. I can see a lump comin' straight out."

Marc was happy to let Cobb guide him the remaining few yards to the familiar veranda. "Did you get a good look at him?" he said.

"Matter of fact, Major, I did. But I was some ways off. Soon as I seen the club in the air, I let out a holler and the bugger skedaddled. I had to stop and make sure you was all right before I set off after him. By then he'd got clean away."

"What did you see of him?"

"Medium build, dark clothes head to toe, and a woolly sailor's cap pulled down to his eyebrows."

"The stock-in-trade of the street robber," Marc said.

"But this one had a great bushy black beard on 'im."

Marc sat huddled in a clump of lilac a few yards from the house of Abner Clegg, with a thundering headache and a bruised shoulder, staring at the disc of sun just rising over the Don River and thinking about the attack on his life the previous evening. According to Cobb – who surely must be trusted implicitly from now on – Rumsey had been seen in the Tinker's Dam with a dark-capped man sporting a bushy beard. Could the person who had paid Rumsey to shoot Moncreiff have come after the man investigating the crime? Cobb had explained that Rumsey himself was thin and more than six feet tall, so he could not have been the assailant. But why try to murder the investigator when anything he knew or surmised would have been passed along to his superiors? Murdering him would not stop the investigation. This was as far as Marc got with that conundrum, for the front door of Clegg's shack swung open and the courier himself emerged. He looked carefully about him in all directions. But Marc, wearing a simple blue shirt with grey trousers, could not be seen. Feeling himself safe, Clegg – an angular, loping man – moved swiftly down Front Street towards the market.

Marc waited until Clegg was fifty yards ahead before he came out on to the roadside and sidled along, whistling nonchalantly. One advantage he held over Cobb's effort last week was that the market on a Friday was only a quarter the size of the one on Saturday. It would be hard for Clegg to elude him there. When he saw Clegg nearing the market, Marc ducked between two houses and, as he had anticipated, his quarry took that moment to glance around for anyone following on his trail. Satisfied that he was home free, Clegg strolled in among the stalls.

Meantime, Marc raced up George Street to the lane that ran behind the row of houses on the north side of Front Street, then wheeled west onto it and reached the market in time to see that Clegg had similar notions – except that he had sprinted past Colborne Street and then deked onto the lane that backed the stores on the south side of King Street. Marc followed. But when he turned onto the lane, no one was in sight. Stacks of boxes and crates and rotting refuse lay everywhere. A rat waddled from one pile to the next. Then Marc heard the crack of wood breaking, about thirty yards ahead and to his left. Clegg had slipped into an alley and was headed south back towards Colborne. Marc decided to take a narrower alley to the same destination. Stumbling over debris and scattering rats as he went, Marc emerged not on Colborne but farther south on Market Street. As he peered around the building at the end of the alley, he saw Clegg gazing his way, scrutinizing every bump in the road. Again satisfied, the courier began a more leisurely pace west on Market.

By now Marc knew exactly when Clegg was most likely to turn and stare back behind him. What puzzled him still, though, was the motive behind all this clandestine movement. Despite the Governor's intemperate ranting, there was nothing in any way seditious about the letters. If anything, they were muted and rational in comparison with the regular press on either the left or the right. Why, then, would Farmer's Friend go to such melodramatic lengths to maintain his anonymity? He felt he was very close to finding that out.

Marc trailed Clegg west along Market, across Yonge, and then north to the tradesman's lane that again backed the businesses on the south side of King. The courier suddenly slowed down, and Marc slipped behind a tall packing crate. There was no one else in the lane at this time of day. Few people would be up yet, and no business opened before eight, if then. It was just Marc and Clegg and the empty lane.

Marc watched with some amusement as the courier flattened himself against the wall of a brick building, then edged along towards a door at the back of one of the businesses. He eased one hand around the jamb and rapped – once. A few seconds later, the door was opened slightly, a beige envelope appeared and was grasped, then a large coin followed suit.

Clegg tucked the envelope inside his shirt, scoured the lane both ways for the enemy, then moved past Marc at a brisk trot – heading no doubt for Church Street and the *Constitution*.

Marc did not follow. With his heart now thumping more vigorously than his head, he walked up to the door and knocked quietly. When it opened, he merely said, "Hello, Beth."

"You mustn't blame Abner Clegg for leading me here," Marc said. "He did everything to lose me but turn himself inside out."

They were in the small back room again, but this time there was no tea or scones, and they had to keep their voices low because Aunt Catherine was still asleep and unaware of the identity of Farmer's Friend.

"My letters must be havin' more influence than I thought," Beth said. "The Governor's put his top investigator on the trail."

"I didn't ask for this assignment. And I had no inkling that you could have been the author. I still can't believe it."

"Thanks very much."

"No, I didn't mean to imply that –"

"– a woman isn't smart enough to write letters like that?"

"I don't know what I thought when I realized Clegg was at your door," Marc said lamely, as a stab of pain struck him between the eyes.

"You've been hurt," Beth said with concern.

"It's part of being a soldier. But this bump had nothing to do with you or Clegg. Besides, I've been told I've got a thick skull." He smiled warily.

"Tell me more about my letters. Please."

"Well, they've stirred up quite a lot of admiration and an equal dram of umbrage and condemnation."

"I think that's about right, don't you?"

"When the Governor got to London, Mackenzie's people had printed your individual letters as broadsheets and sprinkled them like hailstones all over the political landscape. Sir Francis was not amused."

"Well, that is praise enough, is it not?"

"He was enraged, actually, and ordered me to bring him the name of Farmer's Friend or the perpetrator himself by noon today."

"Have you read them?" Beth said softly.

"Yes, I have."

"And?"

"And I think they are telling and true and written from the heart."

Beth caught her breath, and looked down at Marc for a long moment. "Thank you," she said. "That means a lot to me." Then in a different voice, she added, "So what are we to do now? Are you duty bound to turn me in?"

Marc did not answer right away. The question had been clawing at his heart. "Why not let the world out there know who you are? Let them be astounded to learn that the author is a woman who was also a farmer, who suffered exactly as those in her stories suffered, or whose sufferings she took on, on their behalf? Don't you see how much more power and authority could be gained?"

"That isn't possible . . ."

"What is the worst that could happen? You've done nothing illegal. The Governor can rant and rave, but then he'll be just like the rest of the politicians he despises." The words were just flowing out of Marc before he was fully aware of the deep forces propelling them. "It might do him good to feel powerless for a change."

"But I can't, don't you see?"

"No, I don't."

"It's got little to do with me and everythin' to do with Aunt Catherine."

Marc was baffled and, as it showed in his face, he could feel Beth beginning to withdraw, and he suddenly felt cold, very cold, in the pit of his stomach and in the region where his heart stammered and stalled.

"How many customers do you think we would have left if they found out I was the author of those letters?"

"Then to hell with them! They can go – stuff themselves!"

"Be quiet. I won't have her wakened. And try to think of someone besides yourself for a minute."

"Marry me, and I'll get transferred back to England and –"

"You must not talk such foolishness. I was the one who encouraged my aunt to sell everythin', leave her friends, and come up here to start a new life. I never should've written those letters, but my husband, who could've written them in blood, isn't here to do it. So I had to take the chance, don't you see? And now only Abner and you know who Farmer's Friend is. And it must stay that way. It must." She was on the verge of tears, and she fought them back fiercely.

"But I swore an oath," Marc said, "to serve my King and obey my superiors. I made a solemn vow."

"Then the time's come for you to choose between love and your duty," she said in a voice that chilled the air in the cramped room.

Marc got up and, without looking back, walked out into the alley. A pair of rats eyed him till he was safely out of sight.

Marc was still in a daze when he got back to Mrs. Standish's. He was barely aware of changing into his uniform and making polite conversation with the Widow and Maisie over late-breakfast tea in the parlour. In walking out on Beth – forever, unless he could conjure some morally dubious compromise – he had instinctively, reflexively, chosen to do his duty as a soldier, and that meant giving Sir Francis Beth's name. But when he arrived at Government House, he found he was not prepared to do so and came up with a plan of sorts to delay the inevitable. Unable to equivocate face to face with Sir Francis, Marc wrote him a note explaining that he had tracked the courier to King Street and Bay, where he had temporarily lost him, only to meet him returning with the letter in hand. Hence, the writer was located in that block of King Street between Bay and Yonge. Therefore, all he had to do was place himself there next Friday or Saturday and wait for Clegg to come to him. His fingers shook as he penned the lie and saw it staring back up at him.

With the polling about to begin on Monday and with last-minute rallies to be arranged – as well as the grand gala tomorrow night – Marc was hoping that Sir Francis might have his attention redirected long enough for him to forget about Farmer's Friend or, in the least, downplay its significance. That was all Marc could think of at the moment. Even so, he was so torn with conflicting and irreconcilable emotions that he had to get out of Government House entirely.

He soon found himself walking in the afternoon sunshine down to Bay Street and the Crooked Anchor. Perhaps Cobb would be there. He desperately needed someone to talk to. To his disappointment, the constable was not in. Marc stood at the bar anyway and sipped on a dark ale. No one spoke to him.

He was just turning to leave when Cobb stumbled through the doorway, out of breath and wide-eyed.

"What is it?"

"Rumsey," Cobb said. "He's been spotted near the Tinker's Dam – headin' due north. On foot. For Danby's Crossing."

At last, Marc thought.

Chapter Eleven

"I'll get a horse and come with you," Cobb said.

He and Marc were in the stables of Government House, and a groom had just finished saddling Marc's chestnut mare.

"Not right now," Marc said as he swung into the saddle. "I want you to go up to the House and alert Willoughby and the Governor. Have him call out as many troops as he thinks necessary. I'll need some backup at Danby's, but we've got to be prepared to initiate a pursuit and a full search if the bastard gets away on me."

"If he does, Major, then he'll head fer the wharf. I'm sure of it."

"I'll leave that part to Hilliard or Willoughby. But if Rumsey's making for his cabin on foot, he's only got a half-hour head start, so I'm certain I can get up there about the same time as he does."

"Don't underestimate shank's mare," Cobb said.

But Marc was already on his way.

He rode furiously north up Simcoe Street, shouting and waving aside donkey-carts, drays, vegetable wagons, and cheering youngsters. He swung briefly along Lot Street and then onto College Avenue, where he was suddenly alone with the horse-chestnut trees on either side and the vista of the university park ahead. He urged the mare to her best gallop and, pounding east again, reached Yonge Street in a blaze of speed and sweat.

But the mare soon began to flag, and he was forced to pull her back to a sustainable canter. At the Bloor turnpike, he let her drink a little and had to pull her roughly away before she did herself some damage. A dead horse under him would be an ignominious end to his second investigation. In fact, he thought, it was time to start using more brains than bravado. He couldn't just blunder into the square at Danby's Crossing and announce his military presence to all and sundry. He still had no idea how many allies among the locals up there Rumsey might actually have, despite Cobb's repeated assurances that the fellow was a loner. And Rumsey would be armed with a long-range rifle and a sharpshooter's eye.

With a start Marc realized that he might be riding into true danger for the first time. This was not the case of a panicked man in pathetic flight, as Crazy Dan had been. Rumsey was a cold-blooded killer. He had hidden himself successfully for ten days, living off his wits, no doubt. He knew every stick and stone in the woods around Danby's. As a celebrated deer hunter, he would have stealth and patience on his side, should he need to call on them. You didn't fell a twenty-point stag by letting him see you first.

Marc did not slow down at the Eglinton tollgate, and was in full gallop as he passed the startled onlookers outside Montgomery's tavern. He decided to approach the hamlet from the north, where he would be least expected to arrive. So he rode on past the crossroad to Danby's. A quarter-mile farther on he veered east into the woods. It wasn't thick or swampy here, so he made good headway and soon came to the rugged trail that he had ridden in pursuit of Crazy Dan. Only this time he followed it south until he could see smoke rising from the chimneys from the hamlet just ahead. He eased the exhausted mare a few yards off the trail into the brush, dismounted, and tethered her. He took down his Brown Bess musket, bit the paper off a bullet, and loaded it. For good luck he touched the haft of the sabre that Uncle Frederick had given him upon his graduation from Sandhurst (a weapon Frederick himself had used at Waterloo). Then he picked his way through the trees towards what he hoped was the vicinity of the Rumsey cabin.

Marc was soon soaked with sweat, which he attributed entirely to the heat of the overhead sun. Surely Rumsey would not stump boldly into his cabin, even if he felt there had been as yet no general alarm raised against him: his instincts would lead him to scout the near environs first, and only then would he slip safely home. At this very moment Rumsey could be on the prowl nearby – quiet as a cat, deadly as a rattler. Every four or five steps now, Marc stopped, stood still, and listened intently, while making certain there was always a thick tree trunk between him and what he took to be the path to the cabin. His progress was much slower and more erratic than he had intended, and for a moment he was certain he was lost. While he had been inching his way southward, he might well have passed by the cabin to the left or the right. He stopped walking and leaned against a birch tree. He was dizzy. He couldn't keep the sweat from stinging his eyes and blurring his vision. His bladder throbbed with the residue of the ale he had drunk at the Crooked Anchor. There was no sound anywhere except his own laboured breathing.

Then he saw it: a mere thread of smoke curling up into the humid haze and lolling there just above the treeline to his right. The cabin could be no more than thirty yards away. He was still trying to decide whether to sneak up on it or simply march through the front door and trust that the sight of a uniform and a primed musket would do the rest when he heard a shout and then a cry. Running low and as swiftly as he could, Marc made directly for the source of those very human sounds. One had been uttered in rage, the other in distress. And they were now being repeated, louder and more terrible.

The cabin came up so quickly before him that Marc almost ran right into it. He found himself at the windowless wall opposite the entrance on the west side. He sped along the north wall and swung around into the clearing in front of the cabin. Rumsey was already in full flight towards an opening in the woods to the south – the path he no doubt used to get him to the Tinker's Dam. Marc raised his gun, caught the blue blur of Rumsey's overalls in his sight, and fired. Rumsey stumbled at the abrupt blast of sound, twisted briefly in Marc's direction, started to raise his own gun, then whirled and fled.

Marc cursed and began reloading. He knew it was hopeless to pursue Rumsey on his own terrain, a tactic more likely to prove fatal to the hunter than the hunted. But then he realized that Rumsey could have stood there at the edge of the woods and dropped the meddling soldier like a fawn frozen in fear. Rumsey must have assumed that the soldier was not alone, for they rarely were (few being as foolhardy as this one, Marc thought). So, he was more likely to flee than to counterattack. All Marc had to do, then, was follow after him as noisily and clumsily as he could – calling out as if to comrades and perhaps even firing off a shot or two for dramatic effect. If Rumsey continued south, Willoughby or Hilliard would be able to intercept him at the Tinker's Dam or at the city docks, his most probable destination, where Cobb was sure to be waiting with a squad of deputized constables.

Marc never got to put his plan into action.

"My God, somebody help me! *Please!*"

It was Margaret Rumsey, calling out from inside the cabin. Marc put his gun down and rushed in.

Margaret Rumsey lay where she had fallen under her husband's savage blows – on the dirt floor next to a rickety bedstead. One side of her face was already beginning to swell, and her lower lip was split open and bleeding profusely. Her right arm hung limply at her side, bruised or broken. She had apparently used it to ward off Rumsey's fists. Her pathetic grey shift was torn down the front, and when Marc came up to her in the smoky light, she clutched its shreds together to cover her breasts.

"It's all right, Mrs. Rumsey. I'm Lieutenant Edwards. I was here last week. I'm here to help you. Don't be alarmed."

The terror in Margaret Rumsey's eyes began to fade, though the tears – now able to flow – made it difficult to determine what other emotions might lay there. She was trying to speak through blooded spittle: "Elmer . . . Elmer."

"Your boy?"

She nodded, then groaned and closed her eyes.

Marc looked around for the children. Up in the loft at the east end of the big room, he saw the whites of a pair of eyes. "It's all right, Elmer. You can come down now."

Slowly, a boy of ten or eleven descended the ladder and stood, unmoving – traumatized either by the violence he had witnessed or his mother's sobbing. Marc went over to him. "You must try to be brave, Elmer. Run quickly to Mr. Kimble's shop and bring Mr. and Mrs. Kimble back here right away."

The boy simply stood and trembled.

"Your father has gone off into the woods. He won't come back."

The boy began to shake his head, but whether yes or no, Marc could not tell. "It's all right. I'm a soldier. I've got a sabre and a gun. Nobody will hurt you or your mother. But your mama needs help. Now *go*!"

At this curt command, Elmer Rumsey dashed out the door. He did not look at his mother.

Marc found several cloths and a pail of ice-cold well water and began daubing at Margaret's cuts and welts. Gently he raised her right arm and rotated it. She winced but did not cry out.

"Good," he said, "it's not broken. Now hold this cold cloth against that swelling on your cheek. He may have cracked it, but we'll wait for the doctor's opinion on that."

Despite the pain it caused, Margaret shook her head vigorously.

"It's all right. I'll pay the doctor. You've suffered enough."

She began to weep, though the sobbing had stopped, and Marc sensed that these were not tears of pain now but of a deeper anguish no physician could touch. Marc managed to create a soft place for her to lie down by arranging every threadbare blanket he could find to form a sort of nest on the bedstead. He lifted her up and placed her down upon it, covering her nakedness with a grimy sheet.

"Are the other children safe?"

"Yes," she said huskily. "At Mrs. Kimble's."

"Mrs. Kimble will be here in a minute. Then I'll arrange for the doctor to come. Now, can you tell me what happened?"

Margaret pushed herself up onto her good elbow. Her eyes widened, as if her mind had unexpectedly cleared and she had remembered things she must say, pain or no pain. "He went crazy. He was out of his mind. He never hit me before, never. But he was so angry, so angry. 'I killed a man fer nothin',' he kept yellin' and screamin', and I couldn't stop him. 'I killed a man fer ten dollars,' was all he said."

"Did Philo shoot Councillor Moncreiff in the square last week?" Marc asked.

"That man told him he'd make us rich. Philo said he could earn us fifty dollars, we could move back to Buffalo, buy us a house, and I said, 'But how can you get fifty dollars?' and Philo said, 'You'll see,' and when that old feller got shot out there and Philo sneaks in here the next day with his mama just dead and then sneaks out again and tells me to say he's still in Buffalo, then I knew how he was gonna get us fifty dollars."

"Then why was he so angry, Mrs. Rumsey?"

"He was screamin' like a wild man that the rich fella paid him ten dollars at first, but then wouldn't give him the rest of it."

"Did Philo know who this man was?"

"Fella with a big black beard, Philo said. Someone pretendin' to be what he wasn't. But Philo found out who he was, and he said he was gonna get his money, one way or t'other. But he was so angry, so angry. He was writin' the fella a letter. 'This'll make the bugger pay,' he yelled, but I kept tryin' to get him just to up and leave now fer Buffalo, and be satisfied with ten dollars, and he goes all purple in the face and his eyes bulge out somethin' terrible, and I'm real scared, and he up and hits me, and when I get up he hits me again and again, and all the time he's yellin', 'I'm gonna take my gun and get my forty dollars, you hear!' Then he throws the letter into the fire and runs out, and I hear a gun go off, and I don't know what's happenin'."

Marc eased her back down just as the door opened and Mrs. Kimble came bustling in. She had a basket of salves, bandages, and a towel full of ice. "There, there, luv, it's gonna be okay."

Marc moved away to let her minister to Margaret Rumsey. As he did so he noticed for the first time the fire smouldering in the grate of the big stone fireplace. He crouched down and with a thumb and forefinger lifted free a crumpled sheet of paper. It was singed around the edges, and smudged with soot and ash. Marc blew off as much of this as he could, then unfolded it and walked out into the sunlight to read what Philo Rumsey had been writing by way of threat to the man who had instigated the murder of Langdon Moncreiff.

This is what remained for him to read:

tried to carrie out my part of the
pay me in full fer doin yore

not my fallt Guv Head dropt hi

or I'll go to the magistra

Marc was deeply disappointed that the person being threatened was not named, but the substance of the rest of the letter was stark enough. Rumsey had been given an initial payment of ten dollars, with another forty promised, no doubt, when the deed was done. *But Rumsey had shot the wrong man!* Sir Francis had – as Marc had relived the action every night in his dreams – bent down to pick up the notes for his speech, and the bullet had missed him and struck Moncreiff. In the letter Rumsey was pleading that it was not his fault that Sir Francis had bent down without warning, and was demanding full payment or else he would go to the magistrates. That seemed a hollow threat, however, and Rumsey must have realized it as he wrote it, and decided in a rage to take more direct action. Perhaps they would be lucky enough to trail him to the doorstep of the real villain of this affair. Besides confirming Rumsey's guilt, the note explained also why he had been hanging about York County since the shooting instead of seeking asylum in Buffalo: he wanted his forty dollars.

Most important, in Marc's view, was the confirmation of his initial hunch that Sir Francis had been the assassin's target! The unthinkable had almost happened. And Marc himself must bear the grim news to the Governor as soon as possible. His life and the fate of the province might hang in the balance.

Marc picked up his musket and poked his head into the cabin. "I have urgent business with the Governor," he said to Mrs. Kimble, still at Margaret's side. "I must leave."

"Everythin'll be okay here. Mr. Kimble'll see to it."

"Have him bring a doctor. I'll take care of the fee."

Margaret Rumsey sat up, stared hard at Marc, and cried, "You won't hurt him, will you?"

When Marc finally found his way back to the spot where he had tethered the mare, he discovered only a pile of fly-ridden horse-dung. The branch to which she had been tied was not broken, so it appeared someone had stolen her. Philo? No, he had headed south, where his only chance of escape or revenge lay. But it was still possible that Philo had an accomplice. Possible also that Cobb's assessment of Phineas Kimble had been premature. Sarah-Mae Kimble seemed a genuinely kind person, and she had readily admitted hearing the shot that had killed Moncreiff. But her husband had not. Moreover, he had given Philo occasional work long after he had had to fire him for the good of his business. Why? Did he, like his wife, feel sorry for the Rumsey children? Or was there a darker, more ulterior motive?

These thoughts occupied Marc as he crashed through the bush back towards the square and the livery stables. There he would commandeer the best horse in the name of the King, and ride on to Government House. Sir Francis must be shown Rumsey's letter and told the unsettling truth. By the time Marc managed to find the trail and make his way to Danby's, he estimated he had lost close to an hour since the initial encounter with Rumsey. In a state of near-panic he stumbled into the livery stables and gasped out his royal command.

The proprietor – a sandy-haired old gent – gave Marc a gap-toothed grin, spat out a gob of tobacco juice, and said, "Well, now, I could do that, sir, but I don't reckon that'll be necessary."

"I am on the Governor's business, sir."

"I don't doubt you on that score. But seein' as yer own mare is restin' comfortable in one o' my stalls – after some fool run her ragged an' just left her to catch her death in her own sweat – I figured you'd want to ride *her* back to town."

It was late afternoon, with shadows lengthening across the streets, when Marc at last rode up to Government House with the scrap of Rumsey's alarming letter in his pocket. He expected to find the place alive with bustling troops and excited clerks, but only the duty-corporal greeted him in the hall and, with no especial concern, ushered him in to the Governor's office. There he found not only Sir Francis but also Willoughby, Hilliard, and Titus Burns. They were in the midst of a toast, and it looked as if it were not the first.

"Come in, come in," Sir Francis beamed, all smiles. Willoughby and Hilliard looked like a pair of cats who had just shared a canary. "We were beginning to worry about you, Lieutenant. In fact, I sent Parker and a unit up to Danby's to make sure Rumsey hadn't shot you before we got him."

"You *got* him?"

"Not I. It is Willoughby and Hilliard here who deserve the credit."

"But it had to have been Lieutenant Edwards who flushed the blackguard out and sent him scuttling our way," Colin said generously.

"You *did* encounter him, then?" Sir Francis asked Marc.

Marc was still trying to take in what was happening here. He had news that surely superseded anything else, but his instincts told him that it was Sir Francis alone who should hear it. "Yes, sir. I took a shot at him near his cabin, and he was fleeing south. I got down here as fast as I could to raise the alarm."

"Then once again you have done me and the province a great service," Sir Francis said, choosing to ignore the obvious question as to why it had taken Marc almost two hours to make a forty-minute journey.

"Has Rumsey confessed?" Marc asked.

"No, he hasn't," Hilliard said with a curious grin on his face, somewhere between a smug and a smirk.

"Well, it doesn't matter," Marc said to Sir Francis. "I've got proof that he did it."

"We won't need it," Hilliard said.

"He's dead," Colin said.

"Dead?"

"Yes, Lieutenant," Sir Francis said. "That's what we've been toasting: the just outcome of a heinous crime. Hilliard and Willoughby here were led to a pier near Turner's brewery by Constable Cobb. They and their platoon hid in the long grass down there and simply waited. About an hour ago, Rumsey arrived and, thinking himself unobserved, started to make his way towards an old fishing boat tied up there. When challenged by Hilliard here, Rumsey turned and fired, wounding an infantryman in the leg. A moment later, the villain went down in a hail of bullets."

"And good riddance," Hilliard said.

"The rifle that killed poor Moncreiff was found in his hand," Sir Francis said.

"And that's the end of it," Colin said.

"But now you'll never know who hired him," Marc said.

"But we don't know for sure that anybody did," Hilliard said.

"I agree," Sir Francis said. "As far as I am concerned, the whole sorry business is over. We have an election to deal with, and the fact that the killer turned out to be a malcontent Yankee will certainly not work against us. And now we have the extra fillip of having brought him to justice – swiftly and remorselessly."

"And we have a gala tomorrow night to spread the good news and celebrate," Hilliard said.

Marc held his peace.

It was early evening before Marc was given his private audience with the Governor. The parade of well-wishers traipsing in to congratulate him on his triumph in the London district and upon the quick and tidy resolution to the "Moncreiff business" not only prevented Marc from seeing the Governor alone but made the revelation he had to make all the more distressing.

Marc began by saying, "Sir, I wanted most urgently to see you alone the minute I arrived here from Danby's Crossing. But it has proved impossible –"

"Don't blame yourself, young man. Just get on with what you seem to have an incurable urge to say." Sir Francis was still in a euphoric mood.

"I'll get right to the nub of the matter, then. I have here in my hand incontrovertible proof that it was not Langdon Moncreiff whom Rumsey was hired to kill."

"I thought that missive might be a letter of promotion, as you've been squeezing it to death for the past minute."

"Rumsey was hired to kill *you*, sir."

"You must be joking," Sir Francis said, but the twinkle in

his eye had already vanished. "I told you last week that no one would dare assassinate the King's representative abroad."

Briefly, Marc outlined what had happened earlier that afternoon. He repeated Margaret Rumsey's words verbatim.

"I see why you are so agitated, Marc. But, even so, we must take a long, objective look at this evidence. I'm sure Mrs. Rumsey had no cause to lie to you about her husband's claims. After all, they were incriminating, not exculpatory, and a woman in that dreadful state is not likely to be dissembling. However, how can we be sure that Rumsey did not feed her such false information in order to justify his own seditious actions?"

Marc held out the charred letter. "I found this in the fireplace, where Rumsey tossed it before running off."

Sir Francis took the scrap of paper and read it carefully – growing paler by the second. He read it again, and the paper trembled in his grip.

"You do recall dropping your notes, sir? And Moncreiff was almost directly behind you along the line of fire. I checked these details last week. There can be no doubt that as you bent down suddenly, the bullet meant for you struck Mr. Moncreiff."

Sir Francis sat down stiffly in the wingback chair beside his desk. All colour had drained from his face. His eyes were glassy, and for a second Marc was afraid the Governor was going to faint. But he drew in a single, gasping breath to bring himself around. Both hands still shook in his lap.

"There is more, sir."

"Then spit it out, dammit!"

The Governor's sudden anger shocked Marc, but he gritted his teeth and carried on with his duty. "This letter confirms what Rumsey's rantings to his wife implied: that he was a *paid* killer, and that the one who engaged him appeared in disguise. What is more, he was seen by a witness to have given money to Rumsey, and that witness described the man as having the posture and bearing of a swell or a bigwig – by which we may infer that he meant a gentleman."

"Somebody in the government? Or the Family Compact? That's . . . *absurd*. It has to have been some Reformer with the bearing of a gentleman."

"Perhaps, sir. But we must consider both possibilities. I hate to say it, even to think it, but we may well have a traitor amongst us. And we do not know but that he may try again."

Sir Francis stared at the letter as it lay on his desk before him. The truths that it bore were inescapable, and that reality had taken a cold grip upon him: anger, fear, confusion, indecision, brief bravado – all were clearly readable in his posture and expression.

"Shall I leave you alone, sir?"

"No, Marc, I think not." A cunning, calculating look had come over his face. "You see, don't you, that I cannot make this evidence public. I dare not even tell my most trusted allies in the Executive and Legislative Councils. Such news would create panic on a grand scale – a traitor among the upper echelons of government or respectable society? The Governor's life in jeopardy and no way of dealing with it short of a witch hunt through the ranks of the social register? Or posting a regiment of troops around Government House?"

"But would this news not stir up sympathy for you . . . and your cause?" Marc had intended to say "our" cause, but the thought had come out otherwise.

"Maybe so, but the confusion and alarm among our own supporters would be disastrous. I've run the entire campaign around the notions of loyalty, lawfulness, and peaceful public order."

"What are you suggesting, sir?"

Sir Francis rose and strode as bravely as he could to the window. With his back turned to Marc, he said with chilling calculation: "Only you and I know the contents of this troublesome letter." The paper crackled in his grip.

"That is why I waited so patiently to see you alone, sir."

"And once again your judgment was unerring, Marc. And so, if I were to destroy the evidence – as I am doing now – no one outside this room would know any different, would they?" Slowly and deliberately Sir Francis ripped Rumsey's letter to pieces. They fluttered to the floor like dust off a dead moth's wings.

"But, sir, your life may be in danger –"

"I do not really think so. Rumsey botched the initial attempt. He is now dead. The public will be fully satisfied that Councillor Moncreiff's killer was himself justly killed. The momentum we have gained in the campaign is now self-evident, and the Moncreiff business – sad as it may be – has already worked to our advantage and will continue to do so. Why would anyone risk another attempt on my life so near to the election?" As he spoke, Sir Francis seemed to be trying to convince himself of what he was saying as much as he was Marc. A residual and persistent fear still lurked – like a bright, throbbing thorn – in the corner of each eye. "The political motive, you see, has been virtually eliminated. And since you and I know that it was *not* a lone madman who tried to kill me, but rather an intelligent if misguided gentleman, then it follows that I am in no imminent danger."

The Governor's gaze narrowed. "In fact, there will be nothing to stop us now – not Mackenzie, not Bidwell, not Perry, not the demagogues from the American republic, not even Farmer's Friend and all his ilk."

Marc did not reply.

"So you see, Marc, we cannot ever divulge what has just passed between us," Sir Francis said quietly. "The Moncreiff affair is closed."

"You know you can count on me," Marc said. "My loyalty to the Crown is absolute." Well, almost absolute, he thought, even as he prayed that the Governor's obsession with the identity of Farmer's Friend would continue to fade.

"Yes, yes I can," Sir Francis said, as he went over to his bookcase, fumbled with some books, and came up with a Bible. He slapped it on the desk, face up. "Put your hand on this Bible and swear a solemn oath that you will never reveal the contents of Rumsey's letter to a living soul." His eyes danced manically.

"But, sir –"

"Swear it! *Now!*"

Marc did as he was told.

The solstice sun had sunk down somewhere beyond Fort York, but there was still light in the sky: hazy, insubstantial, ghostly. Marc walked, and walked. He had no idea where he was going or why. A day that should have been replete with triumph and satisfaction had turned into a nightmare, whose images floated unmitigated before his mind's eye – taunting and terrible: Beth's face as he had turned and left her sitting in that cramped room, stunned and alone; the battered face of Margaret Rumsey and her pathetic plea for her worthless husband's life; a hired killer shot to pieces by a soldier's volley, just as Crazy Dan had been; the gloating visages of Hilliard and Willoughby; the half-mad stare of Governor Head, who was, it seemed, dangerously unstable.

It had been a day that had begun with the wrenching argument at Beth's over vows of love and duty, and it had ended with yet another vow that was just as compromised and conflicted as the others. For he had had more than enough time to march into the Governor's office and admit that he had done his duty by discovering who had written those telling and true letters on behalf of the voiceless citizens of the province, and then confess that he could not reveal the name because of a matter of honour that was more compelling than duty, a trust too solemn to be broken. In short, it came down to a choice between loyalties. But, of course, he had not done the honourable thing; he had taken the coward's route and had been rewarded with the unforeseen possibility that the Governor had lost interest in his vendetta against Farmer's Friend. With luck, he would soon abandon it entirely – letting Marc wriggle off the hook like a pusillanimous worm.

Of course, he could still crawl back to Beth in a week or so and boast that the Governor had not forced the author's name from his lips and never would, implying craftily that her lover had, with passing nobility, chosen her over his soldierly duty. But just minutes ago he had put his hand on the Holy Bible at the irrational behest of a man he no longer respected and had sworn yet another binding oath of allegiance – when he ought to have turned and marched from the room. So, even if he were now to go back to the crazed Governor and openly refuse to betray Farmer's Friend, it would be an act of supreme hypocrisy. He could not do it. His tongue would turn to stone.

He walked on and let the last of the twilight settle around him, blurring the painful edges of everything before him. Only one thing was now certain: he could never look Beth Smallman in the face again.

Eliza opened the front door before he reached the top step. She laughed softly. "I've been watching for you since supper." The fragrance of night flowers hung about her as she reached down to him.

They entered the unlit vestibule, and when she took his hand to lead him into her sitting room, he was so grateful he almost burst into tears. "Is your uncle at home?" he managed to say.

This time Eliza giggled, a rippling little-girl laugh that cut through Marc's misery as a baby's smile might mellow a cynic. "He's taken the steamer to Kingston. We have the whole place and what's left of the evening to ourselves."

He sat down on the sofa in what had become over the past few weeks their intimate room. She took a candelabrum off the mantel and brought it over to the table beside the sofa. "This is more comfortable than the settee in the parlour," she said, sitting down and patting the cushion beside her. She was wearing a simple pale-linen dress over her chemise, and the flickering gleam of the candles caught the tender hollows of her neck and shoulders and highlighted the darkening surge of her unbound hair. No stays reconfigured the sensual droop of her breasts.

The light shone also upon Marc's face.

"My God, what's happened, my darling? You look . . . devastated."

"I am," Marc said, and when she drew his head consolingly to her breast, he did not resist.

"Then you must tell me why."

So he did. In rushed, incoherent phrases he poured out the day's disappointments and humiliations, editing out only those portions sanctified by oath. Farmer's Friend was "someone dear" but, in this version, resolutely male. The Moncreiff case had not been properly concluded, but, of course, it could only be hinted as to why. The sad episode at Danby's Crossing could be fully exhumed and recounted, including even the chagrin at losing his horse and being patronized by a hostler.

Eliza fetched the brandy decanter and poured them each two fingers. "Sip slowly, darling, you'll singe your tonsils." She ran her fingers through his hair with such casual caress that it seemed as natural as breathing.

Marc looked up from his nestling place and said, "Will you marry me?"

Eliza uttered a tiny laugh – half-nervous, half-amused. She pulled back so that his head came up and she could look at him directly. "You've only had one brandy."

"But I'm serious, *darling*." It was the first time he had used the word in her presence. He took her hand formally in his and said, "I want you to be my wife. Now. As soon as we can arrange it."

Eliza looked at him with a solemn, almost wistful, expression on her face. "But I can't," she said softly. "Please, believe me, it's not that I'm not genuinely fond of you. I am. The time we've shared these past weeks has been the best thing that has ever happened to me."

"Then, why? I don't understand."

"Well, for one thing, there's Beth Smallman."

Marc showed his amazement. "You know about her?"

"Enough. This is a very small town." She smiled as best she could and added, "And those candid descriptions of your exploits in Crawford's Corners in January left little to the imagination."

"But that's over," Marc said, feeling foolish at having dropped to one knee. He got up awkwardly to sit beside her. "It's finished."

"Perhaps. But I do wonder if such things are ever finished." Her expression darkened. "The man I tried to leave, back in England, followed me here."

"He did? Why didn't you tell me? Has he been bothering you?"

She stroked his cheek in a decidedly motherly gesture. "He's managed to keep his distance – so far."

"You must tell me who he is!"

"So you can play guardian?" she said, not unkindly.

Marc sat back. "So you won't marry me, then?"

"I don't think I'll marry anyone, so don't feel sorry for yourself."

Marc reached for her hand. "It's Uncle Sebastian, isn't it?"

"In a way, yes."

"Then there's nothing to worry about. I'll just –"

"We're going to New York," Eliza said, not letting go of his hand.

"I don't follow –"

"Uncle Sebastian is on his way to Montreal to meet Uncle Samuel and escort him and a shipment of port to Toronto. Uncle Samuel is going to take over the business here. Uncle Sebastian and I are moving to New York to set up shop there."

She let go of his hand. "It was Uncle Samuel who was supposed to go to New York, but Uncle Sebastian suddenly changed the plans. He says I may stay here if I wish . . ."

"But?"

She looked him square in the eye with a glance that conveyed pain and resignation in equal measure. "I won't leave him," she whispered. "He cannot do without me."

Marc was pretty certain why Sebastian Dewart-Smythe had altered the plans, but all he could say was, "When do you . . . leave?"

"In a week or so. As soon as Uncle Samuel gets settled in."

Marc was numb. There was nothing to say.

Eliza said, "But we don't have to marry. You could come with us to New York. I could teach you the wine business. We could travel to the continent, to France, to Italy –" She stopped. She reached out again and ran her fingers down one side of his head and cupped them about the nape of his neck. She sighed. "That was foolish of me. I'm starting to sound like the little girl who wants to eat her cake and have the baker too."

She knew, as he did, that he could not leave the army any more than she could leave Uncle Sebastian and the wine business she was born to.

"This is goodbye, then?"

"You could come again tomorrow. He'll still be away."

"I've got to attend the gala at Somerset House," Marc said, "and you've already refused to come with me."

"I'm sorry, but there may be someone there I don't wish to meet."

"Oh, I see," Marc said, not sure that he did. "Your rejected suitor?"

She smiled cryptically and said, "So, we've got only tonight to ourselves, then?"

"Yes."

"I want you to do one thing for me, if you will," she said with mock solemnity. "A sort of last request."

"Anything."

She pulled his face into the hollow between her breasts. "I want you to make love to me. Now."

And there in their intimate room, in the uncertainty of candlelight and its insubstantial shadow, Marc made love to the woman who had just refused to marry him. The discovery that she was not inexperienced in conjugal matters was, initially, somewhat disconcerting, but, on the other hand, she left him scant opportunity to mull over such moral niceties.

It was dawn before he found the will to leave.

Chapter Twelve

On Saturdays Marc often went over to the garrison to take part in the morning parade, not because he had to (as aide-de-camp to the Governor and attaché to Government House he was excused such routine manoeuvres), but because it made him feel more of a constituent part of the regular army. On this particular Saturday morning, he needed the tonic of military ritual and rigour more than ever. The prospect of filling the idle hours between breakfast and the gala at Somerset House in the evening with nothing but replays of the images and actions of what had happened since Thursday was intolerable. After the parade, Marc had lunched with Colonel Margison and Quartermaster Jenkin in the officers' mess, where talk of his heroic exploits in flushing out Philo Rumsey was both flattering and galling. At mid-afternoon, he made his way back to the boarding house, and there he found a note waiting for him, from Horatio Cobb.

In the Crooked Anchor, Cobb seemed uncharacteristically eager to tell Marc about Rumsey's death at the pier near Turner's brewery. He had barely touched the fried trout in front of him.

"It was me that led the troops down there and told 'em where to hide in the grass so's them ridiculous costumes wouldn't show," he was saying.

"I know, and I'm sure you'll receive due credit," Marc said.

Cobb was anxious to talk, but he was also eyeing Marc closely, as if sensing that there had been some sea change in his outwardly unflappable superior. "That don't matter a pig's arse," he said and jabbed a fork into his plate. "So, like I was sayin', after I talk them into skulkin' down there like a pack of bird dogs, I start to sneak back up the embankment to see if I can spot Rumsey before he gets too close to all them popguns. I know it's important to take Rumsey alive as he's got a lot of talkin' to do before we hang him, but, dammit-all, the bugger'd already outcircled me. The first thing I know, I turn to see him almost on the wharf and scuttlin' fer a fishin' boat with a little cabin on it. So I give out a holler, but the troop is already liftin' out of the grass like flushed pheasants, and Rumsey of course sees 'em." Cobb took a deep breath but did not raise his flagon. "I swear to God, Major, one of them crazy soldiers shoots before Rumsey can say shit or surrender. Naturally, he misses, but Rumsey ups and fires back, and I hear a mighty yelp and see one of the soldiers grab his leg and go down. Then there's a roar like a ten-gun salute and the poor bastard flies backwards with the guts shot out of him before he hits the water."

Cobb now hoisted his flagon and drank greedily. "I ain't ever seen anythin' like it, and I hope to Christ I never do again."

Almost absently Marc said, "Any idea who fired that first shot?"

Cobb picked up on the tone instantly. He looked at Marc for a long second before answering. "Could've been any one of 'em. They ain't got a brain to divvy up amongst 'em."

"Rumsey's dead," Marc said. "And that's all that seems to matter."

Cobb picked at the bones of his trout. "Well, it ain't really none of my business, I suppose, but I recall you figured Rumsey couldn't've been actin' on his own. Don't we have an instigator of some kind maybe runnin' around loose somewheres? Or don't that matter no more either?"

"As far as the Governor is concerned, the case is closed."

"And as far as *you're* concerned?"

"I do what the Governor commands me to do."

Cobb flashed Marc an enigmatic grin. "Well, then, I best get back to my humble patrol."

Marc rose and held out his hand. "It's been a pleasure working with you, Constable."

Cobb did not respond, but he watched Marc as he slowly made his way out of the tavern.

Marc returned to Mrs. Standish's after eating supper at the officers' mess, where all the talk was about the upcoming gala at Somerset House, the life-and-death decisions regarding dance cards and partners, the relative merits of one colonial beauty over another, and the irresistible allure of the British officer in his ceremonial accoutrements. There was much teasing of Ensign Roderick Hilliard, who, having won inestimable favour in the Governor's eye during their trek through the western hustings, had been rewarded with the honour of escorting Angeline Hartley to the ball and dancing both the lancers and the galop with her. It was almost eight o'clock when Marc stepped onto the veranda and greeted his landlady, who was sweeping the dust of the day off her threshold.

"Is Colin home?" Marc asked her.

The Widow Standish leaned forward with both hands on her broomstick. "He was, Lieutenant. But he's left – and in such a state!"

"He'd not been drinking?"

She sighed: "No, sir, I could not say he had. But he was unforgivably rude to me, he threw his clothes all over his room, and on his way out he give Maisie such a snub as left her sobbing for an hour in the laundry shed."

Marc was beginning to tire of defending the young man he had taken under his wing, but he said, "Colin's had a frustrating week chaperoning the Governor's ward when he was promised better things. Then yesterday, as you've heard, he was part of the heroic troop that tracked down and shot Mr. Moncreiff's killer. Now he has nothing before him but returning to his routine duties at Government House on Monday morning. And he tends to get upset over such disappointments –"

"More like a little boy throwing a tantrum, I'd say."

"And I daresay you are right, Mrs. Standish."

As he began dressing for the gala, Marc realized that he had sleepwalked through the day's events. His failure to live up to Beth's expectations, Eliza's rejection of his proposal (did she know more about him and Beth than he had supposed? Could she herself have arranged to leave *because* of what she knew?), his abject behaviour before a superior whose ethics (not to speak of his dubious sanity) he found repugnant, and his cowardly acquiescence in the whole sordid cover-up of the Rumsey affair – all these less than sterling actions had left him benumbed, devoid of passion and commitment.

Even worse was the fact that both his superior officers and those he commanded viewed him as an exemplary soldier, and could not stop pouring praise in his direction. It had been *his* efforts, they had said repeatedly, that had pointed the finger at Rumsey on the very day of the murder, *his* strategy that had set up the spy system at Danby's Crossing and the Tinker's Dam, leading to Rumsey's being spotted yesterday (Cobb was a mere cipher in all of this), *his* quick thinking and courage at the cabin that had spooked the fugitive and sent him scuttling to the docks, and *his* intuition that had forecast the precise pier to which the villain would flee. He might even be made a captain.

It was little wonder, then, that Marc found he was unable to concern himself with Colin's moods, perceived slights, and childish disappointments. Willoughby would just have to face the stern realities of being adult and conscionable like everybody else. After all, what had he to complain about compared to someone like Beth Smallman, who had lost a husband and a much-loved father-in-law in the same year, who had been left with a farm and a crippled brother to raise alone in the semi-wilderness? Or Eliza Dewart-Smythe, rich heiress that she was, who had been orphaned at three and raised by a succession of uncles more attached to the wine business than parenting, and who had been bitterly disappointed in love (had it been a fortune-hunter pretending to be a lover?) and had come two thousand miles to an outpost of civilization to learn a man's business and compete in a man's world? To hell with Willoughby! Let him take care of himself.

On his way out, he gave Maisie a warm smile, and was rewarded when her face lit up and she blushed prettily.

The provincial aristocracy was out in full force and gay panoply. Tory gentlemen and their wives from London, Brantford, Cobourg, and every place in between had come in to the capital a day or two before the event and set themselves up in comfort at the best Toronto hotels and inns or had descended upon wary relatives with spacious abodes in town. In one way or another, all this had been part of Sir Francis Head's strategy for the elite to take back the political powers of which they had been indignantly deprived in the elections of 1834 and upon which they had hereditary claim. Every carriage and horse-drawn vehicle in York County and beyond had been commandeered for the purpose of conveying the eighty-some guests to the magnificent residence of Mr. and Mrs. Ignatius Maxwell (and daughter) along a route that would give them the widest exposure for their ostentation and the least discomfort for their behinds. Most of them connived to promenade at least part of the way westward along fashionable King Street, where the hoi polloi cheered and jeered them with equal vigour. And since more than a dozen handsome officers of the 24th Regiment of Foot had been included in the guest list and since such officers were necessarily resplendent in scarlet or green and gold with high, feathered shako caps, those with the most important carriages and the showiest horses contrived to pick up one or more of these trophies, adding both colour and sex appeal to their equipage.

Marc chose to walk. He went down Peter Street to Front, where, dangling from a flagpole in front of the Toronto Hotel, was a crude effigy of Philo Rumsey, his neck well wrung by a hangman's noose. They would, it appeared, be celebrating more than a patently successful electoral campaign tonight. For a block around Somerset House, the streets were bustling with stomping horses, beleaguered grooms and footmen, and of course gorgeously arrayed women and rigidly handsome gentlemen moving in stately file up the stone steps of the great neo-Gothic house. Sir Francis stood beside Prudence and Ignatius Maxwell on its lush portico and accepted fealty in the form of curtsy and bow from the guests. All this house needs is a moat, Marc thought uncharitably. He was surprised to see several moderate Reformers among the guests, including Robert Baldwin and Francis Hincks.

As he made his way politely along the reception line, Prudence Maxwell leaned over to him and whispered, "I've put you down for the waltz later on, Lieutenant – when the party's had a chance to warm up."

Marc was a natural and, on most occasions, an enthusiastic dancer. He was glad this was so, for it enabled him to coast through the main part of the evening in a not-unpleasant, near-narcotic state. Riding the rhythms of the music (the orchestra in the ornate mezzanine of the enormous, tall-windowed ballroom was the best money could assemble) and tripping through the formal configurations of the set-piece dances, he was able to smile and utter brief, meaningless pleasantries as fingers touched and hips brushed and eyes locked – while his thoughts and feelings floated free in their own misery-laden ether. Indeed, it was only by reference to his dance card that he could be sure he had actually partnered Angeline Hartley, Chastity Maxwell, and half a dozen other belles whose names he was expected to remember. When he somewhat reluctantly went over to Prudence to fulfill his commitment to the waltz, he was surprised that she glided out onto the floor like a proper chatelaine, made light but coherent conversation, and barely looked him in the eye. Her own eyes, however, were beginning to sparkle like the champagne fuelling them, and Marc hoped for her sake that she would make it through the evening with her hostess's dignity intact.

When the requisite and preordained dances were complete, the orchestra took a break, and the grand ladies and gentlemen repaired variously to the sweetmeats-and-champagne tables or to the powder rooms tucked away behind a huge screen of intersecting Persian rugs. Within minutes, natural groupings had formed and were from time to time reformed as boredom or more avid passions took precedence.

Without a lot of real interest, Marc stood well aside and observed the to-ing and fro-ing. He noticed that Willoughby (who had arrived late and scrupulously avoided him all evening) was paying much attention to Chastity Maxwell. Could *Colin* have been the officer secretly courting her? It was possible.

Colin had definitely been seeing some woman or women in the past week or so: Mrs. Standish's instincts in that regard were near infallible. Hilliard, who had arrived with Angeline, had danced with her at least three times and was now plying her recklessly with champagne while the Governor's gaze was averted. Marc decided to keep his own watch on the couple. He liked Hilliard, who was as ambitious as he himself was, and did not wish to see him jeopardize his career so foolishly. Prudence Maxwell, tulip glass in hand, was chatting with Chief Justice Robinson and his sturdy wife, while her own husband was in a far corner, his mutton chops caressing the cleavage of a debutante from the hinterland. When Justice and spouse took their leave, Prudence made a wobbly beeline for the drinks table.

When the orchestra returned and struck up a lancers tune, those guests with youthful energies took up the challenge. Without the strictures of the dance card, men and women were free to partner as caprice propelled them. Liaisons or the promise of such were made, coyly retracted, then reinstated with a coquettish smile or an extra squeeze of hip or fingertip. Hilliard stuck close to Angeline (or she to him, it was hard to tell). Willoughby had disappeared but not, Marc was relieved to see, with Chastity – who was keeping a daughterly eye on her mother. For Prudence, still counting herself among the vigorous, had tottered into a square, tumbled against a startled ensign, and, in breaking her fall, had latched onto a part of him generally reserved for his own use. Chastity and another woman – whom Marc took to be Flora Moncreiff, her aunt – assisted Prudence towards the powder rooms, but she put up such a fuss that they had to be satisfied with sitting her down on a chair, where she slumped like a punched puppet. Ignatius Maxwell was nowhere in sight. Nor was the debutante.

Marc wanted very much to leave all of this – the superficiality and the melodrama and the picayune conflicts. But he was genuinely concerned about Prudence, and Chastity too. God knows where Maxwell had spirited his young woman or what he was planning to do with her. Prudence was undoubtedly aware of her husband's philandering, but the humiliation of his carrying on at a gala of which he was host and which the Governor himself had sanctioned as a celebration of sorts could well prove too much. He expected her at any moment to start proclaiming her mate's apostasy before the assembled pillars of the community. And with a voice like hers, the deafest dowager in the hall would soon know all.

Fortunately, the frolic was almost over. The last dance had been announced. Marc took the opportunity to sidle over to Chastity and say quickly, "If you need any help with your mother, please call on me. I'll stay till the end, if you like."

Chastity smiled gratefully. "Thank you. She's almost asleep in her chair, thank God." Marc moved a discreet distance away, and noticed that Chastity was looking anxiously around the ballroom for someone – her truant father, or Willoughby?

The dance was now over, and the revellers began to make their way to the vestibule with its dazzling chandelier and majestic oaken doors. The commotion of footmen, grooms, and restless horses could be heard outside in the summer air. The butler, Jacques, and his conscripted underlings were busy sorting out wraps and hats and gloves, and bowing curtly at increasingly rapid intervals. Several of the regular servants had begun snuffing out the candles, and the big room began to darken by degrees. Looking weary and bored, Sir Francis stood on the porch and bade farewell to all and sundry. Marc hung back until he saw Chastity and her black-robed aunt lift the near-comatose Prudence towards the rear exit, which led to the women's apartments beyond.

He was just about to depart when Ignatius Maxwell clapped him on the shoulder and said heartily, "Do join the Governor and me for a nightcap and a cigar, young man. We hear you are the toast of the town!"

If Sir Francis was worried about his eccentric behaviour yesterday evening, he showed no sign of it during the twenty minutes or so that he and Marc and Maxwell spent in casual conversation in the Receiver General's den in the wing of Somerset House reserved for his use – and any privacy he might require from time to time. Obviously, the Governor still had full confidence in his aide-de-camp. Marc endured their compliments as best he could, taking refuge in the French brandy and a West Indian cigar.

"And I must tell you, Ignatius – confidentially, of course – that I intend to make this young Turk here my military secretary as well as principal aide-de-camp. Poor old Burns will be ready for half-pay within the month. But Marc here –"

Marc was on the verge of a protest – just how he might have worded it he would never know – when Sir Francis suddenly pitched forward in his chair. Maxwell caught him before he toppled to the floor.

"It's nothing, nothing," the Governor mumbled. "A bit too much champagne and one too many cigars."

"You're sure you're all right?" Maxwell said with some alarm.

Marc's alarm was as real as Maxwell's but had more sinister sources: Was this another attempt? Was the madman still loose and determined to have his way? Marc cursed himself for having been so caught up in his own personal problems that he had not bothered to keep a close eye on the very man whose safety was his foremost responsibility. How simple it would have been for an assassin to slip something poisonous into one of Sir Francis's drinks amid the noise and bustle of the gala!

They both bent over the stricken Governor.

"I'm just . . . very tired," he said in a voice frighteningly weak. He was also grey around the gills.

Maxwell nodded at Marc and said to Sir Francis, "You'll stay in my apartments tonight, Governor. I'll ring for Jacques, and we'll have you tucked in, in a wink."

Sir Francis made no protest, and Marc was relieved to see the colour returning to his cheeks.

"Would you mind informing the Governor's footman, Lieutenant, that his master will not be needing the carriage tonight?"

Marc agreed, then quietly withdrew. He put on his jacket and shako cap, and made his way through a maze of hallways towards the ballroom. He had just stepped into it when he met a concerned man in livery, looking for Sir Francis. He seemed much relieved at the news Marc conveyed, and trotted out through the massive doors, still manned by two stout servants. Otherwise the vast space was empty, silent, and growing dark as the final few candles burned themselves out. Marc had taken just one step towards the exit when he heard Jacques's voice behind him.

"Excuse me, sir. Mrs. Maxwell's in a bad way. I've been summoned to the master's rooms. Would you mind just keeping an eye on her till I am able to get back to her?"

"Where is *Miss* Maxwell?"

"She has gone to her room, and my knock failed to rouse her, sir. I'm afraid she is fast asleep. And Mrs. Moncreiff has gone home with her daughters."

"Should I go for a doctor? Is she seriously ill?"

Jacques actually blushed, then stared at his shoes as he said, barely above a whisper, "Not exactly, sir."

Dead drunk and about to stir up a ruckus of some sort, he might just as well have said. But the message was clear nonetheless, and Marc had no choice but to go in the direction

Jacques pointed out, while the butler headed towards the safer domain of the male Maxwell. The corridors were unlit, so Marc had to tiptoe along until he spotted a door partly ajar with a flickering light of some sort behind it. With a mixture of disgust and pity, he eased the door open and stepped inside.

At first he could see little, as the only source of illumination seemed to be a candle-lamp on a small table set against the far wall. Cautiously he edged towards it.

"Over this way, lover." The voice was that of Prudence Maxwell, slightly slurred but showing little sign of physical distress.

As Marc drew nearer, he noticed – with a start – that he was not in a sitting room or antechamber: he was in the lady's boudoir. A canopied four-poster bed stood before him in vivid outline. In the pool of light splashed across it, he could see a rumpled, rose-embossed comforter, and the pale, rougeless face and sprawling coiffure of Prudence herself, who peered up at him with blurry-eyed curiosity.

Marc started to backpedal: "Please excuse me, Mrs. Maxwell, I had no idea you were abed when Jacques asked me to look in."

"Oh, it's you, Lieutenant," Prudence breathed, and blinked sharply, as if that might somehow bring him more fully into focus. "You'll do just fine."

"I'll have Jacques wake one of the maids."

"Jacques has already done what he was told to do. Now be a good lad and come sit beside me. I've a dreadful –"

"Please don't do anything you'll regret in the morning."

"– itch. Way down here!" She threw back the comforter with a single sweep of her hand. "And I never regret anything in the morning."

Prudence Maxwell was as naked as Godiva, though the image she presented upon the silk sheets of her feather bed was more akin to a Rubens nude – all pink and plump and enticingly hollowed. Her prodigious breasts stared up at Marc with their stiff, blind eyelets.

"Climb aboard, sailor. This brig needs her sails trimmed."

The second and a half that it took Marc to avert his gaze was all the time Prudence needed. She lunged halfway off the bed, braced her plummeting weight on one outstretched hand, caught her balance, and seized Marc by the left wrist. Thinking she was about to crash unaided onto the hardwood floor, he had sprung forward to assist her, and the combination of his leap and her seizing precipitated them both back onto the bed. Whereupon she began to tear at his clothes as if she were plucking a warm chicken. He felt his shirt ripping, but the more he tried to find a decent and workable purchase on his assailant, the more he inadvertently stirred her ardour by brief clutches of breast, hip, thigh, or buttock.

"I've got to have you, you beautiful man!"

"But think of your husband –"

"I *am* thinking of the son of a bitch!"

She had almost succeeded in trapping his thighs in a scissors hold when they heard a noise in the hall (the door was still ajar), as if someone heavy had just stumbled.

"That's him now!" Marc gasped as he attempted to pry her nearest thigh away from his pant leg without having the manoeuvre misinterpreted.

"He never leaves his apartment," she hissed and, to refocus her lover's attention, made a grab for his privates. "He's in there now screwing that little bitch from Brantford!"

The next stumble was not only louder, it was right outside the door. And it was followed by a singularly primal, male grunt.

"Jesus! I thought he'd gone. You better get out of here fast."

"How?" Marc said. He looked wildly about him. There were one door and two windows too high and narrow to be of use. Under the bed was a possibility, but hiding there could be more daunting than merely confronting a cuckolded husband.

"He gets into such terrible rages," Prudence said, and there was genuine fear in her voice.

Just before blind panic seized him, Marc had one rational thought: at least the Governor must have recovered.

"The closet!" Prudence screamed through her teeth. "It runs all along that wall over there. Get inside. Quick! Please!"

Marc sprinted for the closet, deep in the far shadows of the room, pulling his tattered uniform together as best he could. He fumbled about for a door handle, found one, yanked the door open, and practically somersaulted into the silks and brocades and other gauzy attire exclusive to the female sex. He eased the door shut just as the interloper clumped into the room.

"Ah, darling. You see how ready I am for you? What took you so long?"

Marc had to admire the lady's aplomb.

Maxwell – no doubt thwarted earlier in his pathetic attempt to seduce the young woman from Brantford – had apparently decided to offer his favours to his long-suffering wife. Marc heard a thick body thump onto the bed, followed quickly by a slurred moan, then a muffled male gurgle: "My God, you *are* ready!"

Well, Marc thought, as he thrashed softly among dresses and shifts and petticoats like a bumblebee in a web and tried not to listen to the groans and wheeze of the aging fornicators: this is surely the ultimate humiliation. It was at that moment that he realized the latch on the outside of the closet door had slipped back into place during his frantic entry. He was trapped.

"Ah, yes, lover, yes, *yes*!"

The room beyond fell suddenly and blessedly silent. Moments later a pair of mismatched snores vied for supremacy.

Desperately, Marc searched along the length of the closet, trampling on dresses as he did, but none of the other doors had been left unlatched, and none could be opened from the inside. He could force one of them open, but the noise might waken one of the spent lovers, and with his luck he knew which one it would be.

He was here for the night. Or longer.

Deciding that he might as well try to sleep – at least it would be Prudence or her maid who would open one of these doors in the morning – he sat down and lay back against the rear wall and was just beginning to take note of the fact that his bladder was alarmingly full when the wall abruptly gave way. He found himself lying flat on his back and staring up at what had to be the ceiling of another room. The adjoining room! He nearly laughed aloud for joy! Prudence's closet obviously served the occupants of both chambers. He had fallen through an unlatched door on the opposite side.

A tight but definitely female squeal brought him upright and twisting around to see whose privacy he had now invaded. The squeal erupted again, as if a maid had just identified a mouse in her bed.

Marc slammed his eyes shut, but not before – in the light of several candles – they had taken in the essentials of a young woman standing naked in front of her four-poster bed.

"I'm sorry, Miss Maxwell," Marc whispered, though he wasn't sure why. "I can explain everything tomorrow, if you'll just pull a robe on and show me the door."

There was no answer. Was she terrified? With good cause, he thought. Finally he detected a faint rustling noise, waited for thirty seconds, then opened his eyes just a slit.

Chastity Maxwell remained frozen not ten feet away, her youthful beauty caught nicely in the candle's glow. She was staring at him. There was fear or concern of some kind in her gaze, but she made no move to cover her breasts or the golden thatch at the vee of her thighs. What on earth did she want? Marc's heart sank. Not *again*!

Still she said nothing but began to jerk her head furiously and roll her eyes to a low window on the outer wall, which was wide open to the midnight breeze. On the third or fourth swivelling of head and rolled eyes, Marc got the point. She wanted him to go out through the window quietly, afraid no doubt that her mother might have heard her suppressed shrieks and taken it upon herself to come staggering in from the hall to beat back the barbarous threat to her daughter's maidenhead. Marc smiled his understanding, and Chastity continued to watch him silently as he crept over to the window, hoisted himself up onto the wide ledge, twisted around so that his legs hung down outside, ready to cushion his drop to the ground, and began to lower the trunk of his body over the outside sill – while trying not to stare at the beautiful young woman standing there like Galatea, nude before Pygmalion. Just as Marc was about to drop, Chastity moved back to the bed. At the same time, a second unclothed figure unfolded itself from under the flounce around the lower part of the four-poster and rose up over her.

It was Hilliard.

Marc was so shocked he forgot to brace his legs and feet, and as a result he crashed heavily to the ground twelve feet below.

A needle-sharp pain shot up the length of his right leg, and he collapsed in a heap. The unmuted scream he let out might have awakened the soundest of sleepers. Grimacing and cursing silently, he listened for any signs of disturbance within the great house, but all was quiet. He rolled over into a sitting position. He was in a garden, and somewhere close by he could make out a street lamp. He was home free. But when he tried to get up, his right ankle rebelled, and gave way under his weight. It was seriously sprained. He was not sure he could walk, or even limp. My God, was this the final humiliation? Was he going to have to crawl to Mrs. Standish's on his hands and knees?

"Require some assistance from the local police?"

Marc looked up into the shadowy face peering down at him. The nose glowed like a beacon, and never had Marc been so happy to see it. "Cobb?"

"That's what the wife calls me when she's in the mood," Cobb said, tucking his truncheon back into his belt. "I pert near split yer noggin with this here, Major. Took you fer the burglar that's been upsettin' rich folks down here."

"Would you mind helping me to my feet?" Marc said. "I've turned my ankle."

Cobb leaned down and pulled Marc up, then held him as he tottered and swayed.

"I don't think I can get home on my own," Marc said.

Cobb was appraising the dishevelled state of Marc's clothes. "You do this often, Major? Drop out of strange windows in the middle of the night?"

"Only when I can't find the door."

"No need to be sarcastic, Major. Why don't you just put an arm around my shoulder and we'll see if we can find the door to the Widow's place."

"Thank you, Constable."

"'Course, with me gone, the burglars down here'll think Boxin' Day's come early."

They had barely shuffled half a block when Cobb paused to catch his breath, then said, "Say now, Major, where'd you leave yer hat?"

Chapter Thirteen

It was nine o'clock on Sunday morning when Marc woke up after a deep, dreamless sleep. Even so, his whole body ached. He realized now how utterly exhausted he had become in the ten days since the Governor had narrowly missed being assassinated. The throbbing in his right ankle reminded him, despite his best efforts to blot out the memory, of the débâcle at Somerset House, and his astonishment that it was Hilliard, not Colin Willoughby, who had been courting both Chastity (the second misnomer in that family) and disaster. With a supreme exercise of will, Marc raised himself up and stepped down onto the rug below. His yelp was piercing enough to bring both Mrs. Standish and Maisie flying to his rescue.

"It's all right," he insisted, not a little abashed at being observed standing at his bedside in his cotton nightshirt. "I twisted my ankle last night."

"That must've been some dance," Mrs. Standish said. "Maisie, run down to the wharf and buy some ice." To Marc she said, "You'll have to ice that swelling for a couple of hours at least. You should've had it looked to when you come in last night."

"I didn't want to disturb you – ouch!"

Mrs. Standish had both hands on his wounded ankle. "Well, it ain't broken – just sprained. So we won't need the doctor."

"Did Colin come in after me?"

"Ain't put his head to the pillow yet," Mrs. Standish said reprovingly, and waved Maisie off on her errand.

Marc was not unhappy with that news: whoever Willoughby's lover was, she would provide some necessary consolation, diversion, and, possibly, perspective.

Later, Marc was served breakfast in bed by an enthusiastic Maisie, who peered up at him with worshipping eyes whenever she felt he was not looking. Then the two women dressed and went off to St. James to hear "the dear Reverend Strachan" fulminate against the enemies of the Mother Church. Marc fell asleep again.

By mid-afternoon he felt strong enough to limp gingerly about the house and, eager to find something to occupy his mind so that he would not start mulling over "what if's" and "might've been's" in regard to his feelings for Beth and his attraction to Eliza, he decided to go to the officers' mess at the garrison and while away the Sabbath in the pleasure of male companionship (and where he would learn whether Sir Francis had fully recovered from his temporary dyspepsia). He had initially considered going over to see Eliza, as her uncle was still away, but remembered in time his solemn promise to her Friday night that he would see her only once again: on the day of her departure. Anything else would have been unbearable for her, and probably for him. So, Maisie was sent to the stables at Government House to arrange for the chestnut mare to be brought down to him, and by four o'clock, with minimal assistance, Marc mounted and rode off towards the fort, less than a mile from the city.

It was dusk when he mounted again and, pleasantly drowsy with good wine and serviceable food, trotted east along Front Street towards the town. In fact, he had fallen into a doze in the saddle, and the mare, without specific instruction, headed up John Street for the stables, and her stall. When Marc was finally jerked awake, he looked up to see that he was in front of Government House.

"Good girl," he murmured. "You took yourself home." He nudged her around towards the stables, where he hoped to find a groom to lead the horse to his boarding house and return with her here. But just then the duty-corporal came hustling down the front steps to intercept him.

"An urgent message for you, sir!" he puffed, holding out a sealed envelope.

"From whom?"

"I think it's from Lieutenant Willoughby, sir. A lad from the city was paid to run it up here, and he says it is very urgent. I was just about to send a rider down to the garrison to find you."

"How long ago did it arrive?"

"Maybe half an hour ago."

"Thank you, Corporal," Marc said, taking the note and dismissing the messenger. As he opened the envelope and recognized the handwriting as Colin's, Marc speculated as to the nature of any "urgency" his wayward friend might have got himself into: an irate husband with a primed pistol was the best bet. He read the note, but it was not what he expected. Not at all.

Marc:
Wilkie and Cobb are down at Enoch Turner's brewery near the mouth of the Don. They apprehended three thieves breaking into the premises. While they were

questioning them, one of them, a fellow named Campbell or Kimble, suddenly said that he had some knowledge of Rumsey and the Moncreiff shooting. When Cobb pressed him, he clammed up and swore he would only talk to somebody high up with more authority. Cobb suggested you, and the villain agreed. Wilkie was dispatched to fetch you immediately. When he appeared at the Widow's house, he found me coming out. I told him I would go up to Turner's while he went looking for you – and scribbled this note for him. Come as quickly as you can. This may be our only chance to find out who was behind the assassination.

Colin

Marc did not hesitate. He urged the mare to a full gallop and was soon speeding east down Front Street towards the brewery. The sun had almost set, but there was still plenty of misty, high-summer light.

So, Rumsey had had an accomplice after all, Marc thought. He was not surprised, as he had suspected Kimble from the outset. Cobb had reported that Kimble had money troubles, and so his involvement with the murder and with these break-ins was no doubt driven by the need for cash. And it seemed certain that the information he could provide would lead to the naming of the instigator and the discovery of his motive. That this person was in all likelihood a member of the elite class, whatever his politics, would explain why Kimble was demanding to speak to a high-ranking official: the knowledge he possessed was deadly dangerous. For a brief moment, Marc felt a pang of jealousy: what if Willoughby – also a member of the Governor's staff – should prove to be that high-ranking person and get credit for solving the murder? Marc shook off the thought and dug his good heel into the mare's left flank. Justice was the paramount concern.

As Marc galloped past the last houses on Front Street, he looked up to see the great Gooderham windmill that marked the eastern entrance to the capital. It was turning slowly and steadily, a symbol, Marc thought, of humanity's persistence and quest for permanence in an otherwise inhospitable wilderness. Marc was almost beginning to feel at home here. Soon Turner's brewery stood before him, shadowed and unlit anywhere inside or out. It was Sunday, and no one would be about – except the police and the thieves they had caught in the act. Good old Cobb: he had proved himself yet again. Marc felt a twinge of guilt at having ever doubted his absolute loyalty.

The brewery offices faced the road, and beside them was the warehouse complete with large double doors, where the teamsters would park their wagons for loading casks of beer and unloading barley, hops, and other supplies. On the far side of the warehouse, Marc knew, there was a platform that served as a pier on the Don River itself, where shipments of beer were loaded onto barges and drifted down to the Gooderham wharf on the lake. There they could be hauled aboard steamers or schooners bound for Cobourg or Burlington. To the west, and rising up two or more storeys, was the brewhouse proper, with its half-dozen chimneys above the malting kilns. Marc assumed that the thieves had been caught in the warehouse section, where they could, as soon as darkness came, load casks and kegs onto a boat of their own with little fear of being disturbed. Marc tied up the mare and hopped up onto the platform facing the river. It was very dark here on the eastern side of the brewery, even though in the west there was still light in the sky. He pushed open one of the doors and limped in, one hand on his sabre. His ankle throbbed like a headache but held his weight.

"Cobb!" he called out in a loud stage whisper.

No answer.

He limped farther inside, but saw little except the blotchy outlines of kegs stacked one upon the other. Perhaps they were in the office section where there were lamps and chairs to aid interrogation. He tried to walk faster, but the pain in his ankle meant he was barely able to hobble down the dark hallway towards the owner's office. When he finally got there, he found the room empty and silent. Which meant they must be in the brewhouse, where, he recalled, there were spacious windows that provided both sunlight to work by and cool air to make the men's labour tolerable in the summer. Cobb must have taken them up there for the interrogation for some reason.

With his limp growing more agonizing at every step, Marc made his way to the brewhouse doors and eased them open. A hazy mote-filled light permeated the vaulted room around and above him. Marc could make out the enormous oaken vats where the beer, in its final stage, was fermenting on its own time, and the series of wooden catwalks that connected them and allowed the brewmaster and his assistants to observe the progress of the wort. In behind them, but not visible, were the kilns – now cold and dark. The air was musky with the odour of yeast and hops, and the pleasant sting of fermentation.

"Up here!"

It was Willoughby. Marc breathed a sigh of relief, and headed for a ladder that would take him up to the first level of the catwalk system, where Willoughby's voice had come from. Climbing up caused him excruciating pain, but he was determined to be in on the conclusion of this investigation: it had cost him more than any honest man should ever have to bear.

"We're up here, Marc. Everything's under control."

Oh, no. Had they already got the information they needed? If so, then why was he being asked to climb up here? He got the answer a second later when something hard, blunt, and angry struck him on the forehead. He gasped, felt his limbs turn to water, and crumpled on the catwalk.

When he woke up, it was dark. The light from a single lantern swayed a few inches before his eyes, making whatever was behind it blacker still. He was propped up against something wooden. His head now throbbed in concert with his ankle. His feet were tightly bound together with twine, and his hands likewise, in front of him.

"I knew you'd come," Willoughby said. "And come alone. You'd never pass up a chance to further your overweening ambitions – at the expense of those you have the effrontery to call your friends." The disembodied voice was hoarse, at the edge of exhaustion or uncontrollable excitation. It was seeded with incalculable bitterness and something far more feral, far more lethal. It was scarcely recognizable.

"What the hell is happening?" Marc moaned and twisted futilely at his bonds. "What have you done with Cobb and Wilkie?" he asked softly and, for the first time, fearfully.

"They're a long way from here, you'll be pleased to know." Willoughby laughed, a low chortle. "And there are no thieves here. Just you and me. And in a few minutes, there'll only be me." Willoughby moved the lantern so that it illuminated both his face and Marc's, as if he wanted to make sure that Marc could see the cold derision in his eyes that was already so vivid in his voice.

Marc had no more doubts as to his fate. He was staring into the face of a madman; of one who was past all reason, all caution, all caring; of one who, for whatever perverted motive, had deemed revenge the only course of action that would satisfy.

"Why have you tied me up? What are you planning to do?" Marc tried to keep the tremor out of his voice but failed.

"I'm going to kill you, Lieutenant. I'm going to tip you into that vat there, bound hand and foot, and then I'm going to watch you drown, second by second."

"You're mad! You can't expect to get away with this!"

"Oh, but I will. I did the first time, didn't I?" And again he laughed, holding the lantern up so that Marc could share his tormentor's enjoyment.

Marc couldn't believe what he had just heard. "You hired Rumsey to shoot *me*?"

"That was my only mistake. The son of a bitch missed and killed dear old Moncreiff. But that was your doing, too, wasn't it? You bent down, like the fawning sycophant you are, to help the almighty Governor pick up a scrap of paper!"

"And it was you who took that first shot at Rumsey down on the docks."

"I missed, though, didn't I? The others did the rest."

"You're mad."

"And you're repeating yourself, Lieutenant. But I'm not mad, you see, only angry. And twice as clever as you who've set yourself up as regimental know-it-all. Otherwise I wouldn't be here listening to you whine and beg. You'll be astonished to learn that I've known every pathetic move you've made in your so-called investigation – sometimes before you yourself did. You made it particularly easy for me to have Crazy Dan conveniently killed: it was you, remember, who failed to give the proper order, not me."

Willoughby certainly had been in a position to clarify the order, and had chosen not to. Crazy Dan, then, had been Willoughby's deliberate attempt to have Dan blamed for Moncreiff's murder – and conveniently silenced. When Rumsey was fingered, Colin must have been in quite a panic, even though he'd taken pains to disguise his identity in his dealings with him at the Tinker's Dam. But with Rumsey dead and the

Governor happy, Willoughby would be in the clear. Only Marc stood in his way. And all that "remorse" he'd suffered had been for the inadvertent murder of Moncreiff, not the mangled corpse of the innocent and harmless Crazy Dan.

"You're the fool," Marc said, realizing that his only hope of survival was to keep Willoughby talking until some plan or other suggested itself to him. "I hadn't the slightest suspicion it was you who hired Rumsey. I even had evidence from Rumsey that seemed to point to the Governor as his target. You've risked this charade for nothing!"

Willoughby merely laughed. "So you think that's what this *charade* is all about, do you? I can't for the life of me see why the Governor chose you to investigate a murder."

"Why am I here, then?"

"Because I hate your guts, that's why. I hired Rumsey to blow your brains out, and when he failed I thought of nothing except of ways to do the deed myself. But first I had to make sure I wasn't found out. Then, when the chance of taking your job for a week came up, I thought, well, perhaps I can show Sir Francis Bonehead after all that I am your superior in every way, perhaps I'll even get what I was promised when the old fart took me on back in London: *I* was to be his aide-de-camp! He made a promise to my father! *A solemn vow!* And he reneged on it."

"You cannot blame Sir Francis –"

"I blame only you! That's why you're trussed up like a capon for the pot! I want you to know exactly why I hate you, what I have suffered at your hands, and why I need to watch you cringe and cower and beg like a dog for your miserable life, and then watch you die slowly like a fly in porridge."

The odour from the vat that Marc was resting against was suddenly overpowering. He felt his stomach heave. "All this just because I was commanded to take your job – against my will?"

Willoughby did not answer. He pushed the lantern forward into Marc's face so that his own features were obscured. Only his voice – bitter, enraged, irrational – now carried his venom to its target. "You really have no idea, do you? Well, then, sit back and listen while I tell you a story. It'll be the last one you'll ever hear."

"But I've tried to be your friend, I –"

"Quite true. My anger over the Governor's betrayal was intense when I arrived with him in January. He told me you were recommended by Sir John and his hands were tied, and so on. But I was already suffering, and it took little to drive me back to drink and whoring. It was you who kept me from going under when you got back from Cobourg."

"And I knew you'd had a bad love affair in –"

The lantern was drawn back marginally so that only the sleep-deprived, whisky-slitted, bloodshot eyes could be seen. "But you didn't know, Mr. Investigator, did you, that the woman who jilted me was here in Toronto?"

"That's impossible, you came –"

"I came out here, four months after she abandoned me and left me to perish in the sewers of London. She herself came out here in November – to escape me!"

Marc could hear the maniacal chuckle deep in Willoughby's throat as he watched the truth register in his victim's face.

"You can't mean Eliza?"

"She might've been Eliza to you, but she was Rosy to me – always."

"You're making this up, you're –"

"– mad. So you've said. But it *was* Miss Dewart-Smythe, my darling Rosy, my dear, dear pink rose."

Eliza, who was forever surrounded by flowers, by pink roses, Marc thought . . .

"You will be amazed to learn – arrogant fool that you are –

that she was besotted with me even when she suspected me of being dissolute and unfaithful, even when I came to her bed stinking of other women. It was her meddling uncle who undid me, who found out what I was up to in the stews and opium dens – and that my father was threatening to disinherit me. Well, that news put paid to the engagement, *after the second banns had been publicly proclaimed!* I was ruined."

"That's why your father arranged for you to come out here." Marc continued to twist at the rope binding his hands, as he strove to keep Willoughby talking. The pain in his ankle prevented even the slightest attempt to loosen the bonds down there.

"He didn't know, but *I* did, that Rosy was heading this way also."

"But why did you –"

"Because I still loved her, you fool! You insensitive fool! And as soon as my feet hit the wharf here, I made straight for her house." A chilling, brutal tone took over the voice and its twisted narrative. "You can't begin to imagine how that cold bitch treated me! She made me stand on the porch in the snow, she ordered me to stay five blocks from her house or else she would go directly to the Governor and destroy any hopes I had of advancement here."

"And you managed to keep away, even though –"

"*I had to!* But, Christ Almighty, I now hated and loved the bitch at the same time. I wouldn't expect a cold-hearted, egotistical bastard like you to understand, but I loved her from afar more than ever, even as I plotted ways to avenge her snub." He chuckled softly and added, "I found a couple of scoundrels at the Tinker's Dam only too willing to burgle St. Sebastian's precious wine cellar."

Willoughby had no idea just how closely Marc could identify with the remark about loving from afar.

"Then back *you* come, taking my job away from me, and then, suddenly, in April I see you with my Rosy, and I see the looks you give each other, and I can't believe my eyes: you rob me of my rightful appointment and *then* you steal the only woman I've ever loved."

"But I didn't know, you should have –"

"Shut up! I don't want to hear another word from you or I'll dump you into this vat right now."

Marc said nothing, but his mind was alive with thought. Willoughby could be no more than three or four feet away. He had been crouching low so as to stare his victim down and reap the rewards of his slow, mental torture. If Marc could get him talking again, perhaps he could use his bound legs as a battering ram – painful as that might be – and topple Willoughby off the catwalk. It did not seem likely that he could free his hands: already he could feel blood trickling down his palms.

"Taking my Rosy was the last straw. I began to plot my revenge. I heard about this Rumsey fellow at the Blue Ox and I sent a note to him in a roundabout way, and we met at the Tinker's Dam. He had no idea who I was, but when he saw ten dollars in his palm, he came on-board. I sent him the information about the Governor's trip to Danby's Crossing. A murder on the hustings, I calculate, will throw everything into confusion: people will naturally think the Governor was the target. Who'd want to kill a no-account like you, eh? And the beauty of it is, I will be standing near the platform when the shooting takes place, so I can't be suspected. I'll even get to turn around and pretend to be shocked at your face blown apart, while I'll be laughing inside. But you always find a way to bugger things up, don't you? You even managed to get your buggy tipped over on King Street and that foolishness got the Governor all sweated up about Angeline – who's no angel, by the way – and that got me assigned to guarding the little ball-breaker for a week instead of leading the *Governor's* guard and showing him I was better at the job than you, the incompetent that got Crazy Dan killed. If you hadn't tried to play Sir Lancelot on King Street, I might have gotten what I truly deserved. I might've even tried to forget about Eliza. So, you see, in your own blundering way, you ensured your own death."

Willoughby started coughing. And Marc noticed that some of his words were slurred: he had doubtlessly been awake since yesterday, and had probably been drinking rotgut whisky in some dive. That meant he was beyond exhaustion and, most likely, in that state of final euphoria just before the mind and body collapse around each other. If only . . .

"And here's the best of it, you conniving, immoral bastard. Angeline's driving me crazy with her juvenile chittering, and after a quick poke on our outing to Streetsville, she won't let me near her, so I go looking for solace elsewhere, and I remember Lady Maxwell batting her lashes at me in February at the Grange, so I sneak into her bed and she goes off like a bombshell, and I'm feeling so mellow I even begin to think maybe you're not a hypocritical arsehole after all."

"But you tried to club me to death!"

"I got myself drunk at some blind pig and went a little crazy. And I damn near got caught – it gave me quite a fright. So I sneak back to Lady Lascivious, and she wraps those fat stumps around me and lets me stay till morning. I begin to feel generous again, the world doesn't seem so bad when you're getting it regular – I even have thoughts of replacing Hilliard between Chastity's thighs. But then you go and do it again – seal your own fate. For what do I find when I slip back into Somerset House last night after everybody's gone and the master's tucked away with his own doxy, but a hot-blooded woman already primed for her lover – except when I wake up in the morning, there's something interesting on the floor beside the bed –"

"My shako . . ." So it had been Willoughby at Prudence's door, not her husband. "But, Colin, I was only –"

"I told you to shut up and listen! What I want you to know – to take with you as the muck clogs your throat – is that the hardest part of all this was not outfoxing you. That was easy because your arrogance knows no bounds and blinds you to what's right in front of your nose. No, the hardest part for me was having to pretend, day in and day out, that we were friends while the very thought of having to smile at you made me want to retch."

Marc braced himself for the one chance that remained. He heard Willoughby begin to stand up, so he swung his legs together in a vicious arc, hoping to catch Willoughby behind the knees. They cracked into the vat, and Marc screamed with the pain of it. Willoughby had leapt nimbly out of the way.

"Nice try, Lieutenant. There's no use struggling. You're a dead man. But if you beg a little, I might let you live a minute longer. If you've got a final prayer, you'd better start saying it now."

Marc said nothing. His prayer was fervent but wordless. His hands went up to his shirt, where he had tucked away Willoughby's note. If he was to die, he was to die, but when the brewers fished him out of the vat, they would find the murderer's incriminating message, and the victim's ghost would have the last –

Willoughby laughed, and there was nothing human left in it. "Looking for this, Lieutenant?" He dangled the note between his thumb and forefinger in the patch of light from his lantern. Then he set the lantern down and tore the paper to shreds. "It'll make a fine addition to the brew, won't it?" And he laughed again: an hysterical cackle. "And so will you. I'm going to get away with the whole thing. As soon as I've seen you suck in your last breath, I'm going down to the warehouse and roll a few casks off the dock, so when they find your body contaminating their beer, they'll think you surprised the booze burglars and got surprised yourself. And who knows, some people may even think you died a hero!"

Marc felt Willoughby's powerful, vengeful arms begin to lift him up, as one does a cripple. He twisted feverishly, and even tried to bite his tormentor. He felt his injured foot strike the iron edge of the open vat, the wort bubbling and lethal just below.

"Stand where you are, sir! You're under arrest!" The voice was loud, coming from somewhere in the darkness below.

Cobb's commands struck Willoughby with the force of a truncheon, and he dropped Marc in a heap onto the catwalk. Willoughby wavered as if he had been stunned, or perhaps the effects of sleeplessness, rage, and drink were taking their toll. Marc rolled away towards the vat (he didn't relish tumbling on his own off the catwalk and cracking his skull open on the stone floor of the brewhouse). Cobb was climbing the ladder with the aid of a lantern, making him an easy target for Willoughby, who, seeing exactly who the challenger was and that he was alone and unarmed, staggered towards the spot where the ladder met the catwalk floor. On his way, he knocked over his own lantern, and it shone upwards enough for Marc to see that he was drawing a pistol from his belt and cocking it.

Marc could hear Cobb's feet clumping on the rungs of the ladder as he climbed bravely and foolishly up. In desperation, Marc started rolling over and over towards Willoughby. At any moment he expected Colin to wheel and put a bullet into him, but he seemed fixated like a snake, waiting for Cobb's face to rise up above the ladder before shooting him point-blank.

Marc struck Willoughby just behind the knees. He toppled instantly: first forward, then, in trying to right his balance, sideways – kicking the lantern as he did. There was a short, pathetic shriek, a splash, and then silence. Marc hauled himself up – two-handed – to the rim of the vat into which Willoughby had pitched. He reached down for the lantern, fumbled with it, got its handle between his teeth, and held it up over the surface of the vat. He could see nothing. Cobb could be heard huffing up the final few steps of the ladder.

Suddenly there was a whoosh and a frantic splashing, as Willoughby broke through the murky surface and began flailing at the froth with the palms of both hands. Marc could make out only the hollows of his eyes and mouth.

"Reach your arm up this way!" Marc cried, realizing as he called out that he could not raise his bound wrists above the iron edging of the vat. However, the sound of Marc's voice – the familiar ring of its command – seemed to cut momentarily through the absolute shock that had gripped Willoughby, and he stopped thrashing about for a second and stretched out his right hand – still gripping the pistol – towards the safety of the vat's rim. At the same moment, Cobb thumped up beside Marc. In the unsteady gleam from Marc's lantern, the constable thrust his arm out over the bubbling wort. As he began to sink back down, Willoughby managed to clutch Cobb's wrist in a death-grip, and the pistol plopped harmlessly away. Cobb grunted, and then started to haul Willoughby slowly but surely towards him. Willoughby's head and shoulders rose up out of the yeasty mass, like a stag out of quicksand.

"Hang on, Colin! Everything'll be all right!" Marc shouted.

And it looked as if it should have been, for Cobb, with his breath coming in great gusting pants, was in the act of clasping his left hand over Willoughby's wrist so that he could lever him up and over the rim. But at the sound of Marc's voice, Willoughby let go of Cobb's wrist. The whites of his eyes flared in their dark hollows, and their pupils seized upon something directly before them, widened with recognition or dismay, and squeezed shut against whatever could not be borne. Cobb's other hand clutched at air. Willoughby drifted down into the comforting ooze, his Byronic curls floating in the froth for a long second before they, too, vanished.

Marc groaned and slumped to the catwalk floor, reaching down in a vain effort to coddle his throbbing ankle.

Cobb picked up his lantern, turned its light fully upon him, and said, "Well, Major, you seem to get yerself into the goddamnedest predicaments."

Chapter Fourteen

As it turned out, Cobb had to carry Marc down the ladder, while juggling his lantern, and through the brewery to the door that opened onto the road. There stood a two-wheeled, tumbledown donkey-cart and a grizzled donkey, who looked as if he hadn't been separated from it since birth.

"You must have quite a story to tell, Major," Cobb said dryly as he unhitched the donkey and stroked its muzzle. "Lean on the butcher-cart fer a second – I'm goin' 'round the back to fetch yer horse."

The sky above Marc was pitch-black, but the full moon had arisen already in the southeastern sky, shimmering far out on the lake and bathing the landscape with a surreal light. Strangely, Marc felt as if he were in St. Paul's Cathedral and that, despite the trials of the past two weeks and the horror of watching Colin Willoughby let himself drown, he was, against all odds, being blessed. Then a cloud passed briefly over the moon, and he felt his heart darken with the suddenness of night.

Cobb returned, leading the mare. "I'll put you in the cart,

Major – where ya aren't liable to fall out – and do my best to walk this donkey gently home."

"The mare will follow along," Marc said as he allowed Cobb to hoist him into the box of the cart. There was no driver's bench, as the butcher who owned it simply led the donkey through the narrowest of alleys in the town, delivering his wares to the back doors of inns and taverns. Cobb grasped the halter, and the tiny entourage started down the road towards the city limits.

"So, Major, how in Heaven's name did you succeed in comin' all the way out here to try and get yerself killed?"

"Your story first," Marc said. He was still too numb to talk with any semblance of coherence. "How did you manage to arrive just in time to save me – again?"

"It's a bit of a tall tale, Major, but at the rate this ass is hoofin' it, we got all the time we need." Without turning his head, Cobb told his story. "It all started around five o'clock. Me and the missus and the little Cobbs was just tuckin' into a joint of rare beef when Wilkie comes poundin' on our door. 'Mistress Cobb,' I say, 'we're in fer trouble, mark my words.' And so it come about. Seems that young Maisie Pollock'd come rushin' into the station house with her hair a-flyin' and her eyes as big as a guinea hen's, and when she catches her breath, she sobs out a tale of terror and violence."

Cobb paused to give Marc the opportunity to say sharply, "Has anything happened to Mrs. Standish?"

"Calm yerself, sir. Everybody's okay – now. Seems that Lieutenant Willoughby come home about four-thirty in a wild and unmannerly state, which is a polite way of sayin' he was pissed and belligerent. He was swearin' like a Trojan and talkin' to himself, and when the Widow tried to calm him down, he pushed her into a laundry hamper and called Maisie a lewd name, which she refuses to repeat, and then stomped off to his room. And just when they think he might be gonna sleep it off, they hear the most godawful crashin' sounds and the most dreadful cursin' – mostly yer name bein' taken in vain – and by the time they get up a nerve to have a gander, he comes staggerin' out of there like a ravin' loonie, knocks Maisie on the cheek with an elbow, and roars out of the house. The room is a shambles – bedclothes ripped and scattered, drawers pulled out and smashed, feathers tore out of the mattress. Wilkie and me saw this fer ourselves when we got there. So there's nothin' to be done but to give up the best part of our Sabbath and go huntin' fer the lunatic."

"Is Maisie all right?"

"Nothin' a kindly nod from yer direction won't cure," Cobb said, still looking ahead at the moon-washed fields between them and town. A few paces later, he took up his story again. "In the state he was in, we thought Willoughby could do some awful harm to anyone in his way. We know most of the taverns he frequents, so Wilkie and me divvy them up and go lookin' in them one by one. But there's not a whiff of him anywheres, and nobody admits to seein' him. So we finally give up, and Wilkie goes home to his family, but I figure I ought to take one more peek to see if the Widow's okay, figurin' that Willoughby might've circled back there. But everythin's calm, the women're tidyin' up the room, and they mention you're up at the barracks, so I plan on hikin' out there to let you know what's happened and ask you to keep a close eye on the Widow and Maisie. But, of course, I spot you gallopin' past me like a runaway colt, and I holler after you, but you're spooked or somethin' – and I start thinkin' maybe you and Willoughby have been bad boys together, so I commandeer the nearest vehicle, this butcher-cart parked outside Gandy Griffith's house, and I light out after you. Except it's damned hard to get a donkey to trot and to steer him whilst jouncin' in the back. I see you're keepin' to Front Street, so I tag along as best I can. Then I lose sight of you, but when I get to the end of Front Street, I can see yer dust way down the brewery road, and I figure you're headin' fer Turner's or the wharf. When I get here, with half my teeth loose, I mosey about and finally spot yer horse tied up behind. I go in, and hear voices. I light a lantern and head fer the noise. And that's about it."

"Thank you," was all Marc could say, knowing it was not half-enough.

"But you ain't heard the best part yet," Cobb said, and Marc could hear the wink in his voice. "The Widow found *this* while she was tidyin' up."

Out of the big pocket of his coat, Cobb drew a bushy, black beard.

"Well, that's the precise piece of physical evidence we need," Marc said. His mind had miraculously cleared, and he was thinking hard – despite the drum roll of a colossal headache.

"It's an actor's beard," Cobb added. "You can feel the glue 'round the edges. I'm told you *gentry-men* back 'ome are given to puttin' on theatricals."

Marc decided it was time to fill Cobb in on as many of the details about the murder as he could ethically reveal. He began by suggesting Willoughby's almost certain but unprovable complicity in the unfortunate death of Crazy Dan. He then explained – to Cobb's intermittent "ums" and "ahs" of surprise or confirmation – that he himself had been the target of Rumsey's bullet, but that when he and Sir Francis had both bent down to retrieve his speech, the bullet had struck Moncreiff instead. Marc did not mention that he had assumed, for a day, that the Governor had been the intended victim. (But only now did he realize that both he and Sir Francis had misread Rumsey's note: it had referred to Sir Francis dropping his speech, but the scorched line after that must have gone on to say that this unforeseen action had led to *Marc's* bending down as well and thus escaping death.)

"I thought you two was friends," Cobb said when Marc's narrative stalled.

Marc told him about Willoughby's jealousy, touching briefly on his reluctant romp with Prudence Maxwell and not at all on his encounter with the misnamed Chastity. He also let Cobb know that Sir Francis was the one who had ordered the investigation closed, being happy with the results as they stood and pooh-poohing any suggestion that Rumsey was a paid assassin.

"Well, now we know he *was* paid," Marc concluded, "and by whom. And we have all the proof we need in that regard, and the attempt on my life here will confirm that it was I who was the target all along. We shall go together to Government House, wake up Sir Francis, and give him the complete story, the whole unvarnished truth."

Cobb was silent for a long while. They were drawing near to the first houses on Front Street, where windows glowed with the warm light of the lamps within.

"I don't see that we got proof of anythin'," Cobb said at last.

Marc was flabbergasted. "But you are my witness, Constable. You saw Colin Willoughby try to kill me. You found me bound hand and foot with this goose egg on my skull!"

"What I seen, Major, and what I believe are not quite the same."

"In what way? What on earth are you driving at?"

"Just this, Major. All I actually *saw* from the floor of the brewery was someone who might've been Willoughby standin' wild-eyed over you. You were tied up, as I found out when I got up there. I yelled at *every*body to stop whatever they was doin'

– until I could climb up and see fer myself. Then I start up the ladder and I can see nothin' but the ladder and the dark. Nobody up there is sayin' a word. Just as I start to peek over the top rung, what do I see but you rollin' like a croquet ball and smackin' Willoughby a crack on the legs that sends him tumblin' into the brew."

"But he had a pistol out and was going to shoot you. I saved your life!"

"I believe you, Major, and I'm grateful, too. I won't forget it."

"But?"

"But all I really *saw* was the black shape of Willoughby fallin' over the rim of the vat. We'll probably find the pistol with him when they drain the vat in the mornin'. Which'll only go to show that he had his officer's pistol with him – not who he was aimin' it at."

"All right, Constable," Marc said coldly. "Tell me what point you're *really* trying to make."

"There's no cause to sulk, Major. But what I'm thinkin' is this. You and me have a pretty clear notion of what happened, then and now. But how might all this look to other people? The Widow sees Willoughby in a lather and cursin' you by name. That suggests there's bad blood between you two. I see you racin' off to the brewery so het up you don't hear me hollerin' at you from thirty feet away. When I get here, half an hour later, I find you two up on the catwalk. You're tied up: by Willoughby or by the robbers you may've surprised. Maybe Willoughby *was* plannin' to get revenge on you, but it's only *your* story that he intended to toss you into the vat: maybe he was aimin' to tickle you within an inch of yer life – in a manner of speakin'. What I do *know* is only what I *seen*: and that was you whiplashin' Willoughby inta the beer-mash where he drowned."

Against his better judgment Marc was beginning to understand where Cobb was taking this scenario. In a curious way he was perhaps trying to protect Marc – the man who had, as he well knew, just saved his life at the risk of his own. Nonetheless, he felt compelled to say, "But it was Willoughby who had the motive. I had no reason to kill *him*."

"Well, I expect Miss Dewart-Smythe will back up that part of the business – should ya want to involve her in this mess – but what about the scrap over Mrs. Maxwell? Would it be wise to air all that dirty laundry? And someone with a suspicious mind might think it was you who was worried about Willoughby takin *yer* job and *yer* woman away from *you*. You said yerself that Willoughby pleased the Governor while you was off investigatin'."

"But nothing happened with Mrs. Maxwell. I've told you that as an officer and a gentleman."

"And I believe you, Major. Still and all, there's a good chance yer fancy hat is lyin' somewheres about Somerset House."

"Prudence Maxwell will deny everything. Her husband is possessive and easily enraged. I think we have little to fear on that score."

"Maybe so. But I've also heard his missus is quite a spiteful lady regardin' matters of the heart. After all, you've gone and killed her lover."

Marc felt a sudden pang of pity for Prudence Maxwell, for her despairing gambits into lust, for her loveless existence. He hoped that Chastity might manage to make something more satisfying of her life.

"And it's said she holds the purse strings in that particular household," Cobb added.

Despite his aching ankle and throbbing head, Marc found Cobb's verbal thrusts bringing out the latent barrister in him. "But all of this assumes that some one person out there with influence or motive will press these matters. Is there any reason someone in authority should not believe the sworn testimony of a policeman and a British officer? I can assure you that the Governor himself will be enormously relieved." Of this Marc was certain, knowing as he did that Sir Francis still thought he himself might have been the target and that his mortal enemy might yet be plotting a second attempt on his life. The news that his aide-de-camp had been the intended victim and that the motive had been personal jealousy would come as a great relief. He would be able to get on with winning the election.

"It's the Governor I'm anxious about," Cobb said. They were now stopped where the brewery road met Front Street.

"Well, you needn't be. I can't tell you why, but he'll be relieved when I tell him the truth."

"Maybe so. But think of this, Major: the polling starts tomorrow, and in most places goes on fer a couple of weeks. The Governor wants nothin' more than to crush all the folks who don't agree with him. And so far, everythin's gone his way. Law and order and loyalty've been his watchwords. Then along comes the cold-blooded shootin' of Councillor Moncreiff, a man beloved by all, they say. Then, lo and behold, the Governor's personal investigator unmasks the killer, one Philo Rumsey, and he – O lucky stars! – turns out to be a Yankee. Barely a week goes by before the Governor's own troop puts enough lead in him to sink a three-master – a perfect endin' to this sorry tale. The assassin from Buffalo, where democratical demagogues're as thick as herring, is hunted down and given rough justice by the wit and grit of the Governor himself, the King's very own representative."

"Go on," Marc said, but he already knew what was coming, and his heart was turning to ice.

"So along you come, draggin' him out of bed to tell him he's got the story all wrong. It ain't the splendid one he's been proclaiming from a dozen hustings and feedin' blow by blow to the Tory papers. Oh, no, it's a messy saga of love and jealousy between two officers. And these officers, oh my, turn out to be two of his own aides, and one them, alack-a-day, is the chief investigator of the Moncreiff murder, and what does he find out? After Rumsey is gunned down and hanged in effigy in ten counties, he finds out, long after the Governor's fairy tale's been heard and conned by heart, that, by golly, there was no political connection at all. Rumsey was just a poor man with a big family who needed money to feed his starvin' bairns. And these two aides of the Governor – hand-picked by Sir Francis himself – have been hoppin' in and out of the same beds, and end up facin' each other down in a brewhouse, till one of them is tipped into the booze and drowns like a river rat."

Cobb was right. The only physical evidence left was an actor's beard, and that by itself meant nothing. Many of his fellow officers kept such props and, as he had once been, were enthusiastic thespians. The note that had brought him here was in shreds. Suddenly he thought of something he had overlooked. With rising hope, he said, "But the duty-corporal was given the note by a youngster and told it was from Willoughby and directed to me personally."

"And where will we find this lad?" Cobb said, almost apologetically. "And the corporal didn't actually see what was in the letter, did he? So as far as he's concerned, it may've been a message to get you up to the brewery fer a gentleman's showdown: a duel of honour – in a manner of speakin'. Besides, you're still missin' my point. Yer Governor ain't gonna want to hear what you got to say."

Marc felt he had no choice but to break his oath to Sir Francis. "You must swear never to tell a soul, Constable, but the Governor received evidence, now discredited, that *he* might have been the target. And he still thinks so. You are right in surmising that he does not want the Moncreiff-Rumsey version of the murder disturbed in any way. But for his own personal well-being, I feel obligated to tell him – with as much conviction and with what scant evidence we have – that he was not the target. I know him well enough to realize that he will not simply accept my word on that score: I shall have to lay out the full story, sordid as it is, and call on you to assist me. Please understand that I am not asking you to tell Sir Francis anything but the absolute truth – no more and no less."

Cobb appeared to think about this remark for a moment, then said, "And he may believe us. All I'm sayin' is he will never let such a story get out to the voters – or the Reform press."

Again, Cobb was right. Sir Francis was aware of the erratic nature of Willoughby's character and would certainly give Marc the benefit of the doubt regarding the nature of their conflict and its deadly outcome. But he would never, in the present circumstances, allow such tawdry details to become public knowledge. Mackenzie would have a heyday with it. He would no longer need Farmer's Friend.

"And knowin' the Governor," Cobb was saying, "he'll probably make us swear on the Bible never to tell a livin' soul."

Yes – another solemn vow to withhold the truth in the cause of the common good. But Marc could not do it. He had had enough of vows to last him a lifetime. And what was an honest man to do when loyalties clash and cannot be resolved? "But we've got a dead officer drowned in a vat of beer with a cocked pistol," he said wearily, as if such dilemmas were too vast or too minute to be bothered with.

Cobb was stroking the donkey's nose. "I been considerin' that," he said. "If you decide not to tell the Governor what really happened, it wouldn't be hard to set up a story to explain Willoughby bein' at the bottom of a vat."

"And just how would we go about that?"

"Well, Major, after I help you home, return this butcher-cart, and take yer horse up to the stables, I could go back to the brewery, jimmy the warehouse doors a bit, and roll a couple of kegs into the river."

"What on earth for?"

"You'll report Willoughby missin' in the mornin', and as this brewery is part of Wilkie's patrol, he'll be up here to look into the break-in, and whenever Willoughby's body decides to float to the top or the brewers give the wort a good stir, it'll look like Willoughby, drunk or not, came up here, fully armed, and surprised the robbers. And paid fer it with his life. He'll be hailed as a hero. And the Governor'll have another officer to brag about, and Willoughby's poor ol' dad'll be saved the grief of findin' out his son was a perfect monster."

"But what about Willoughby's actions at the Widow's place? His movements tonight will be investigated, surely. Chief Constable Sturges will have heard of Maisie's complaint. And the duty-corporal will remember my taking the note, even if he knew nothing of its contents."

That made Cobb stop and think for a moment or so. Finally he said, "All you gotta do is say the note was an apology to you and Mrs. Standish. I'll say, if anybody bothers to ask, that neither Wilkie nor me found Willoughby in our wanderings, but I did run into Lieutenant Edwards lyin' in a field at the edge of town, a little drunk and a lot woozy from fallin' off his horse. I then dash back to town fer help, borry the donkey-cart, and deliver ya safe to yer bed and board. Ain't that the way it happened, Lieutenant Edwards?"

Despite his amazement, Marc managed to say, "But how would an officer like Willoughby get wind of a robbery?"

Cobb smiled. "I hear tell he spent a lot of time on the King's business in the Blue Ox and other such waterin' holes – where loose talk is as common as loose bowels. Even so, I can't see any of this stuff really bein' necessary. You've got to remember, Major, the folks that run this province are fond of takin' the most agreeable and least irksome story as the truth."

Once again Marc had underestimated the pure cunning of the native-born Upper Canadian. He was too exhausted to work out any specific rationalization for his decision, but he knew, deep down where most things in life really mattered, that he had no choice but to choose as he did. "All right, Constable. Let's do it."

The donkey started up again, matching his pace to Horatio Cobb's.

"I guess now that you and me's started to trade secrets – in a manner of speakin' – I ought to confess somethin' else. Abner Clegg didn't get away from me last week. I tracked the bugger right up to the milliner's door and watched the lady there hand him the package."

"But why did you not tell me this right away? You must've known I'd find the letter-writer eventually."

For a moment only the donkey's harsh breathing was heard. "I knew you was kinda soft on the lady," Cobb said with a blush in his voice.

Marc yawned, but not because he was not intrigued by Cobb's omniscience and, more impressively, by his sensitivity. "Then you must have known she was living here before I did."

"Well, I got kinda chummy with her Aunt Catherine the day after she set up shop on my patrol," Cobb said by way of explanation. "The old gal likes a cup of tea and a good, gossipy chinwag."

"I see. Well, thank you, anyway – Cobb," Mark said. The constable's name on his tongue felt good, and proper. "But I think I have blown my chances with that particular lady."

“That ain’t the story I been told, Major.”

But Marc did not hear this comforting response: he was asleep.

The little procession had turned now onto Front Street – donkey, constable, cart with lieutenant, and chestnut mare. In the eerie half-light of the solstice moon, the entire city lay open before them.

Cobb leaned over and whispered, “Good night, sweet prince.”